Also by Theresa Talbot:

The Lost Children
Keep Her Silent

THE QUIET ONES

Theresa Talbot

HEAD of ZEUS

First published in the UK in 2019 by Head of Zeus Ltd

9 7 5 3 1 2 4 6 8

A catalogue record for this book is available from the British Library.

ISBN: 9781788545341

Typeset by Silicon Chips

Printed and bound in Great Britain by CPI Group (UK) Ltd, Croydon CR0 4YY

Head of Zeus Ltd
First Floor East
5–8 Hardwick Street
London EC1R 4RG

WWW.HEADOFZEUS.COM

For Jeremy

PROLOGUE

'You don't know who I am, do you?'

There wasn't a hint of recognition. It seemed to take him a moment or two to realise where he was. His heels kicked against the floor, but he was too weak to stand up, and the more he struggled, the tighter the ties dug into his flesh. Red welts forming around his wrists and ankles started to weep slightly. Those plastic ties were a godsend. He twisted his head, trying to break free from the gag around his mouth.

'I'm nothing to you, yet you've ruined my entire life.'

He was still drowsy, the sedatives taking their time to wear off.

'But I will mean something to you. Because I'll be the last face you ever see on this planet.'

The gag had slipped down, settling on his chin, but it didn't matter. He was too weak to scream.

'Is it money?' His voice was thick, slurred, barely a whisper. 'Take whatever you want.' He forced his head up;

tears spilled onto his cheeks. At least now he was scared. That was something.

The sheer effort of talking seemed to be too much for him. His head dropped to one side; it sounded as though he was saying please, but it was hard to be sure without getting right up close. It would have been better had he been more alert, fully aware of everything that was going on, but that was too risky. The house was fairly secluded, but screams could carry.

A Tiffany style lamp in the corner bounced a spectrum of colour off the blade. It was beautiful.

'Please, I have a family.'

'You see, phrases like that really upset me.' And they did. As though this were some random attack. As though the fact he had a family were news and could be used as a bargaining tool to curry some favour and get off. Shite like that might work in the courtrooms, but not here. Not in the real world.

'I know you have a family. I know everything about you.'

He closed his eyes. He at least had the decency to look ashamed as the penny dropped.

'I'm sorry.' His voice little more than a whisper.

'No, you're not sorry.'

The hand round his throat stole his breath and his eyes didn't leave the blade as it stabbed into the banister behind him. 'You're sorry that you got caught. There's a difference. A big fucking difference.'

He began to sob.

Snot ran down his nose. He instinctively flicked his tongue out to lick his lips. It was sickening. His crying was starting to grate now.

'I'll tell you what I want from you, and it sure as hell isn't an apology.'

'Anything.' His eyes flickered, a desperate man being given a crumb.

'I want you to tell me what it's like to die.'

Confusion at first. Then fear. It was strange how you could actually see terror in a man's eyes. He began to whimper, a wounded animal. 'What?'

'You heard. Tell me what it's like to die.'

His sobs increasing as his throat tightened, every breath laboured, laced with panic. 'You're mental.'

'Mental? You may well be right.'

'You're fucking crazy.' The insult fell on deaf ears.

'Humour me here. Please. Just talk me through it. Just tell me exactly what it feels like.'

The fear made its way down to his groin and the damp patch spread across the front of his trousers. His whole body trembled, violently shaking now. He dry-retched until the bile rose in his throat and dribbled down his chin.

'I want to know everything. What it feels like, how scared you are. Is it painful?'

'Kill me now. Just get it over with, but I'm telling you fuck all.' The words hiccupped in his throat; it was hard to make them out.

'Listen very carefully to me.'

He tipped his head up, thinking at least there was still some negotiating to be done.

'I'm going to cut out your tongue…'

His screams sliced through the room, his whole body seemed to convulse, the dry retch in his throat made way for vomit and he struggled to stretch his head clear from his clothes. As though that mattered at this stage.

'Shh, shh. Calm down. You didn't let me finish. I'm going to cut out your tongue. If you play ball and tell me what I'd like to know then I'll do that *after* you're dead.'

This seemed to be the best deal he was getting tonight and there was an almost eager nodding in between the uncontrollable shaking.

'If you don't share everything with me, if you don't tell me exactly what's going on as you're breathing your last, then I'll cut out your tongue and I'll cut off your balls too and feed them to you.'

He seemed to get the message. His sobs were pathetic, he'd soiled himself too. The place was starting to stink. He was surprisingly compliant as the noose was put round his neck. It would have been preferable had he done that part himself, but a desperate man was capable of desperate things and there was no telling what he'd have tried had his hands been cut loose.

The rope had been well secured to the banister behind him. Measured to precision to ensure maximum drop without the risk of him actually touching the floor. Once the rope was tight around his throat, only then was it safe to slice through the plastic ties binding his ankles. The ones around his wrists would need to remain until afterwards. He struggled to get to his feet.

'OK, up you go.'

Harry Nugent did as he was told and climbed the stairs of his Houston home for the very last time.

I

Oonagh O'Neil stared at the clock on the newsroom wall; a slow news day was always a drag and today was no different. She looked at the running order of this evening's late bulletin and her heart sank further. A royal pregnancy topped the agenda, followed by some nonsense about council spending, gender neutral toilets in private schools, rounded off with the death of some Scottish football coach she'd barely heard of. Thank Christ she didn't have to read this guff later. That was her only comfort at being sidelined, replaced twice a week by Colin. She couldn't be arsed to remember his second name, but he was young and slick and she guessed he was still paying off the Italian mohair suit that was so obviously made to measure.

'You're not being sidelined,' Alan, her senior editor, had insisted. 'It's just that it's good for the demographics if we have a...' he'd faltered, trying to find another word for *younger*, no doubt, '... ease in another presenter that our new viewers can identify with...' It left Oonagh free to do research and production, he'd said, which in fairness was what she had preferred recently. She had nothing against Colin and his lovely suit, but it was the way things seemed to be happening. And the speed of it too. It seemed like yesterday she was the bright young thing in journalism. When she took her youth and enthusiasm for granted and had no idea of the integral role they'd played in her success. She'd worked hard, no one could ever take that away from her, but there were lots of bright young things who'd worked equally hard.

She browsed the Internet, wondering if it was wise to sign up to another monthly wine delivery, and idled over a few holidays that she had no intention of going on. It had been over a year since she'd actually been away anywhere and she longed to feel the sun on her bones again. It wasn't that she couldn't afford it, but rather that she didn't really fancy going away on her own. Again.

Oonagh wandered over in the direction of the coffee machine, slowing down to peer over her colleague's shoulder. 'What you doing?' She craned her neck to read the screen.

'Bugger off. I'm busy.' Sandy Murray could be a right grumpy sod at times but they'd been pals for a long time and Oonagh liked him. 'I'm doing an obit-pack on Harry Nugent, if you must know.'

Oonagh knitted her brows together.

'Football coach?' The high note of sarcasm was evident in Sandy's voice. 'D'you know nothing about our beautiful game?' Oonagh knew full well who he was referring to. Nugent's death had dropped on the wires earlier that evening and the story was already trending on social media. It all pointed to suicide.

'I can name the Lisbon Lions,' she said, 'but after that I get bored.' She gave him a friendly dunt on the shoulder, 'I know who he is, you cheeky sod, but we don't cover suicides.' And she was right. There were very strict guidelines about reporting such deaths. The fear that some poor soul on the edge could be tipped over if they heard similar deaths reported was all too real. But Oonagh also realised the death of such a high profile figure could hardly go without a mention.

Nugent was the poster-boy for Scottish football. He'd started the Caledonian Boys' Club when he was just twenty years old, and he seemed to have all the right connections. He'd coached kids from the age of nine and very quickly CBC was the feeder academy that boasted the cream of Scotland's youth team. He had it all. Or so it appeared until his devoted wife came home and found him hanging from the banister of their luxury home in Houston.

The full details weren't yet known, but it would appear that he'd killed himself just in time to squeeze the story into their late night bulletin.

'Poor sod.' Oonagh wasn't sure if Sandy was referring to Harry or his wife. Their wedding picture was already plastered all over the on-line early editions of the morning's red-tops.

Oonagh tried not to linger on the image in her head. The bulging eyes, his blue tongue and broken neck. In truth she had no idea what his body would have looked like, but her morbid curiosity flashed gruesome images in her head that she wanted gone.

'What would make him do something like that?' She was thinking out loud, not really expecting an answer.

Sandy shrugged. 'Who knows? Sometimes having it all is just too much.'

Oonagh guessed Sandy was just paying lip-service to get rid of her. Putting together an obit-package for television was a pain in the arse, but it would save him from doing any real work for the rest of the day. There were so many in the can already for senior dignitaries, politicians and every member of the royal family. There wasn't a broadcast journalist in the country that didn't fear accidentally playing out a pre-recorded obituary for the Queen. There were safeguards put in place to prevent that sort of thing. To avert disaster most of the tapes were held under lock and key with two senior station managers being privy to the security code. Oonagh imagined it would be easier to accidentally set off a nuclear warhead.

'I know those houses in Houston,' Oonagh was back idling at her screen, 'They've got high ceilings – would he have jumped from the banister or d'you think he climbed onto a stool or something then kicked it away?' Sandy shot her a look, which she ignored. 'How long does it take to die that way anyway?'

'D'you want to give it a rest, Morticia?' Sandy was losing patience; clearly he wanted to get his pack finished then grab a last pint at The Curler's Rest before closing time. Oonagh mulled over the idea of doing a follow-up feature on this. Male suicide was at an all-time high, practically an epidemic, and Harry Nugent must have been in some state to take his own life knowing his poor wife would find him. Such a high profile figure would be the perfect hook for a programme; speaking to the ones left behind, trying to make sense of this tragedy. She scanned the wires from the past few hours and pulled together all they had on his death. There was no mention of a note, or existing mental-health problems, but a few phone calls would clarify the situation on that. Money worries were usually the next port of call. She'd seen men bigger than Nugent lose everything to a gambling addiction. It wasn't her usual brief, but her hunch told her to stay with this one. Follow the human-interest angle.

She'd already decided to approach his wife, or widow as she now was. But she'd need to tread carefully. Thankfully, it seemed to be one of Oonagh's talents that wasn't diminishing with age: the ability to get perfect strangers to open up to her. She'd make sure she gave her enough breathing space before approaching her. But more than that she'd need to tread carefully with Alan. She'd used up most of her senior editor's goodwill of late. Most people seemed to think presenters had a bit of clout, called the shots, but the truth was Oonagh's jacket was on a very shaky nail and she knew it. There was always someone younger, cheaper – usually these things came in threes – but all it took was someone younger and cheaper and her seat would be filled before her arse reached the door. Right on cue, Colin breezed past clutching a pile of papers to his chest, looking young enough and cheap enough to give anyone the heave-ho.

Oonagh's phone, which was on silent, buzzed and bounced slightly on the desk: DS Jim McVeigh. 'Hey, Jim, how's you?'

'*Might have something for you, Oon.*'

Before she had a chance to answer Alan barged out of his office, pointing his finger at the most senior reporter left in the office. 'You, in here now.' Alan wasn't much for small talk or indeed the niceties of life. Oonagh stood up, and watched as the reporter followed Alan back into his office. 'Jim, can you give me a few seconds here?'

'Yeah, no worries.'

She kept her hand over the mouthpiece and watched as Alan kicked the door over with his heel. It hadn't quite closed and Oonagh peered through the gap. 'Get a camera crew, bring one of the trainees with in case you need a watcher for the van.'

The reporter was scribbling notes and nodding, agreeing to anything and everything Alan was barking at him. He was still nodding as he scurried out of the door. She glanced over at Sandy's empty chair. That bugger always managed to scarper if there was a sniff of a story before closing time.

'Hey, Jim, sorry about that.' She went back to her call.

'We'll be issuing a press release, Oon, but...' Oonagh felt the slight surge of adrenalin, sensing something big was about to unfold. And she was right.

2

DI Alec Davies looked at the body hanging from the oak framed timber balcony and knew he had a major headache on his hands. Harry Nugent was one of the biggest names in Scottish sport, and the Major Investigation Team would be all over this one like a rash. Davies had passed Nugent's wife on his way in; still sitting in the back of a squad car. The flashing lights of the police cars and ambulance shone through the windows, the light catching on Harry's eyes, which were still open. His wife had come home around tea-time and found him. Thought initially it was suicide and ran screaming from the house before calling 999. No one had bothered coming out to see what was wrong. It wasn't that sort of neighbourhood. Davies wondered whether they'd heard Harry's screams and ignored them too. It was only when blue flashing lights appeared that a few heads bobbed out from behind the cedar gates.

When the paramedics had arrived on the scene it had quickly become obvious that Harry Nugent had been murdered, or at least the death was considered 'suspicious'. Very few suicide victims had lesions around their wrists and ankles, and even fewer had their tongues cut off and stuffed down the back of their throats.

The police casualty surgeon had long gone, hadn't taken too much time to pronounce life extinct at the scene. Davies guessed most people would have been able to tell this poor sod was a goner with or without a medical degree. The body was fully clothed – well, almost; one slipper dangled from his right foot, brown leather slip-ons, the other had fallen on the floor. They looked as though they'd cost more than Davies's monthly mortgage repayment. Hellish little good they'd be doing him now.

DS Toria Law came through the front door. The house had been cleared as soon as it had become obvious that it was a crime scene. She was covered from head to foot: white paper overalls, hood up, covering the small cap her hair was tucked underneath, double latex gloves, disposable shoes and a face mask. Only her eyes were visible through the Perspex goggles. She looked like a kid as she nodded over to him, her eyes quickly taking in the scene. This was only her second time as a crime scene manager, but she was turning into a good copper. Davies knew he was in safe hands and left her to it.

Outside the quiet residential street had been cordoned off, with two police cars parked in a 'V' shape, stopping any vehicles entering or leaving. This was an area unused to flashing blue lights or the camera crews that Davies could see were now gathering at the foot of the cul-de-sac.

Nugent's wife was curled up in the back of the car. Frizzy blonde hair sticking out from the top of the grey blanket she'd been wrapped in. Even from this distance, he could see she was shaking. McVeigh sat opposite her, seemed to be nodding in all the right places, no doubt reassuring her that it was just routine that they'd need DNA swabs. He eased himself out of the car, leaving the grieving widow when he saw his boss.

'What's she still doing here?' Davies looked at his watch. Nugent had been dead for the best part of three hours now.

'She wanted back in to collect a few things.' McVeigh anticipated Davies's response. ''S OK, I told her no. She's going back home with her sister now.'

'She up to giving a statement yet?'

McVeigh shook his head, 'Not a chance, sir. She's mogged up to the eyeballs.'

'Who the fuck prescribed tranquilisers before we had a chance to speak to her?'

'I don't think they were quite on prescription, sir.'

'Bloody brilliant.' It was a bitterly cold night and Davies could see his breath against the clear, dark sky. Why did these things always happen at night? Never on a sunny Sunday afternoon, but then Davies could hardly remember a sunny Sunday afternoon in Glasgow, so the odds were already stacked against that scenario. It'd be a long day tomorrow and if he could make a head start tonight then they'd all hit the ground running in the morning. He was about to get back into his car when he saw her.

Oonagh had decided to take a taxi to the scene, knowing full well she wouldn't be able to park anywhere within spitting distance of the house. It dropped her off at the end of the wide, tree-lined cul-de-sac, which was impressive even for Houston. Just three houses in the street, each one with a gravel drive that seemed to stretch on for miles, with enormous gardens offering the owners more privacy than most people could expect this close to the city.

Oonagh caught DS Jim McVeigh walking towards her, no sign of Alec; she guessed he was still inside the house.

'Hey, this is a bit of a turn-up for the books.' In light of recent discoveries, Nugent's obituary had been hastily dropped from the running order. They were leading instead with his murder. Oonagh made to lift the police tape, but Jim stopped her before she could squeeze underneath. 'Didn't take you long.'

'Where's the big boss, then?'

Jim nodded back to the bank of cars in front of the house.

'What's going on?' Oonagh was desperate for answers. 'I thought it was suicide.' She was craning her head past Jim, desperate for a better look, but knew it was useless. Even had she been standing at the garden gate the endless gravel drive meant she'd still be too far away to get a good nosey.

Darkness had descended like a blanket, but without the warmth or comfort. Jim leaned against the street light, hands stuffed into his pockets, legs crossed at the ankles. The irony of the neighbourhood watch sticker peeling on the metal lamppost behind his head wasn't lost on either of them.

'So, come on, Jim, what's the score?'

The place was swarming with police, forensics and reporters. Turned out Nugent's body was still in the house. Harry had not yet left the building.

'So?'

'Nothing yet, Oonagh. No leads.'

She liked Jim, almost thought of him as a pal, and God knew she had hellish few of them she could rely on right now. But tonight he was making her work for her money and wasn't giving much away. News of Nugent's death had come hot on the heels of his wife discovering the body earlier that evening; it had been all over Twitter that he'd killed himself, been found hanging in the hallway of his home. That part by all accounts had been true. Until Jim had called her there had been no suggestion that it had been anything other than that. Oonagh made a mental note to call back into the newsroom to see who, if anyone, had actually checked the suicide angle.

She spotted DI Alec Davies emerge from his car. Even from this distance he looked shattered. He faltered slightly, but seemed to change his mind when he saw her chatting to Jim, and made his way over. Oonagh had got the distinct impression he'd been avoiding her recently. She tried to look casual and gave him a wee wave. Camera bulbs flashed, and several mics were thrust in his general direction. He swatted them away, yelling at the journalists to contact the media relations department, adding that a full statement would be issued in due course. He didn't look to be in the best of moods.

'Haven't seen you for a while.' He looked even worse close up, as though he hadn't slept properly in weeks. His eyes were heavy and the grey stubble stabbing its way through his five o'clock shadow did nothing to enhance his appearance. Now wasn't the time to ask if he'd been avoiding her.

'You look well,' she reached to touch his arm, but he didn't respond. 'So what's the deal? Was he killed right enough?'

Alec held out his arm towards the house swarming with coppers. 'What do you think?'

Oonagh's mind was racing, working overtime. 'Was he robbed? Was the house turned over? Has he been shot?'

'Now, Oonagh.' Davies cut her off mid-stream and ran his hands through his hair. 'You can hardly expect me to give you details of the case.'

She just shrugged; it would all come out eventually. Her mobile phone buzzed; she glanced down and clocked the top-line message. 'Bloody hell!' She looked up. 'Was his tongue cut out? Oh, my God. Is that true?'

Alec's face was like thunder. 'What the fu...? Who told you that?'

Jim raised his hands, palms facing forward. 'Wasn't me...'

Oonagh held up her phone. 'It's all over Twitter.' She knew full well that relying on social media for accuracy was tenuous to say the least, but Alec's reaction said it all. 'So that's a yes, then?'

3

They'd pulled out all the stops with this one. One of Scotland's most prominent businessmen found hanging from a rope with his tongue cut off was major-league, even for Glasgow. Alec Davies stood at the front of the incident room, a mixture of plain-clothed and uniformed cops filling the front two rows, Jim and Toria slightly to his left. He'd already gone over the bare facts, which were scant to say the least, not that that stopped press speculation. Hardly surprising really. They were baying for blood and demanding answers. Davies wondered what the collective name for photographers was. He'd managed to avoid the mob this morning only because he'd stayed overnight at the station, grabbing a couple of hours' shut-eye before trying to drag himself awake with a shower and a shave.

This wasn't going to be easy and the Chief Constable would have his balls on a plate if he didn't shut this one down quick-style. Despite the press speculation that the streets of Glasgow were no longer safe as long as this crazed killer was on the loose, Davies doubted they would strike anywhere else. This killer had targeted Harry Nugent for a reason and was unlikely to be a danger to anyone else. But they were still dangerous – make no mistake. He took a strange comfort in the fact, however, that in the wake of such a horror the streets were indeed safer – for a few nights at least – as revellers cancelled plans, and even the die-hard neds chose instead to stay where they knew they'd be safe.

Behind him, the incident board read like a who's who of Scottish sports stars, as well as the usual suspects. Family, close friends, relatives, anyone who'd been connected with Nugent. But it was now running into hundreds of people.

They were waiting for the full post-mortem report, but he'd spoken to the pathologist earlier. Rosemary Gardner was the best they had. Her initial findings were that Nugent had been drugged, then died from asphyxiation through hanging. Lesions around his wrists and his ankles suggested plastic ties had been used as restraints. Despite a detailed search, the ties had not been found, suggesting the killer took the time to remove them. His tongue too, had been sliced off post-mortem, which would account for the lack of blood and the fact his wife had initially thought it was suicide. This was no frenzied, random attack. Nugent had clearly been up to his neck in something, had clearly pissed off someone big style. This was some fucking grudge which bore all the hallmarks of a gangland-style execution.

'The killer might well have paid some heavies to do his dirty work for him.' Toria looked shattered; Davies guessed she didn't get much sleep last night. 'It's a bit of a high risk strategy doing that lot on your own… and besides…'

'Stating the bleeding obvious…' DS Gilroy shifted in his seat. Davies had worked alongside him in the same station, on and off, for years.

'Yeah,' he replied, 'but she *did* state it, which is more than you've done so far, Gilroy, so can we just work together on this one?' Davies checked Gilroy's smirk as he glanced around the room. You could read a lot into one expression, and from the look on Gilroy's face came the suggestion that Davies fancied Toria and was cutting her more than the usual bit of slack. He felt weary, and not just because of this case. The thought of coming across as a sad old git fancying a girl young enough to be his daughter, or grand-daughter in some parts of Glasgow, left a bitter taste in his mouth. Truth was she was a good copper; she had an unusual way of looking at things and Davies knew that a fresh eye could often see minor details that a jaded eye could miss. Davies caught Gilroy's eye and mouthed *fuck off* under his breath before continuing.

'Right, guys, we need to establish what Nugent was doing in the twenty-four hours before he died. Did he have any enemies?' As he was saying this he knew it sounded corny. 'Anyone with a grudge against him?' He looked at Toria. 'Anything obvious from the scene?'

She shook her head. 'Nothing out of the ordinary, sir. No sign of a break-in or a struggle.'

'Obviously knew the killer.' Gilroy was playing ball now. 'Any CCTV?'

Jim looked at Davies, who gave him the nod to jump in. 'There're no cameras near the estate, nearest ones are almost a mile away.'

Every car that had been driven within a mile of the scene in the previous twenty-four hours was being checked and double-checked on CCTV for number-plate recognition. Davies felt his heart sink further into his gut. As much as he wanted to tell the journalists to fuck off, he knew with this one he needed them on board. They'd be relying heavily on witnesses seeing anything out of the ordinary, and on a Monday night in one of the most salubrious areas in the outskirts of the city that didn't leave much scope.

'What about the usual suspects?' Gilroy was the first to address the elephant in the room. 'There must be some gossip. This has got Glasgow crime wars written all over it. I bet every ned in the east end is boasting about this by now.'

Davies knew he was right. The heavies expected to be able to conduct their business without too much interference, and they'd always throw some fall guy to the wolves who'd be willing to take the rap if the screws were turned tight enough. His budget would be as tight as a drum with this one. There was never too much money thrown at gang wars, but then they didn't usually spill onto victims as high profile as Harry Nugent.

The air was beginning to feel stale in the incident room, and there wasn't much more to be said. They needed to get out and get on with things. Gilroy eased himself out from behind the desk. Davies gestured to Jim and Toria to wait for him outside.

'This is a bastard of a case, Alec.'

'No shit, Sherlock.'

Gilroy stuffed his hands into his pockets and rocked back slightly on his heels. 'You're not seriously going to bust a gut finding this guy?'

Davies raised an eyebrow; he knew what was coming.

'Come on, Alec, this is a gang war. Nugent was up to his oxters in something rotten. I'd bet my pension he was match rigging, or gambling.'

Davies rubbed his hand over his mouth, feeling a patch of stubble he'd missed in his hurry to shave that morning. He knew Gilroy was right. In truth he was an OK guy, just got on Davies's tits at times. But then everyone did from time to time. 'The Chief wants it dealt with.'

Gilroy shrugged, gave that knowing look; they both knew how it worked. If the police turned the heat up, then some rookie gang member would take the rap. He'd be sent down, then released early for being a model prisoner. He'd be well paid for his trouble, his family taken care of, and Davies knew only too well there'd be young guys falling over themselves to do a stretch like this to prove their loyalty to the gang. It'd also earn them a get-out-of-jail-free card for the rest of their criminal career.

The early morning sunshine had given way to rain that smeared across the windows. Everything around him looked grimy.

'No leads, then?'

Davies shot him a look. 'Shit, Frank, if I had a lead d'you not think I'd be sharing it with the team? It's not fucking *Columbo*.' It was only after his outburst he realised it was a rhetorical question.

'Listen...' it was water off a duck's back to Frank Gilroy '... take my advice, don't knock yourself out with this. You'll get little thanks.' He let his hand rest on Davies's shoulder for a second. 'Get yourself some rest, Alec. You look like shit.'

Clearly Gilroy thought he was being helpful, but all it did was make Davies's gut churn more. This wasn't something that would go cold after a few weeks and people would start forgetting. Even the most horrific murders got lost in the cesspit of crime after a certain amount of time, and no one, save for the victim's families, pointed the finger if no arrests were made. But this was different. Harry Nugent would be front page news for some time yet. Davies busied himself sorting papers until Gilroy wandered off down the corridor and out of sight. Only then did he drop his head onto his hands. 'Fuck.'

4

Something wasn't right. Normally celebrities were coming out of the woodwork to throw in their tuppence worth, desperate to big up their part and claim to have had a very special relationship with the deceased, but Oonagh was getting the distinct impression that people were trying to distance themselves from Harry Nugent.

The silence from the cops was deafening. Nugent had been dead for almost thirty-six hours and apart from a rather scant press release telling her what she already knew – that he was dead – they were keeping their cards very close to their chest with this one.

Oonagh needed to speak to his widow, and soon. If *she* played ball, then she'd be better placed to approach Alan for a budget to make a follow up documentary. As it stood he'd given the story to the senior crime correspondent who was a lazy bastard at the best of times, but Oonagh had to admit he had the connections in Glasgow's underworld that she lacked. And it was becoming more and more apparent that this was an organised attack from a professional hit man – which pointed the finger at Nugent being up to his eyes in something brown and smelly.

Mrs Nugent had so far refused to speak to the press, but Oonagh knew she'd need to come at it from a different angle. A human interest angle. Concentrating instead on the impact of violent death on the family left behind. It was what she was good at; getting people to open up, share their stories, tell her their secrets. The public liked her; she knew that. Despite this, Oonagh could feel the nail drive deeper into her professional coffin each year. She was too old to make the leap to print journalism, had priced herself out of the market for most other commercial stations, and knew the screws were tightening where she was now. She knew she was good, but the world was changing and sometimes being good just wasn't enough.

It may not have been her story, but she couldn't let it go. One of Scotland's most prominent public figures killed and mutilated in his own home and the police seemed to be dragging their feet. However, every item she found on Nugent pointed to him being clean. He gave enough money to charity to pay off the national debt of a small country, helped the poor, Christ, this guy even gave up his Christmas Day and dressed up as Santa to visit sick kids in hospital. And there was nothing to suggest that the sports academy was anything other than what it said on the tin – an academy for sporting excellence in Scotland. Well, it said sport, but in Scotland that meant football. But there had to be more behind that goody-two-shoes image. She'd bet her NUJ subscriptions on it. This guy had to be guilty of more than a dodgy hair weave and badly capped teeth. Despite these, Nugent had never missed an opportunity to get his face in the papers.

The summer camps for Caledonian Boys' Club were legendary throughout Scotland. Kids as young as ten were plucked from their working class housing schemes to spend summers in France, Spain, or even Algeria, to be given a chance of a lifetime. The chance of professional coaching, to play their game and make something of themselves. Some even went on to become big names. Not many, granted, but there were a few she recognised as coming up through the ranks, making a decent living for themselves. Local heroes by all accounts.

But it wasn't on the pitch Nugent had made his millions. Sure, that's where he'd earned his reputation, but the money came from his business off-shoots. The more she delved into it the more Oonagh realised just how much Nugent had been worth – whether he was worth even more dead remained to be seen. A spin off business, ingeniously called 'Pitch Perfect', made branded clothing; polo shirts, football strips and blazer badges. It didn't look to Oonagh like a high end business, but it had made more money each year than the all the sporting achievements put together. Oonagh guessed that might just be enough to dry his widow's tears somewhat. Despite his whiter than white public image, Oonagh knew that no one got as far as Harry Nugent had without stepping on a few toes.

The stinging of her eyes told her she'd already spent too long staring at the screen; the stiffness in her back told her she needed more exercise. She logged off, glancing at the clock as she packed up for the night. Not yet eight o'clock and she was shattered. Too many booze filled sleepless nights. She made a mental note that tonight she'd only have the one. One glass to help her relax. She pressed her thumbs into the corner of her eyes.

'Getting too old to be up this late?' Ross Mitchell walked past her desk.

'Fuck off, Ross,' they'd given up any pretence of liking each other a long time ago. A less than average journalist, he'd somehow managed to wheedle his way up to senior management; Oonagh never understood how, but in truth she'd seen it before; arse-licking being a substitute for talent in so many professions.

'I've stuck you down for a presenting shift Sunday evening.' He held a clip-board, which was the newsroom equivalent of wearing a 'please kick me' badge.

Oonagh made a play of fishing in her bag for her phone, refusing to catch his eye. 'The graveyard shift? I don't think so, Ross.' She pulled her jacket on over her shoulders, rounding the desk to where he was standing. Only then did she look him in the eye. 'I'm a senior journalist and senior presenter. I don't work Sundays.'

'We all need to pull our weight. The times they are a changing, Oonagh.'

Whether he'd meant to reference Bob Dylan, or he'd just heard the phrase and thought it sounded clever she wasn't sure. But it pissed her off big style.

'Shift.' He'd wedged himself between two desks, blocking her way. She resisted the temptation to prod him in the gut and instead flashed him a smile.

He stood his ground for a few seconds, then caught whatever look was in her eye and stepped aside. Oonagh felt the colour rise in her cheeks as she wandered through to the sports department, determined not to let her encounter with Ross piss her off more than was necessary. What she needed now was information on Nugent, not to get one over on Ross Mitchell. Information about his career she could find online, but the sports journos would have had more of an inside track on what he was about. And when she spoke to his widow she wanted to be able to hit the ground running.

It was quiet this evening and just one reporter sat in front of a PC battering lumps out of the keyboard.

'Hey, Lovely,' they'd been introduced at one stage, but Oonagh struggled to remember his name and thought this kept her on safe ground, 'you got a minute?'

He grinned when he saw her and swung round in his chair, apparently glad of the break.

'Harry Nugent...?'

'Och, that weirdo.' He butted in before she'd had a chance to pose the question.

'Oh? What d'you mean, weirdo?'

'Everyone knew he was a creep. Hanging about young boys.'

'Really?' Oonagh's heart sank, she was hoping for something more than some Neanderthal theory of a sports journalist who assumes any guy mixing with kids is a weirdo. But so far it was the only thing she had to go on. 'Have you got any evidence... or...'

Rumours being bandied about after someone dies and hard facts are two different things, and Oonagh couldn't believe that the police wouldn't be across this. '... or anyone that knew him well, or...' Oonagh didn't want to come right out and ask the reporter if he was making it up.

'It's just common knowledge,' he offered before his phone rang and he turned his back, taking the call.

If this was true it was a whole new ball game. She knew Alec had been coy these last couple of days. Not answering her texts, giving nothing away about the inquiry. There was no proof yet that Harry Nugent had indeed been guilty as charged, but whatever he'd done had pissed off someone enough to have sliced out his tongue.

5

Initial toxicology reports showed that Nugent had indeed been drugged prior to death, but Forensics were in no doubt he was fully conscious when he fell from the balcony. There was no evidence of a struggle, there were no marks left on the wooden floor, suggesting he'd walked, rather than been dragged, up the stairs, and in fact, had it not been for the plastic tie marks around his wrists and ankles, his death could easily have been mistaken for suicide. Well, those and the fact his tongue had been sliced off.

'He must have been up to his eyes in some shit.'

Davies couldn't disagree with Jim. This was a well thought out execution. Whoever did this was sending out a very clear message. Nonetheless, his heart sank at the fact this appeared to be a classic revenge attack, and professional hit men were buggers to track down.

'No witnesses, no leads, nothing. This case is a bit shit.'

'You're not helping here, McVeigh.' Davies hoped his partner would just button it, but past experience told him that was unlikely.

There was no reason to put on the blue light and siren, but Davies couldn't be arsed with the traffic today so didn't object when McVeigh took the initiative and pulled it out from the glove compartment and stuck it on the roof of the car. It would take the best part of an hour to get to Houston; the morning rush hour was not quite over and the M8 crawled along. Davies eased the car into the outside lane and put his foot down, ignoring his partner's slight look of fear as he gained on the cars in front, relying on them to get their arses in gear and get the hell out of the outside lane. There was a time when just the sight or sound of a police siren was enough to make traffic pull over, but now he was finding that the threat of rear-ending the car in front was a more effective method of clearing the outside lane.

'She'll claim she knows nothing, of course.' McVeigh rarely expected much of a response, which was a good thing. Davies wasn't one for chit-chat this early in the morning. He'd skipped breakfast again and could feel the slight sting of heartburn rise in his chest and settle in his throat. 'But she must know what he'd been up to.'

Ideally they'd have interviewed Nugent's widow at the scene. But as McVeigh had so eloquently put it, she'd been so *mogged out of her head* that had proved impossible. Subsequently, more conventionally administered sedatives prescribed by her GP ensured she'd remained semi-comatose for the best part of thirty-six hours. Now, almost three days into the investigation, they were no closer to finding his killer and rumours were bouncing off the walls in every pub in Scotland as to who carried out the attack – and why. Everything from him being Bible John to being part of a drug deal gone wrong.

'You know there's always been a bit of talk that his interest in those boys weren't just on the pitch?'

Davies let out a sigh and was glad his partner had kept his mouth shut about this during the briefing. They left the motorway and he put his foot down, jumping an amber, squeezing through the lights before they turned red. He nodded. He'd heard all right, but for now had decided to treat it for what it was: a rumour. Davies knew to tread carefully with this one.

'Listen, McVeigh, the fact Nugent is dead means there's a danger every Tom, Dick and Harry will come out of the woodwork and say what they like about him.' Davies and McVeigh both knew the score here.

'Turn right here, just after this pedestrian crossing.'

Davies had his mind on other things and slammed his foot on the brake, the car squealing in protest as he took the corner in fourth gear.

Harry Nugent's widow wasn't at her own home; hardly surprising really. The house had been sealed off as a crime scene. It had taken almost ten hours for Forensics to remove the body, ensuring that the hands, feet and head had been effectively bagged to preserve any evidence prior to the post-mortem examination, and the scene of crime officers had everything they needed from the property.

A uniformed officer remained outside Nugent's house. They could just see him, stamping his feet against the cold as they passed the cul-de-sac on their way, and Davies wondered who he'd pissed off to get landed with such a rotten gig. Sarah Nugent had decamped to her sister's house, which was just a few blocks away. Davies would give her the green light to go home today, but reckoned it might be quite some time before Mrs Nugent cared to venture back into her own house.

'I bet that'll knock thousands off the value.' Jim just had a way with words. 'I mean, who the hell would want to live in a house where someone was slaughtered and hung out to dry?'

Davies tried not to laugh as he pulled up alongside the kerb. 'Yip, nothing like an execution to bring down the neighbourhood.'

'This must be awful for you.' Jim handed Harry Nugent's widow a fresh tissue as they sat at the large wooden table dominating the kitchen. 'It's a godsend you have your family to support you, Sarah. That must be some comfort at least.' Davies was secretly impressed that Jim had remembered her first name. Sure, it had been on the briefing notes, but names and faces blurred into one for him and he was always double-checking personal details. This sort of thing came naturally to Jim and she seemed only too happy to chat to him, unaware that just minutes before Jim McVeigh had been speculating on the value of her property.

'I can't get the image out of my head.'

Sarah Nugent chewed on the skin around her left thumb, worrying a scratch into the table with the index finger of her right hand. All that Davies had seen of her the previous evening had been her frizzy blonde hair peeping out from the regulation grey blanket. Now that had been smoothed down and pulled back into a ponytail and, although Davies wasn't normally one to notice such things, he was impressed that she was fully dressed, right down to the high heels, which seemed rather out of place relaxing in the kitchen. Her make-up, although perfectly applied, did little to cover her grey pallor and the dark shadows beneath her bloodshot eyes. Her breath carried that strong smell of mouthwash, strong enough to suggest she was desperate to cover up the fact she'd been drinking since before breakfast. The half-empty brandy bottle by the sink gave the game away too. This poor woman was shattered.

Jim's very gentle questioning established that she'd been out with friends on Monday afternoon and had come home at the back of six.

'So what're you doing to catch this maniac?'

Her sister wasn't being very helpful here. What did the general public at large actually expect coppers to say to a question like that? *Oh, come on down to the incident room, let me talk you through the briefing and then we'll show you a list of leads.*

'I mean—' she seemed to be on a roll, 'we're not safe in our own homes any more. It's a… it's disgraceful. I blame those video games.' She slammed the tray down on the table slightly harder than intended, by the looks of it, and slops of tea and coffee spilled over the edges of the over-filled mugs.

'Good job there're no biscuits.' McVeigh grabbed his mug from the sopping tray. 'They'd have been ruined.' His sarcasm was lost on everyone but Davies.

'Mrs, eh…'

'Gill.'

'Gill, we've every reason to believe this was a targeted attack.' Davies couldn't be arsed to add that the streets were just as safe now as they'd ever been. Children were just as safe now as they had been in the rose-tinted sixties.

He elected not to recite the murders committed by Manuel in the fifties, the horrors carried out by Brady and Hindley in the sixties or the Yorkshire Ripper's reign of terror in the seventies.

'We need to know why Mr Nugent was targeted.' He looked at Nugent's widow, who'd stopped chewing her thumb long enough to drink her coffee. 'And I'm sorry, Sarah, we'll need to ask you some difficult questions.'

There was no rose-tinted version of the past for Davies, he was only too aware that the world had always been a shit-hole. Sadly for Sarah Nugent, it was only when tragedy came knocking on your door did most people then realise just how shitty it actually was.

6

Tommy Gallagher 1983

There was nothing he could do to stop the nerves in his stomach as he was led through the softly lit corridor. He'd been to the toilet four times that morning already, but still the pressure on the base of his spine returned within minutes.

Trophies lined the glass cabinets and the thick carpet stole any sound of footsteps. Pictures of his heroes, ten feet high, smiled down at him; he was almost scared to catch their eyes. The soft thud of his boots patted against his thigh with every step. They were new. Spotless. He carried them over his shoulder by the laces like a badge of honour. To show the world he'd made it. His mum had insisted on wrapping them in newspaper as she'd placed them carefully in his cheap plastic sports bag, but he'd taken them out and ditched the bag behind a hedge as soon as his mum was out of sight. A slight pang of guilt stung his chest and he hoped to God it would still be there on his way home

'Your dad would be burstin' the day, son. Totally burstin' with pride.' The boots had cost more than the week's messages. He knew that, but his ma never let on. Her eyes had moistened and a tiny tug at the corner of her mouth had betrayed the tears she'd been holding back. The last time he'd seen her cry, in fact the only time he'd seen her cry, was when Dad died. Even then it had been in secret when she'd thought the rest of them were in bed. He'd stood in the hall, peering through the crack at the kitchen door. The thick black wool coat saved for special occasions had already been hung back up in the wardrobe. She'd smoothed her hands over her dark skirt, the one she'd borrowed from Auntie Ina. Ina'd told her to keep it. Given her a black jumper too. Said they didn't fit her any more and his mum would be doing her a favour by taking them. But it had been obvious the clothes were new.

His mum had taken the photograph from her purse. Tommy knew that picture well; he'd seen it loads of times. Just a daft one taken at the booth in Central Station. His dad with a thick moustache, grinning at the camera, his mum squished in on the tiny seat beside him, his arm around her shoulder holding her close. Just teenagers, when they'd been courting. His mum had worried the picture in her hands for a few seconds, then placed it on the kitchen table. 'Oh, Liam, what're we going to do without you?' It was only then that she'd begun to sob. Waves of grief had sent convulsions through her body as she'd dropped her head onto her arms. It had been obvious she was trying to be quiet, but tiny gulps and hiccups had escaped. Tommy had wanted to rush in and throw his arms around her. Make her stop crying and tell her that he'd take care of them. He was the man of the house now. But instead he'd sneaked back into his room, unable to bear it any longer. The sadness in his throat almost choking him. He'd tried to swallow back his tears. Hadn't wanted to wake Ellie sleeping in the bed next to him. So he'd pulled the blankets over his head and pressed the sheet tightly against his eyes to mop his tears.

'You all right, son?' The security man wore a blazer with the club's emblem on the breast pocket.

Tommy nodded, dryness in his mouth catching any words. He coughed slightly and licked his lips. 'Yes, thank you.' His mum had warned him to be polite to everyone, but the nerves in his stomach were now so strong he thought he was going to heave.

The security man ushered him forward, a guiding hand between his shoulder blades. 'Here we are.' He gave Tommy a reassuring nod before knocking on the door.

Tommy wiped the back of his hand across his mouth, making sure there was no grotty spit nestling in the corners, then patted the boots by his side. Running his fingers along the studs on the sole. He looked up. *Thank you, Dad,* he mouthed silently, careful not to let the security man see in case he thought he was a nutter.

His stomach shifted as the door opened. He'd seen him on the telly. On the sidelines at Hampden from a distance. But now here he was, just inches away from Harry Nugent. 'Thanks, Jim.' He nodded to the security man before turning his eyes back to Tommy. Tommy wasn't sure if that was actually the guy's name, or just a nickname to save men as important as Harry Nugent having to remember.

He reached down and ruffled Tommy's hair slightly. 'Come on in, son.'

He tried not to let his mouth gape open as he stepped into Harry's office. It was bigger than his whole house. A giant window on one wall looked right onto Caledonian Park, where Tommy's dad had taken him every week until he'd got ill. *'The green will be greener than any other pitch, son,'* he'd said, *'and even on the coldest days you'll feel warm just by being here.'*

Behind him Harry Nugent closed the door, and Tommy knew his life was about to change.

7

'Say what you've come to say then piss off.'

Oonagh hadn't exactly expected a warm welcome but even she was taken aback by this somewhat frosty reception. It wasn't Sarah Nugent who'd opened the door, but her sister, who evidently wasn't a huge fan of journalists.

'It's OK, Gill, I'm fine.' Sarah Nugent leaned against the door frame at the end of the hall. She nodded to her sister to let Oonagh in then turned and made her way to the kitchen, expecting them both to follow. She pointed to a chair, supposedly to let Oonagh know it was safe to sit down. It seemed a bit late to try and win the family over with the famous O'Neil charm, so Oonagh decided to skip the bit about being sorry for her loss.

'Thanks for seeing me, Sarah... I know how hard this must be...' But her sister jumped in before Oonagh could finish. 'Listen, love, can we cut the crap? We both know you're here to dig the dirt. It's what your mob do, isn't it?'

Perhaps the rumours about Harry's extracurricular activities had reached home. Or perhaps his wife had known already.

'Gill...' Sarah looked like a woman too close to the edge to be left on her own '... can you just give us a few minutes, eh?' Her sister barged out of the room only unfolding her arms long enough to slam the door behind her. 'She's just a bit... protective.'

'That's ehm... understandable,' said Oonagh, thinking how well Gill would do if she ever went into the protection racket. 'Sarah, thanks for agreeing to speak to me.' She'd expected a slight response, but nothing. 'As I said on the phone, Harry's death must have been awful for you. I want to do a special feature on the devastation a violent death can cause to the families left behind.' Sarah Nugent was leaning back against the worktop, arms folded, cup of coffee in one hand. She raised an eyebrow, telling Oonagh she'd need a bit more to go on.

'Have the police offered you any counselling, or...'

'They offered me a twelve year old family liaison officer, does that count?'

Oonagh twisted around in her chair, but they were alone.

'I said thanks but no thanks. I don't need some copper hanging around here. Interfering. Making me feel worse.' Her eyes welled up and she tipped her head back, blinking hard to stem the tears.

'Sarah, I know it can seem like that, but believe me, these officers are well trained, you might find it helpful.' Oonagh wouldn't have got within spitting distance of an interview if a liaison officer was hanging around, but she knew how vital they could be. 'I've worked closely in the past with families of murder victims, the trauma can be...'

'I can take care of myself.'

Sarah Nugent had the look of someone who knew how to handle herself on a good day. Today wasn't that good. She sipped her coffee, clutching the mug with both hands to stop her hands from shaking. Oonagh didn't want to push her too hard; finding your husband swinging from the banister of the marital home was no easy gig. Her eyes had a haunted look, red from crying, the skin underneath tender and creased.

'Clearly someone had a grudge against your husband, Mrs Nugent...'

'Of course someone had a fucking grudge against my husband.' She slammed her mug on the worktop, 'And a serious one at that. D'you think someone took him out because he'd parked in the disabled space at Waitrose?'

Her sudden change of demeanour caught Oonagh on a back foot. The fact she'd said *took him out* and not killed or murdered suggested that Mrs Nugent was no stranger to the polite society often frequented by local thugs. She may well have had her reasons for not wanting the cops hanging around.

'Sarah, what did your sister mean about digging the dirt on Harry?' She needed to start getting some answers here. She'd agreed to an interview, so she must have wanted to give her some information. It was time to toughen up. 'Was Harry...?' She was trying to think of a polite way of asking if her dead husband had been up to his neck in something. 'The cops have got a funny way of turning over the tiniest of stones, and there's no telling what lies beneath them.' Sarah didn't answer her, but at least Oonagh hadn't been told to piss off this time, so she was making some ground. 'If you can come across as the grieving widow…' Shit, that came out wrong. Oonagh raised her hand by way of an apology; Sarah's face was like thunder. 'If something *suspect* is revealed about Harry, then now might be a good time to… to disassociate yourself from whatever or whoever he was involved with.' Oonagh knew only too well how guilt by association worked. That wasn't to say she thought this woman was lily white, but she had nothing to gain at this stage from antagonising her any further. Sarah pulled out a chair and sat opposite her. Apparently ready to talk.

'So what kind of husband was he?' Oonagh actually hated that question – never having had a husband, she wasn't quite sure where the benchmarks were. But it was an opening for Sarah Nugent to say whatever the hell she liked about the man as long as she did a decent PR job on herself.

'The usual type.' She scratched at an imaginary mark on the island unit that served as a table between them. 'Harry was more than happy to give me my…' she paused '… space. We had different interests, you see.'

There was something in the way she said it that gave Oonagh the distinct impression she was already trying to distance herself from her dead husband. If that was the case then she was doing a good job. Setting this up as a typical couple married for two decades but who had grown apart. No longer love's young dream, but they weren't exactly throwing plates at each other either.

'How well did you know Harry's friends? His business associates?'

She shrugged, biting her bottom lip

'Would you agree to go on camera, Sarah?' Oonagh was about to reassure her it would just be a short interview when she saw the flash in her eyes that suggested she would very much like to appear on television. It was the chink she was looking for and Oonagh knew she'd need to work fast on this one. 'It'll obviously be upsetting, but it could help. If people see the human side of this tragedy, what Harry has left behind, then…'

But Sarah Nugent was already one step ahead. 'If you think it could help another woman in the same circumstances…' she looked into her coffee cup, and nodded '… I don't know what Harry was supposed to have done, but he didn't deserve to die this way.'

Bloody hell, this woman was good. She decided to break her in slowly. 'Can we just go over some background here, Sarah?' She didn't say no, which Oonagh took as a yes. 'How did you two meet?'

'I was working,' she said, looking off into the middle distance to nowhere in particular. 'I'd been a model…' she must have caught a look in Oonagh's eye '… obviously not big league. I was never going to make it, I knew that, so I continued my nursing training.' Oonagh had no idea where this was going. 'It's such a rewarding profession…' she paused for effect '… helping others.' Oonagh wasn't sure if she should let her continue or tell her to keep her power dry until she came back with the cameras. She wasn't sure if Mrs Nugent would remember her lines the second time round.

'I first saw Harry at Breakmire.' She caught Oonagh's expression. 'You know, the hospital just past Maryhill?'

'Oh, right, yeah.' The building had lain derelict for years, but from what Oonagh could remember it had been an asylum back in the days when mental health treatment was even grimmer than it was now.

'He'd been doing some charity work there and I was on the wards. He asked me out the second time he saw me. Three weeks later we were engaged, and sixteen weeks after that we were married. I'd already given up nursing by then. Harry said there was no need for me to work.'

'All sounds very romantic,' said Oonagh, who could think of nothing worse and thought the whole thing sounded decidedly sinister.

Sarah Nugent stood up and staggered slightly as she opened the fridge; Oonagh detected the telltale signs of the early morning social drinker. The house was all cream leather and high-end gloss furniture that clearly cost a fortune, but there wasn't an ounce of character in this home. Her sister was obviously doing well. Oonagh wondered if Harry's generosity extended to Sarah's family, but decided against probing too deeply into that one for now.

'Have the police said when you'll be allowed home?' Oonagh guessed it wasn't just the fact that the house was now a crime scene that kept Sarah away.

'Any time really,' she said, tipping the dregs of her coffee into the sink, deciding instead to pour herself a very large glass of wine. 'They were here this morning,' she held the bottle until the glass was precariously full. Oonagh eyed the label and wondered if she was aware it cost over seventy quid a pop. 'They've got what they need.'

Oonagh felt a slight stirring of guilt, but knew the interview would be better if it was filmed in her own home. 'If you'd rather we didn't film there, then that's understandable, we could just…'

Again Sarah Nugent just shrugged, which Oonagh decided was a yes.

If this woman was aware of the rumours surrounding her husband, she was making a good job of hiding it. Despite her designer clothes and flash house, Harry Nugent's widow didn't look like a complete stranger to Glasgow's underworld. Or perhaps it was because of the expensive trappings that she set out to be a tough cookie. Whatever the reason, Oonagh was wary of asking too much at this stage. It wasn't yet lunchtime and Sarah had already made short work of a bottle of wine. It was unlikely she'd get much more sense out of her today. But more than that, Oonagh got the distinct impression that Sarah Nugent wasn't a woman she should cross.

8

The hotel nestled on the banks of Loch Lomond, less than twenty miles outside Glasgow. Oonagh was glad of the excuse to leave the city today. Normally she loved the drive out to this part of the country, the clear air, the loch, Ben Lomond rising from the shoreline, but today was different. She parked up and made her way through to the residents' lounge, waiting just a few moments before being shown to a table by the window.

Oonagh stood when he came into the lounge. He'd long since retired, but still drew a few glances, even somewhere like this. He'd been a hero in his day. The roll of his shoulder gave away the slight limp on his left leg and he placed his hands on the back of each chair he passed, apparently too proud to use a stick. Oonagh clasped his outstretched hand as he neared her table, the perfect excuse to help him ease down onto the soft leather chair.

Jack Nesbit had been a legend in Scottish football, both on and off the pitch. He was old school, from a time when managers commanded respect and his players all called him

Mr Nesbit. Never Jack. Always Mr Nesbit. She'd thought it would take weeks to set up this interview, so hadn't thought twice about cancelling her scheduled meeting with Alan, and had jumped at the chance to come here instead when Mr Nesbit had agreed to meet her this afternoon. She wasn't sure how much she'd get out of him, but so far he was the only one willing to talk to her about Harry Nugent.

'Mr Nesbit.'

'Call me Jack.' He smiled, looked pleased that she'd given him his place. It was rumoured that he was losing it. Too many years heading a ball heavy enough to shatter a human skull left its mark.

'D'you still play?' Oonagh knew the answer to that question, but asked out of politeness. No one wanted to be thought of as past it.

'Oh, yes.' He nodded, then leaned forward to make sure she heard. 'They had to put weights on my Zimmer to give the younger boys a chance to keep up.' Despite his years, Jack Nesbit had lost none of his old charm.

The waiter took their order: Macallan Gold for him, pot of tea for Oonagh. Scotland's new drink drive laws were a nightmare; it was getting so that she was scared to swallow a drop of mouthwash some mornings in case it tipped her over the limit, and she'd already downed so much coffee she was sure her nerves could be heard jangling from the other side of Ben Lomond.

'Bet you've seen some changes in the game in your day.'

There was just a hint of a smile. 'More than you'll ever know, hen.' He took a sip of his Scotch. 'Silly money now. Wasn't like that back in the day. And back in the day the manager was the boss.' He jerked his thumb towards his chest, then grabbed the arm of his chair for support as he leaned forward to place his glass back on the table. 'Not like now, when the players are treated like superstars and the dressing room smells like a tart's boudoir.'

Oonagh stifled a grin. Jack Nesbit really was from a different era right enough. They both knew why she was there, but she still took her time, leading in gently with the question. 'Harry Nugent?' She paused but got little response. 'His death must have been a huge shock to you?'

He shrugged, looking at the bottom of his glass. 'When you get to my age, hen, not much shocks you.'

The window gave a spectacular view over the loch. It wasn't yet three o'clock but the low winter sun was already threatening to dip into the water.

'Stunning, isn't it?' He meant it more as a rhetorical question but Oonagh nodded, Loch Lomond had always been one of her favourite parts of the world. 'I've been luckier than most,' he added. 'This…' He stretched his hand across the view. 'Never thought I could have all this.'

Jack Nesbit had grown up in a mining town in Lanark; this was a world away from his past. She tried to steer the conversation back to Nugent's death. 'Mr Nesbit.' She checked herself. 'Jack.' This was going to be awkward. No one liked to speak ill of the dead, but there had been rumour of a fallout between Nesbit and Nugent. It had been no secret that there was no love lost between the pair. Jack was old school. Nothing flash about him. He'd earned his stripes at a time when footballers earned a living wage, a time when clubs were made up from local lads who either cycled to and from the ground or caught the bus, even for important matches. The big money, the silly money that had come with TV rights and sponsorship, that sort of money had come later, much later.

'How well did you know Harry Nugent?'

'Honestly?' He stretched out his legs, crossing them at the ankles. 'Enough to know I didn't like him.'

This was what she came here for, but Oonagh had to be careful how she handled this. 'Not a fan then?'

'I'll not be rushing to pay my respects, that's for sure.' He finished his drink, eyeing the waiter for a fresh one.

Oonagh stirred her tea, taking a sip to give him enough breathing space to elaborate.

'Did he suffer aye?' He asked, waiting for Oonagh's response before placing his empty glass on the table. 'Good.' A bead of sweat had formed on his top lip.

'This wasn't just a business fall out was it, Jack?'

'Bastard. I hope he rots in hell.'

She rubbed her hand along the back of her neck, conscious of the muscle twitching in her jaw. 'What did he do, Jack? What did he do that was so bad?' She was careful not to put words in his mouth. So far the rumours were just that. Rumours.

The waiter stopped at the table, refreshing his drink, Jack nodded his thanks. 'It wasn't just me. The rest of them knew… they all knew.' His voice rose just enough to cause the waiter to turn back round, but none of the other customers seemed to notice so he let it go, Oonagh gave him a weak smile, letting him know they were good.

'Jack.' She saw the raw emotion in his eyes. It might have been regret; it might have been too many years having a ball batter against his head. Perhaps he truly was losing it, but she couldn't take the risk. She reached over and placed her hand on his. 'What did he do, Jack? And who are "they"? Who're you talking about?'

'I picked him up.' He kept his voice low this time, whether by accident or design Oonagh couldn't tell. 'By the shirt on his back. I grabbed him and dragged him out of that boardroom.' Jack looked exhausted just by the memory, and wiped away the trace of spittle that had gathered on his lips. 'I kicked his arse down those stairs. Bastard.'

Oonagh was trying to piece this together; she had no idea if this was the rambling of a confused old man or a real memory. 'Who are you talking about, Jack?'

'That bastard, Nugent.' Jack Nesbit might have been a frail pensioner, but at that moment he looked ruthless. Oonagh was shocked to see the sheer venom in his eyes. 'The whole lot of them,' he said, 'rotten to the core.'

She breathed deeply. She wasn't going to like whatever was coming next, she guessed. 'Please, Jack. Just tell me what he did.'

He sat back in his chair; suddenly the fight had gone out of him. Replaced instead with sadness. 'He was touching those boys.' He turned his head slightly, looked to the side. Jack Nesbit was from a generation that didn't discuss such things. Certainly not in front of a woman. To him Oonagh looked like a wee lassie. She was younger than his daughter, he'd told her.

How many cover-ups? How many excuses? She wanted to shake him, ask why he hadn't gone to the police, reported Nugent for being a paedophile. For wasting the lives of countless young boys. Kids who'd only wanted to play football but probably had their lives ruined because of pigs like Harry Nugent. Instead she took a deep breath, tried not to blame him, and asked, 'Did you tell the police, Jack?' knowing full well what the answer would be.

He dropped his head. 'No.' His voice was little more than a whisper. 'No, hen, I didn't, and that's something I might regret to my dying day.'

The silence filled the void between them. She had no answer to that. If he expected her to speak first he'd be in for a long bloody wait. Oonagh folded her arms – she was going nowhere – and waited for him to continue. If he came out with some shite like 'things were different in those days' she was sure she'd be able to kick him from where she was sitting.

'Och, we'd no proof. Can you imagine getting those laddies to stand in front of a copper and tell them that a queer had touched him up?' Jack Nesbit clearly hadn't got the email about the twenty-first century being well under way. 'Anyway. We dealt with it. In house, that's the way.'

She couldn't quite see what he was getting at, but the shame of her own attack seeped through her body. She hadn't gone to the police either. Twenty years might have passed but there were still nights when she woke in the wee small hours with the taste of that creep on her mouth. Moments when she could almost feel the weight of him pressing down on her again, forcing his hand between her thighs. She'd managed to fight him off, before he'd gone any further. Before any *real* damage was done – or so she'd thought at the time. Convincing herself that it wasn't *that* bad. But what Nesbit was talking about was different. These kids didn't have a choice.

'But you didn't deal with it. Men like him don't stop because they've had a beating. They bide their time, then start again. The abuse doesn't stop.' Her throat tightened, tears stinging the tip of her nose.

Jack nodded, his eyes clouded over as he glanced down, no longer able to look her in the eye.

'He deserved to be punished.' Oonagh struggled to keep her voice from cracking.

'And he was.' He drew his hand along his mouth. 'End of a rope was where he ended up, and that's where he belonged.'

'But those poor boys.'

'Yes, and think of all the other boys. The ones who lived and breathed football. The club would have been shut down, or worse.'

Oonagh couldn't quite see how a football club being shut down was worse than a boy being abused, but she was no fool. She knew that had this leaked at the time every fan of the club would be under attack from rival fans. Jack Nesbit seemed to read her thoughts. 'There'd have been tribal bloody warfare on the streets of Glasgow.' He clenched his fist against his mouth, as though he was stemming the bile threatening to rise.

'But the business?' Oonagh knew that Pitch Perfect was making a killing. Securing lucrative contracts from every club in Scotland. It had made Nugent a millionaire. 'If he was so despicable, how the hell did his business manage to thrive? He must have had support from teams across the board.'

Nesbit let out a sigh and rested his head back against the chair. 'Friends in high places. That was Nugent.' He turned again to look at the view. 'I made myself a lot of enemies in those days, you know. Cost me dear, too.'

This was news to Oonagh. Nesbit's reputation was legendary, but, now she thought about it, he'd seemed to drop out of the Scottish football scene with dramatic haste. 'How come?'

'Och, I'm not going to pretend. I was past my best. Forty was old in those days. Galloping towards fifty made me seem like an ancient artefact.' He took a handkerchief from his waistcoat pocket and wiped his eyes.

What he said made sense, but usually men in Nesbit's position continued in some form in the game. Either as talent scouts, assistant coaches, even popping up on the media as pundits. For some that was a more lucrative career than on the pitch. But Jack Nesbit had seemed to disappear.

'I was the spanner in the works and they didnae like that, hen. That pig was getting the best publicity for Scottish football since the Lisbon Lions. That summer camp thing of his.' He shook his head and smirked, as though he was the only one in on a very bad joke.

Oonagh had seen enough press clippings to know that Nugent's charitable works enabling young boys from deprived backgrounds to go away each year to football camps in Europe were a PR's wet dream. 'I suppose his good works fooled everyone.' Suddenly the penny dropped. 'The football camps,' she asked, 'the ones abroad?'

'He only ever took the older boys.' Jack Nesbit jabbed his finger in the air to make his point. 'Never the younger ones. They had to be at least fourteen,' he said, as though that had made all the difference.

There hadn't been much football played at the camps by the sounds of it. The boys had been there for one reason and one reason only. To feed Harry Nugent's depravity.

9

It wasn't yet ten o'clock and it was already shaping up to be a crap day. Davies checked his phone. Four missed calls from Oonagh and a text asking him to call. He didn't bother looking at his voicemail, he knew she'd have left as many messages. Rumours that Harry Nugent had been a pervert, a kiddie fiddler, a paedo, had been gaining ground. But now the flood gates were well and truly open.

He twisted the newspaper between his hands and tossed it to the other side of his desk. *'Hero Harry Ruined My Life. My hell at the hands of pervert Nugent.'* There had been lots that had sickened Davies in his career as a copper. Things that had turned his stomach. The stench of death that clung to his clothes, drunk drivers slaughtering an entire family rather than pay for a taxi, and old biddies dying alone from the cold because there was no one there to give a shit about them. But of all the things that he'd had to deal with, child abuse made him sick to the core. He was aware his fist had clenched into a ball as the tension enveloped his entire body.

Someone had come forward claiming he'd been abused by Nugent as a kid. But unfortunately they'd gone to the newspapers first. The double page spread in the tabloid had the typical silhouette of the victim. The guy had elected to remain anonymous and Davies couldn't blame him. These things were a can of worms. Coming forward to admit you have had a grudge against the deceased in an unsolved murder inquiry wouldn't have been the smartest move for anyone. The press would have a field day on this; his balls were well and truly on the line here. He reached down, absent mindedly checking between his legs.

He stretched and tried to ease the crick in his neck, but it was a waste of time. The headache that gripped the base of his skull was crawling down his spine, spreading out through his shoulder blades. The rough stubble against the palm of his hand reminded him he'd forgotten to shave. The same hand running through his hair reminded him he was getting old. Not that he was bald, not by a long chalk, but it definitely felt thinner than it was, unlike his waist. He stuffed his phone into his inside pocket. Oonagh wasn't one to hold grudges, but perhaps this time she'd make an exception.

McVeigh did that annoying thing of knocking lightly then coming in anyway before he'd had a chance to tell him to bugger off.

'Anything?'

McVeigh was chewing on his lip, hard enough to make it bleed if he didn't let up. Davies pointed to the only chair in the office not strewn with papers, folders and other detritus that seemed to accumulate out of nowhere. 'You got a hold of that fucking journalist yet?'

'He's across in Edinburgh, said he'd swing by tomorrow.'

'Swing by? Swing by? This is a fucking murder investigation. Not a vicar's tea party.' It was no use shouting at McVeigh, but right now he was the only one in his line of fire.

'You know how these things work sir.' McVeigh reached down and picked up the newspaper which had fallen on the floor, 'there's nothing in there we can hold him on. Said the interview with the alleged victim was done on the phone, he has no idea who the guy is,' He smoothed the crumpled pages across the desk with both hands, 'the whole thing's peppered with *alleged, claims, maintains*. He'll have had it legalled before going to print.'

Davies put his hand up, telling him he'd heard enough. 'I still want his arse in here. Little shit.'

The article only went to print this morning, and social media was already swarming with allegations of a cover-up. Three more victims had now made themselves known to the police. Davies suspected there would be more. Many more. Those ones that could provide an alibi and wouldn't be hauled up as a suspect. God knew they'd have had the motive. He couldn't rid himself of the gnawing feeling in his gut that he'd taken his eye off the ball somewhere along the line.

'Have you managed to track down any of the old witness statements?'

McVeigh shook his head. 'Nothing.'

'And every force has been checked?'

'Aye. There's nothing, boss.'

'Fuck.'

Those who had come forward claimed they'd notified the police about the abuse when it had happened. This was going back decades. Of the three, two had been in their late teens, one boy just thirteen, but despite this there was no record of any complaints being filed. McVeigh rested his elbows on his knees, ran his hands through his hair. 'It's not as though the complaints were all from the same station, boss. That way, then perhaps...' Davies nodded. That way it could be put down to sloppy station management, but the victims say they all spoke to different police officers at different times and yet still there wasn't a trace of any sort of complaint against Nugent. The guy hadn't even been slapped with a speeding ticket in the past twenty years.

'If they did make formal complaints against him...' McVeigh was choosing his words carefully '... it either means they weren't taken seriously and the complaint was binned...'

'Or?' Davies hardly needed him to elaborate.

'Or it *was* taken seriously and *deliberately* hidden.'

'Whatever this fucker was doing, he wasn't doing it alone.' Davies struggled to keep the emotion from his voice, wondering how much more shit he could take. Crime was changing and he wasn't sure he still wanted to be on the side of the good guys. The guys who had to play by the rules. 'Who else knows about this?' If there was a cover-up, he needed to play his cards very close to his chest.

'No one. I came to you first.' Despite his initial misgiving's, McVeigh was a good partner. Loyal too. 'We've still to take full witness statements, sir, but so far all three stories are consistent and the guys are all different ages, so from what they've told me, I reckon it would have happened over a fifteen year period.'

Despite Nugent's murder having the hallmarks of another gangland killing, this case wouldn't be swept under the carpet. A high profile figure like Nugent ensured this would be headline news every day and the emerging allegations of abuse against him just added to the shit pile.

It wasn't always easy to separate rumour from hard facts in historic abuse, but the evidence was now stacking up. Davies rounded the desk, patting his pocket to make sure he had his keys.

'Want me to drive, sir?' McVeigh was already one step ahead.

He nodded as he dropped the keys into his partner's hand, hoping to God that Mrs Nugent had stayed sober long enough this morning for them to get some sense out of her.

Sarah Nugent let her mobile ring four times, picking it up before it went onto voicemail. Number withheld but she guessed who it was even before she heard him speak. Gripping the phone in both hands she squeezed her eyes closed and swallowed hard, but nothing could stop that familiar shift in her gut.

'*I hope you're not ignoring me.*'

She slumped down on the hard kitchen chair, grabbing hold of the table, 'I'm warning you, stay away from me,' the slight tremor in her voice betrayed the strength of her words.

He laughed, '*or what?*'

The kitchen was suddenly stifling and her thin sweater clung to her back. 'I never want to see or hear from you again.'

'I'm afraid it's not that easy, Sarah.' He paused, just for a moment, '*We had a deal, remember.*'

She wanted to scream at him to stay away. Get out of her life forever, but the words choked white-hot in her throat.

'I'll be in touch.' Was all he said, then the line went dead.

He was watching the house. She was sure of it. Gill had only been gone five minutes. She hadn't wanted to leave her at all today, but Sarah had insisted she'd be fine on her own for half an hour. Three times now, and he only ever contacted her when she was alone. She pulled the blinds down in the kitchen, then double checked the lock on both back and front doors. This house would never feel like home again. She took the picture of Harry from the frame, looking closely, closer than she'd looked when he was alive. Seeing behind the smile, behind his eyes. They were as empty as he had been. The phone buzzed on the table, making her jump; a text from her sister reassuring her she'd be home in twenty minutes.

The bottle of single malt on the table was almost full. She unscrewed the cap, pouring half the contents down the sink. She needed a clear head today. Her scalp tightened at the sound of a car on the gravel driveway; it was too early for Gill. Racing through the hall, she grabbed at the door handle, shaking it, testing it again. It was still firmly locked. Her breath caught in her chest, her pulse throbbing in her throat as she peered out of the side window. Two cops got out of the car. The same two as before. She pressed her forehead against the wall, allowing herself a moment to get her breath back. The tightness in her chest eased as she made her way back to the kitchen. Hardly surprising they were back sniffing around. She knew how these things worked.

The knock was loud, that copper's knock. Sarah fished a small plastic bottle from her handbag and sprayed some whisky in her mouth, gagging slightly as it hit the back of her throat. They knocked again. She counted to ten, spritzing just a touch more alcohol before making her way to the front door. Playing the hopeless drunk was even more important to her survival now than when she was living with Harry.

10

Oonagh woke with that telltale thump on her temple. Her resolve to only drink at the weekends was continually wavering. Thursday was almost the weekend, and if she worked Saturday morning, which she sometimes did, then that meant Monday could be considered a day in lieu. Today was Wednesday and she'd been pissed last night. She couldn't remember how much she'd drunk but knew it had very probably been gin from the headache. Oonagh took a very small degree of pride in being able to distinguish between different types of hangovers. She wondered if that set her slightly apart from the other drunks in the village. Gave her a certain standing in the drunky community.

She swung her legs over the side of the bed, steadying herself on the bedside table, not quite trusting herself to stand up. The lamp was lying on the floor, the shade detached from the bulb. She must have knocked it off some time last night. She glanced briefly back to the bed – at least she was alone. The shame of her one and only one night stand came flooding back and she had no desire to ever repeat that night. She pulled on a pair of jammie trousers and a vest top before noticing her bra was still wrapped round her waist. She tugged at it several times, unable to loosen the catch, before deciding to shove the flipping thing down her legs and step out of it. The heating had been on since yesterday and the house was stifling, catching the back of her throat as she made her way down the stairs. Walking sideways, one step at a time, clinging to the banister as though it was her only friend, and, given that she had very little recollection of what happened last night, it probably was. She had a vague recollection of stopping off for one drink late yesterday afternoon after seeing Jack Nesbit.

Her purse was at the foot of the stairs, lying next to her bag on the floor, suggesting she'd at least had the sense to get a taxi home. Her kitchen was bright and clean and shiny. She so wished she felt that clean and sparkly, but she didn't. She felt dirty, grimy, contaminated. The misery of other people, the evil that people inflicted, had bored deep inside her and she was struggling more and more to shake it off. There had been a time when this had all been a big game. Journalists fighting to get their teeth into a juicy story, the more salacious the better, then punching the air when that really big one came good. The one that made people sit up and take notice. But now? Now it made her skin crawl, and she anaesthetised the horror by obliterating every vile image with booze.

What had started as a rumour was now starting to take shape and it looked very much as though Nugent had abused the boys in his care. But how he'd managed to do that for so long without one person stepping up to help those poor kids was a mystery. How the fuck had this man, this monster, been allowed to reign supreme over the misery of others for so long? Oonagh sincerely hoped they found his killer; she'd really like to shake the hand of the man who'd slaughtered that beast.

The coffee was hot and bitter and she was glad she'd splashed out on the state-of-the-art machine as it hissed a refill into the tiny cup that held barely a mouthful. She didn't know how the Italians coped with just one cup each morning and knew that the hangover along with what was now her third cup meant she'd be wired all day. But that was what she needed.

'Good morning, lady.'

The voice came from nowhere and she dropped her cup; it smashed against the granite sink as she spun round. 'Mum,' she said, clutching her chest, 'where the hell did you come from?'

Fran made her way across the kitchen and did that thing she did of wiping down an already immaculate surface and making as much noise as possible armed with nothing more than a J-cloth. She moved to the sink and picked out Oonagh's shattered coffee cup, putting the broken pieces in her hand.

'Mum, leave that, please.'

But she just ignored her, lips set in a tight line as she dropped the broken crockery into the bin, clearly hacked off at Oonagh's obvious hangover.

Oonagh looked towards the front door then back to her mum. 'Did you let yourself in?'

'Good job I did, you were in no state to answer the door.'

Oonagh lowered herself down onto a chair and let Fran's voice wash over her. She caught every third or fourth word and nodded whilst holding her head in her hands. She'd completely forgotten they were supposed to be meeting for coffee this morning.

'It's not the fact that I was waiting almost half of a full hour…' Oonagh wondered why Fran never just said half an hour like other people '… but I was out of my mind with worry when you never answered the phone.' She was now emptying the dishwasher with intent, holding up various items of crockery like weapons as Oonagh slumped further into her chair and pointed in the vague direction of whichever cupboard or shelf they'd be best placed.

'Can we not do this now, Mum?' What age would she need to be before she stopped getting a row from her mum for being drunk on a school night? Fran ignored her pleas and threw each item of cutlery into the drawer. Every clang making Oonagh's nerves jump to attention.

'I don't know what your father—' She stopped, then softened. 'Sweetheart, I don't like seeing you like this.'

Oonagh was tempted to tell her not to come round uninvited then, but she bit her tongue and instead just groaned further. 'Actually, Mum, I think I have a bug.' She rubbed her tummy, going for the sympathy vote.

'I wish you would meet someone. Someone nice,' Fran added, sensing that Oonagh was no stranger to total utter bastards.

'Mum, I don't need a man. I just need some coffee and a lie-down.' Oonagh had had enough. All she wanted now was for her mum to stop making noise, stop asking questions, stop judging her.

'Please, Mum.'

Fran reached out her hand; Oonagh could feel the warmth on her shoulder. 'Sweetheart, I'm not saying it's about time you got married, but...' her voice sounded heavy with regret '... you need someone to share your life with. This isn't good for you. Just...'

Oonagh reached up and patted her hand. Said nothing. It was enough. Fran leaned and kissed the back of her head, threading a strand of hair behind her ear the way she used to when Oonagh was a kid, then gave her shoulder a little squeeze before putting her coat on. She had the good grace to close the door quietly on the way out. Looking around, Oonagh knew most people would give their eye teeth to have her life. A good job, money in the bank, nice things. She rested her head on the table and cried.

The shower was hotter than was probably good for her in her state, but she clenched her toes, feeling the roughness of the mosaic floor underfoot and allowed the hot jets to hit her skin, bringing her slowly back to somewhere on the right side of normal.

The morning was bleeding into the afternoon by the time she got online to see what the latest about Nugent was. It wasn't a huge surprise to see someone had now come forward claiming he'd abused them as a young boy. Nesbit had refused to go on record, but he gave her enough to know this story wasn't going to go away.

She punched the number into her phone, and tried to shake any remaining sleep from her voice. 'Hey, Alec.'

He picked up after only two rings. 'At last. I was wondering how long it would take you to call me again.'

He didn't sound pissed off. Just matter-of-fact. He clearly knew exactly what it was about.

'There are claims, Alec, that abuse allegations against Nugent were never investigated.' She tried to keep any accusatory tone out of her voice. 'I know it was before your time, but still...' At the end of the day, Alec might have been a pal, but he was a copper first and she'd need to skirt round this one very carefully.

'We're looking into that, Oonagh.'

'So, was it an open secret right enough?' She busied around the kitchen, making another coffee to replace the one she'd dropped. 'Was Nugent abusing young boys?' The machine hissed in the background. 'Shit,' she added, giving nothing away about her meeting with Nesbit. 'I was so sure it was gangland.'

'Oonagh, I'm up to my eyes in it here... I can't...'

She knew better than to push him when he was like this and didn't argue when he made his excuses and hung up.

She scanned the tabloid story again; it had one person's name written all over it. Matt Bradley had worked beside her years ago in local radio; they'd started off as cub reporters together. Even without the byline, Oonagh could recognise his handiwork. She decided to chance her luck.

'Hey, Matt...'

'Don't even ask me to name names...' Matt thought he was one step ahead of her.

'Oh, c'mon, I'm only asking you for a heads up here.' She could hear him rolling his eyes down the phone. 'Is it genuine or are you hoping to smoke out any other victims?' Oonagh didn't quite ask him if the whole story was made up, but she was no fool. There were enough rumours flying around now to roast Harry Nugent, but nothing that anyone could actually prove. Rumours just weren't enough in hard news and police investigations. Matt had always been a bit of a maverick and operated on the shady side of legal. He'd been threatened by so many Glasgow gangsters over the years it was a miracle he still had ten fingers and ten toes intact, although in fairness she'd never seen him wearing a pair of sandals. Despite Matt's apparent fearless reputation, he was no Bernstein or Woodward. He had a contact list as long as his arm, so for every gangster who'd threatened him, there were two more heavies who'd be happy to throw their weight around if he needed some protection.

Looking at this story, Oonagh had a good idea what he was doing. 'So, did you really get that interview?'

'You saying I made this up?' He was smiling, she could hear it.

'Did you?' She knew how he operated. The dead can't be defamed, the cops couldn't force him to hand over any contacts if he claimed the interview was done anonymously, and meanwhile it could smoke out other victims, men who may come forward under the protection of safety in numbers.

'Listen, Oonagh, we all know that creep was up to his neck in something.' In effect Matt had created this story. But it didn't mean it didn't have a grain of truth.

'I'm surprised that with your contacts, Matt, you've not come up with a gangland connection.' She heard him take a sharp breath, but it was just a bit too theatrical for her liking. 'So nothing to suggest he'd stepped on the toes of one too many hardmen?'

'You should know more than me – you've already spoken to the merry widow.'

'Yeah, well, I'm clearly losing my touch because I didn't have a clue.' She cradled the phone between her ear and her shoulder, pouring more coffee. She needed to sober up quick-style. 'D'you honestly believe he was abusing those boys?'

'Absolutely. But proving it's another matter. That guy's slippier than Teflon.'

That was all Oonagh needed to know what Matt's game was. She pondered whether a career on the red tops would be an easier bet than the broadcasting editorial guidelines she was currently stymied by.

Nugent's away games were fast becoming public knowledge. Football clubs and celebrities across the country were distancing themselves from him, and the pressure would now be on the police to investigate any claims made by victims. As far as she knew, none of the victims had actually been brave enough to come forward in person yet. It didn't do well to put yourself in the frame of a murder investigation, but as soon as an arrest was made and the killer of Harry Nugent made public, *then* there would be a queue forming. She was sure of that.

11

Oonagh flicked off the edited interview of Sarah Nugent. There was no doubt about it, that woman knew how to work a room, and the camera loved her. The feature had gone out last night as part of the evening news programme. It was hardly the thirty minute programme Oonagh had pitched for, but given today's wee nugget in the press about Nugent it was just as well.

On screen, Sarah had struck just the right balance of grieving widow mixed with victim. In the last shot she'd looked straight into the camera and appealed for anyone with any information about the death of her husband to come forward. As agreed, Oonagh had thrown in a few pictures of Sarah in her glory days, which had seemed to give her an added incentive to open up more. The fact that Harry had been married to a former model, albeit a lesser known former model, gave some credence to his public image of a normal guy with no interest in young boys. And perhaps for that reason Sarah had wanted to big up her part as a model, skimming over her nursing career.

But now Nugent's reputation was in tatters. Social media was in overdrive with everyone throwing their tuppence worth in, and Sarah Nugent was well and truly in the firing line. The main stream media was still playing it a tad too softly-softly for her liking. Journalists could be a petty lot. Not wanting to admit that Matt Bradley had broken the story. So for now it was all very much '*police are refusing to comment on rumours*.' Oonagh looked again at the screen, she'd not quite so much stepped on the toes of the crime correspondent as danced all over his feet by getting the interview on what was effectively his story. He'd initially gone bleating to Alan, but Oonagh had just claimed that Mrs Nugent had made the first move and refused to talk to anyone else. He was livid and had stormed out of the newsroom muttering something about Oonagh being a lightweight. But his tail was now well and truly between his legs. Oonagh didn't really care; her skin had grown thick and somewhat impenetrable over the years. Alan didn't seem to care much either. As long as the interview was in the can, he'd let them slug it out among themselves. The police were no closer to an arrest, and had no real leads to go on, as far as she could tell. For Oonagh that was the best news ever. As soon as an arrest was made and the case became live, they'd stop any future reporting or speculation until the case went to court. But until then, Oonagh was free to investigate how she liked. Within reason.

Despite growing speculation that Nugent was in fact an abusive psychopath, she had nothing more concrete than that to go on. But somewhere along the way he'd crossed a line, and his luck had run out.

Her phone buzzed in her bag. She looked down; it was her mum. She was going to ignore it, but a pang of guilt got the better of her; she owed her an apology for yesterday. It stopped ringing just as she stretched down to get it. Within seconds a text pinged through. How the hell did her mum do that? Manage to type so quickly? She glanced at the screen.

> Hi darling, just seeing what you're up to. Do you fancy coming for dinner one night this week? Loads to catch up on. I've got some news. Mrs Reilly died. GBH. That's not my news. Well it is news, but that's not what I want to tell you. Let me know when you're free darling. And let me know if you can come along to Mrs Reilly's funeral. It's on Friday. She was a poor old soul at the end. LMAO.

As ever, Fran's text was long enough to be entered for the Booker Prize. It took Oonagh a few seconds to realise that poor Mrs Reilly didn't die from grievous bodily harm, or that her mum wasn't laughing her arse off at the thought of her final send off. It didn't matter how many times Oonagh explained, Fran didn't quite get why she shouldn't abbreviate *God Bless Her* or *Love Mum And Owen*. Oonagh didn't have time for this right now, but replied with a single kiss, otherwise Fran would continue texting – each one longer than the last – until she could be sure that her daughter wasn't lying dead in a ditch.

A very slight feeling of unease niggled at the back of Oonagh's mind. She had too much work to do right now and tried to push the thought out. But it kept coming back bigger and stronger than ever. Her mum's news. It could only mean one thing. She and Owen were getting married. Oonagh rested her forehead in her hand and slumped down in the chair. Memories of how she'd behaved when she'd first met Owen burned crimson through her body. It wasn't that she didn't like the guy. And it wasn't as though she didn't want her mum to be happy. None of that. Turned out he was a decent bloke and she'd actually quite warmed to him now. It was just that she missed her dad so much that seeing her mum with another man was sore.

It was gone nine. Once again, she hadn't intended to stay so late. She printed off a load of research notes and threw them, along with her handbag, into an archive box, deciding to call it a day. It had been dark for hours and there was no one left in this part of the building. Shivering, she made her way to the corridor which led to the stairwell and wished to god they'd stretch to a decent heating system as she flicked the light off on her way out.

The sound from the room was muffled. The door was closed and the dim light escaping from underneath it seemed to be coming from a computer screen. Whoever was in that office was clearly having more fun than she'd had in a long time. Oonagh carried the box in both hands, pushing open the double doors with her back. Again, it was faint, but a very slight squeal pierced through the sound, and it triggered that sickening feeling in the pit of her stomach. She might be wrong but couldn't take the risk. The carpet tiles swallowed the noise of her footsteps as she placed her box down on the nearest desk, and, easing the handle gently, Oonagh opened the door as quietly as she could.

Sophie was half perched, half pressed against the desk, her hands steadying her as she dropped her head to one side. Ross had his back to her, but Oonagh didn't have to see his face to know it was him. Oonagh had had enough run-ins with the fat bastard in the past. He leaned over Sophie, his thighs pinning both her legs in place, his arms at either side. Even in the poor light Oonagh could see Sophie looked scared and her chin gave little involuntary spasms as she tried to fake a smile.

'Let her go, you fucking monster.' Oonagh wasn't sure if she meant to grab Ross by the hair, or if it was the first thing that came to hand, but once there it felt good between her fingers and she gave it a twist before yanking as hard as she could, pulling him off Sophie.

The young girl darted from the desk and stood at the open door. 'I'm sorry, I'm sorry.' She reached a hand out, looked panicked as Oonagh let go of Ross's hair.

'You've nothing to be sorry for, Sophie, you've done nothing wrong.' Oonagh put a protective arm around her, ignoring Ross cursing in the background.

'And neither have I.' Ross just wasn't getting it and refused to give up. 'You're a fucking maniac, O'Neil,' he said, rubbing his head.

'Sophie, sit outside for a few moments, sweetheart, leave the door open and please make sure you can see me at all times.' Sophie did as Oonagh asked, and purposely avoided Ross's eye as his rant continued.

'She's nothing but a jealous old bag,' he shouted through the open door, before turning back to Oonagh. 'You're a has-been, O'Neil, a jealous, pathetic has-been.'

Oonagh ignored him momentarily as she scrolled through the staff contacts list on the desk-top monitor. Picking up the phone on his desk, she tucked the receiver between her chin and her shoulder and spoke to Ross almost as an afterthought. 'Being part of your sad little wank-fantasy wasn't really high up on my agenda.' She glanced at Sophie and gave her a reassuring nod. The poor girl looked petrified as the exchange escalated.

'You gonna call the police? Go on, make an arse of yourself, why don't you? Think they'll come running because I was chatting to a colleague after hours?' Ross jabbed his thumb vaguely in the direction of Sophie, then gave that little snigger that brought out the bad girl in Oonagh and made her want to smash his face in.

'No, Ross,' she punched the numbers into the keypad, 'I'm not phoning the police.' Even Oonagh knew that would be pointless – she'd been in this game long enough. 'I'm calling your wife, you worthless piece of shit.'

'You fucking dare.' He lunged towards her but she held her ground and squared up to him but her right leg trembled and she was secretly grateful for the desk between them.

'Quit while you're ahead, Ross.' She brandished the receiver in front of his face. 'Don't take another inch towards me. I'm not some twenty-three year old trainee you can bully.' Whatever look was in her eye, it did the trick. He stopped dead in his tracks. Changed tack.

'Listen, come on, it was a misunderstanding.' He turned in Sophie's direction, pleaded slightly. 'Sophie, tell her.'

Oonagh keyed in the last number and waited for someone to answer. 'Hi, Jennifer. It's Oonagh O'Neil at the office here.' A beat while the other woman spoke. 'No, no, nothing's wrong. Ross asked me to give you a call. His mobile's out of battery and he needs a lift home.' Again another pause. 'No, some little shit's trashed his car. Slashed the tyres and keyed the doors.' Ross was trying to take this in. 'I know, terrible, isn't it...? I'll tell him to get a taxi, then. Hope to see you soon. Lovely... yip, bye.' She dropped the receiver back on its cradle.

'Jennifer's put the baby to bed, so you'll need to get a taxi.'

'What the fuck are you playing at?'

Oonagh came round from behind the desk. 'Listen to me, Ross. If it weren't for the fact that I don't want to upset Jennifer, you'd be in the brown smelly stuff by now. If I even hear a whiff of you throwing your fat gut around and intimidating female colleagues who're trying to do their job, I'll have your balls on a plate.'

'I never touched her!'

She walked out of the office and to Sophie, whose mouth was hanging open. 'You OK?'

Sophie nodded, still saying nothing. Ross was hovering in the doorway.

'Look, I'm not the bad guy here. I misread the signs.'

'Signs?' Oonagh swung round to face him. 'What signs?' This guy just didn't know when to give up.

He looked genuinely confused, took on the role of the injured party. 'She was always flirting with me, making me tea and stuff.'

'Will you just give it up?' Ross's wounded expression was getting on her tits. 'She was nice to you because she's a nice person. She made you tea because you're her boss, and she laughed at your pathetic jokes because she was too embarrassed to do anything else.'

Oonagh put out her hand and pulled Sophie up to her feet. 'You can take this further, you know. I can still call the police. You don't need to accept this.' To her shame, Oonagh hoped Sophie would indeed accept this particular form of rough justice. She knew she'd be slaughtered if she spoke out. They'd hang her out to dry; blacklisted from every media outlet in Scotland. Branded a troublemaker who couldn't have a laugh with the boys. She'd been there herself. Knew the score. And despite all the press coverage, Oonagh knew the *Me Too* movement hadn't quite made it far enough down the food chain to include trainees in a Glasgow newsroom. It still had a long way to go.

Sophie forced a smile that didn't quite reach her eyes. 'No, I'm fine, honestly.'

Oonagh draped her arm around her shoulder and gave her a little hug. 'D'you know how to let tyres down on a car?' Sophie shook her head. 'What the hell do they teach you at journalist college nowadays?' She laughed and Oonagh was glad to see the colour come back to her cheeks.

'Hey!' Ross shouted from the office, 'You're not really going to trash my car?'

'Just let the tyres down, and maybe a wee scratch – need to make it look authentic.' Oonagh picked up her box from the desk and Sophie held open the swing doors. She turned to Ross before they left. 'Switch off the lights on your way out, eh, love.'

*

Oonagh got the drinks in, embarrassed to see the gratitude in Sophie's eyes as she placed them on the table. She could almost have written the script to what was coming next. 'Thanks, but you know...' Sophie hesitated slightly; Oonagh gave her space to finish '... it really wasn't *that* bad.'

'No, Sophie, but it really wasn't that good either, was it?' Oonagh had done the same herself. Countless times. Brushed off misogynistic, sexual pressure as not being *that bad*. 'The thing is, where do we draw the line?' She meant it as a statement, wasn't really expecting an answer.

'But he didn't actually... I mean, I feel terrible.' Poor Sophie, feeling bad, feeling guilty, feeling like shit.

'Trouble is, Sophe, guys like him never see themselves as sex pests. If they don't leave you battered and bruised and dumped in a back court somewhere, then they've done nothing wrong.'

Sophie relaxed slightly, gave a wee nod to let Oonagh know she agreed with her, then sipped her drink. 'Thanks again.'

'It's a tough world, Sophie, and you need to choose your battles.' Oonagh wished someone had told her that sooner. She felt as though she'd been fighting with someone or other her whole life.

'What does that mean?'

Oonagh suddenly realised that Sophie looked upon her as the sensible older woman. 'I don't exactly know, if truth be told. I think it means, decide which fights you want to take on. Or maybe only take on the ones you know you'll win.'

'Is that what you do?'

'I will from now on!'

'D'you think Ross'll be cross when he sees his car?'

'Maybe I shouldn't have kicked the back door. Nearly broke my heel.' They both burst out laughing. Oonagh thought for a moment. 'Listen, Sophe, I'll have a word with Alan about this. Ross needs to be—

'No.' Sophie reached out and grabbed her wrist. 'Please don't. Don't tell anyone.'

The thought of that little shit getting off with little more than a broken wing mirror was sticking in her throat. But it was Sophie's call. 'OK, but you need to be really strong the next time you see Ross. It'll be hard, but hold your head high and be the consummate professional.'

Sophie was nodding furiously, hanging on Oonagh's every word. She had no idea Oonagh was winging it, as she did most days.

12

'Shit.' Oonagh threw her phone down on the bed. It wasn't a huge shock that Sarah Nugent was refusing to answer her calls. She decided to leave it for a day or two then turn up at her door. Despite the horror stories about Harry Nugent, less than a handful of men had come forward, none of whom were prepared to speak to the press. That much she'd managed to get out of Jim McVeigh. She could hardly blame them. Historical abuse was a flipping nightmare to prove, and sadly for men, the support just wasn't there. They were expected to '*man up*'. Oonagh guessed that many of his victims would never speak out. Burying the trauma deep inside, the shame of the abuse burning whilst pretending that life goes on as normal. There was no way of telling how many men were affected. Could be thousands, even tens of thousands, given the amount of boys Nugent had come into contact with over the years. Oonagh couldn't be certain, but guessed his wife had had her suspicions all along.

If she could find at least one man who would go on the record, she could use that as the core for her programme.

The support for men remained shockingly inadequate, she'd already intended to approach charities and government ministers for interviews. But she needed this one in the can first. The easiest place to start would probably be the summer camps. At least there would be a record of which boys attended. There was also enough press coverage that she might be able to recognise more than the handful that she'd seen earlier. There was nothing else for it other than to go down the list trying to find contact details for each one. Sophie could help, and the rest would be down to legwork and old fashioned door knocking – the type of thing she'd initially loved when she'd started out in journalism, but had quickly grown to hate when she'd realised how much she was intruding on people's grief, their lives, their privacy.

Oonagh considered the money she'd forked out for a decent voice coach and a presentation skills course all those years ago as a wise investment. Trainee journalists were being churned out of college at a rate of knots, and it was astonishing how little in-house training there still was in the Scottish media. She'd long recognised that to stand out from the crowd she'd need to hone her skills. That had helped her move up the ladder quicker than most – well, that and knowing how to exploit an opportunity. But her voice, which was now her trademark, and her ease in front of the camera had set her apart from the thousands of other hopeful young journalists battling to make it in the media. She'd taken out a loan and lived off her credit cards and overdraft for the best part of a year just to pay it off, but it hadn't been long before she'd started to reap the benefits. Recently it had crossed her mind that a new set of tits and a course of Botox would probably be a better investment in the current climate.

She bit the bullet and rang the number of one of the most famous boys on the list. George Alexander had been one of the country's best loved players. In a game that cleaved through the heart of Glasgow with religious bigotry, Alexander was loved by both Catholics and Protestants alike. He'd been spotted and picked up by one of the big clubs down south before he could be affiliated to either one of his city's native teams, then capped for Scotland. So he was loved by everyone. Oonagh had met him once or twice through the years. Whoever was in charge of managing his PR did a blinding job. Polite and courteous, he lived up to his nickname Gentle George. Admittedly a cliché, but sports pundits weren't known for their prowess with words. One of the best things about working at the station was that Oonagh never had to do all the painstaking legwork of looking for contact details. Even the number of the most coveted politician, sports star or celebrity was in the system.

He answered his phone somewhat gingerly. He clearly didn't recognise the number, perhaps fearing it was yet another call trying to help him after his recent accident that wasn't his fault, or to claim back all that PPI that he'd forked out for over the years. She'd met him a few times before, but they weren't exactly on best mate territory yet. He recognised her name, and if he was suspicious of her call he didn't show it in his voice. Oonagh didn't come right out and say what she wanted to talk to him about – that wasn't the sort of thing one blurted out in an initial phone call. Gentle George Alexander was now a sports pundit on talk radio, so was well used to handling interviews. He'd kept himself fit too, unlike many former footballers who'd crashed and burned so quickly after their career on the pitch was over.

Oonagh kept the initial call very vague, said she was doing a piece on Glasgow boys made good and asked if he'd be up for an interview. He paused slightly before saying yes. There was no escaping the stories surrounding Nugent, but if he was suspicious about Oonagh's motives he didn't let on. He seemed less keen however, when she explained there wouldn't be a fee. Here was a man as sharp off the pitch as he had been on it. Newspapers could pay through the nose for a decent interview. An exposé with banner headlines. Television and radio just weren't like that. Contributor fees were usually pretty basic, and for someone already rolling in it amounted to no more than a decent coffee. But George Alexander was well versed in the workings of broadcasting, as Oonagh had gently reminded him, so he plumped for her buying him lunch instead.

A flurry of adrenalin stirred inside; he was unlikely to reveal all to her, but over lunch, with a few glasses of wine, people often said more than they'd intended to. Not that she'd use anything in an underhand way, but he might give her a pointer as to where she could dig a little deeper, as so far she felt she'd been banging her head off a brick wall with this one.

'OK, I'm free this Thursday and Friday, after that I'm booked solid for the next month.'

Oonagh didn't even bother to look at her diary, deciding in advance that whatever she had planned could be cancelled. 'Fabulous, shall we say, Friday?' It was usually easier to persuade someone to have a few extra drinks on a Friday afternoon. Thursdays could be tricky that way. 'You name the place – where are you based?'

'Formby.'

'Is that near Clydebank?' Oonagh's heart sank. She'd imagined him living somewhere a little more salubrious, and wondered if he wasn't quite as successful as he appeared.

'No, you're thinking of Faifley.' He sniggered, slightly more than was polite, then said, 'Formby… near Southport…' He was obviously waiting for some sort of recognition from Oonagh. 'Just outside Liverpool?'

Shit! 'Oh, *that* Formby?'

What a pain in the tonsils this was going to be. Liverpool was one of the hardest areas to get to from Glasgow. No direct flights and a train journey that could take up to four hours with two changes in between. Although the last time she'd been it had taken her almost seven hours as she'd drunk too much prosecco, fallen asleep and missed her connection at Wigan. She had no choice but to pitch up in Liverpool tomorrow, otherwise she'd need to get up too early on Friday morning.

Alexander was clearly doing all right for himself. House prices in Formby were not for the faint hearted and, although Oonagh was footing the bill, she'd asked him to book the table for lunch. Oonagh was no stranger to a decent eatery, but even she had to admit to being impressed. Understated elegance was how it would most probably be described; she tried not to look too gobsmacked as the waiter took her coat and led her to where he was sitting. Without looking at the menu she knew this was going to cost a bloody fortune.

Alexander stood up as she approached, clearly a regular here, she let him choose the wine, pandering to his male ego. Her heart sank just that little bit further when his eyes glanced to the bottom of the list and she wanted to wipe the smug smile off the waiter's face when he nodded in agreement. No house white for him. What with the rail fare, the overnight stay and now lunch at this poncey place, this meeting was costing more than her first car. She hoped her smile passed as genuine and started to actually enjoy his company. A bit. Until the conversation got round to Nugent and the summer camp. Then Gentle George Alexander froze slightly.

'You must be devastated at what's emerging. I mean you, like so many other boys in Scotland, have so much to thank Harry Nugent for,' Oonagh edged a stray crumb back into the corner of her mouth with her pinkie. 'He was such an inspiration, really, a hero, and now this.' Daft-manning it was second nature to Oonagh – she found it easy to get her opponents on the back foot before pushing them against the ropes. But Alexander was no adversary. He'd agreed to chat, that was all, but as soon as she'd seen him that day she'd realised this was not a man about to open up and pour his heart out to a stranger. Here was a man who had worked at his public image for the best part of five decades and wasn't going to show anyone his Achilles heel now. Certainly not a daft wee lassie like Oonagh O'Neil. He hadn't said as much, but Oonagh was used to the patronising way the old-school sport's pundits regarded her.

'Don't remember much about the man, to be honest.' George eased back, slinging one arm casually across the chair. His years off the pitch had done nothing to reduce his stature, his shirt straining very slightly across the muscles on his shoulders and biceps.

'He'd had a run-in with Jack Nesbit, that was all very strange...' Oonagh waited for a response, but she'd have a long bloody wait. He was polishing off a ninety quid bottle of wine and eyeing the waiter to bring them another one. She'd need to strike soon, before she ended up bankrupt here.

'George I need to ask...' He looked as though he knew what was coming. A tiny muscle twitched along his jaw. 'Did *you* ever have your suspicions about Nugent?'

'No.' His answer came back too fast and too certain. He gestured to the waiter just to pour the wine, dispensing with the pantomime of tasting it first.

'Look, George, I'll level with you, this is now way past the unsubstantiated rumour stage.' She told him about her meeting with Jack Nesbit. Let him know exactly what he'd said.

The waiter approached their table, but Alexander dismissed him with just a slight gesture of his hand. 'Listen to me. D'you think for one moment I was stupid enough to believe the pile of shite you were spouting?'

Oonagh took a sip of wine, her mouth suddenly dry.

'In the midst of all this, you think I believed you were actually doing a story on local boys made good?'

The colour burned through her cheeks, what the fuck had she been thinking? 'Why did you agree to meet me then?'

'I wanted to know what your game was.' The same slight hand gesture told the waiter it was now OK for him to pour the rest of the wine. 'And what I have to say is best said face to face.'

Oonagh hadn't assumed that this was ever going to be an easy conversation to have, but she'd reckoned that in a public place, with a man whose reputation was his lifeblood, she was on relatively safe ground. Just showed how wrong you could be.

George had bypassed the sweet trolley, but was by all accounts partial to a nice piece of Cheddar. 'Listen to me.' he sliced through the wedge on the board, not faltering for a moment. 'If I ever catch you saying that I was some sort of pathetic victim. If you even suggest that queer touched me up…' he popped the piece of cheese into his mouth, chewed twice and then licked his lips '… I'll have your fucking head on a plate.' He spoke very quietly, without a trace of aggression.

She tried to swallow but her throat had tightened, 'George, being a victim of abuse doesn't make you…'

'Drop it.'

She knew she was adding to his pain but couldn't back down now. 'Did you know he was abusing those boys?'

But he butted in before she could finish. 'Are you deaf?'

'I'm not saying he did it to you. I'm just asking, did you know?'

He leaned over, just inches from her face. 'Fucking drop it. And never contact me again.'

Gentle George Alexander was a big guy, but still surprisingly light on his feet. He swung out of his chair and left the table without giving her a second glance.

'Please just tell me,' her voice trailed after him. 'Tell me what you know.' But he was already out of the door, his silence telling her everything.

13

Oonagh pressed her finger on the bell for a second time, letting it ring for a little longer this time, refusing to give up. She rang a third time, then rapped her knuckles on the door. She'd been waiting so long she actually jumped when it eventually opened. The guy on the other side draped himself across the door and looked far from impressed.

'What?'

She recognised him from somewhere but couldn't quite place him. Looked as if he might have been a boxer in his day. There was something about that flat faced, broken nosed appearance that made all ex-fighters look the same to her. Oonagh peered over his shoulder. 'I'd like to see Sarah, please.' She stood on tiptoe to get a better view. 'Is she in?' The ground floor of the house was open plan. The vast hallway had a wall of glass that opened up to the back of the house where someone doing a remarkably good impression of Sarah Nugent was perched on the edge of a leather sofa.

'Who wants to know?'

Shit, she had no time for these stupid games. 'I think you know who I am.'

There was a genuine look of confusion on his face. 'Eh, I don't actually.'

Oonagh felt a slight blush rise through her cheeks and was glad of the cool November breeze as she told the guy her name. He closed the door and left her standing on the step before going off to check if the merry widow was at home to guests that day.

The police had allowed Sarah Nugent back into her home and Oonagh had to admit to being somewhat impressed that she'd actually chosen to spend a single moment in a house where her abiding memory must be that of her husband swinging from the balcony. Forensics had clearly done their job, and as Oonagh was ushered through to the living room there wasn't a trace of the horror that had taken place there. But she could feel the spectre of Harry Nugent as she passed through the hall. Imagined his dead body swinging from the banister above.

'Is that your…?' Oonagh was about to ask if the guy with the broken-looking face was her minder.

'My brother, yes.' The penny dropped. The guy was Chaz Walker, had been almost famous in his day. Handy with his fists, not a bad fighter, but not good enough to go further than local heats. 'But then I'm surprised you don't know that already, given how much you like to pry into other people's affairs.'

Oonagh was a bit surprised herself. She'd obviously taken her eye off the ball for a moment. Sarah remained standing, clutching a wine glass the size of a small fish bowl. She caught Oonagh glancing at the clock; it wasn't yet midday. 'Don't judge me,' she said, tipping back the last mouthful.

Oh, you've got me so wrong, thought Oonagh, dying for some herself, certain that the hair of the dog would settle her more than the two paracetamol she'd taken before leaving the house.

'How're you bearing up?'

'How am I bearing up?' Sarah flopped down onto a leather armchair. 'You've got a fucking nerve asking me that.'

A copy of a newspaper with Harry's face blazoned across the front page lay crumpled on the floor beside the settee. A somewhat blurred picture of Sarah, looking glamorous and giggly at an award ceremony, was inset beside it. The mud was well and truly being slung. *'Nugent ruined my life'* was the headline. It was now open season on Harry Nugent; he was trending on Twitter and an online support group had already been set up for his victims.

'Sarah...' Oonagh had to reason with her '... this had nothing to do with me.'

'You're the only journalist I spoke to.' Her voice was quiet now. The tears catching in the back of her throat.

'Is there anything, anything at all, in that paper that alludes to what we talked about?'

Sarah sniffed, wiping her cheek with her fingers. She shook her head but said nothing. Oonagh noticed she was no longer wearing her wedding ring.

'I didn't even steer the interview along these lines.'

'I told you that Harry and I lived separate lives. I told you that.'

Given that Oonagh and Sarah were no long best buddies, the fact that she had a prize fighter in the next room and the fact that she was pissed and looked as though she could pass out at any moment, Oonagh decided to try for some damage limitation.

'If that had been my angle…' she waited until Sarah looked at her '… I'd have put it in the interview. I'd have put that in the voice-over. Believe me, it's easily done.' And it was. Oonagh knew only too well how easy it could be to manipulate the media. 'But I didn't, Sarah. And I'm not here to take the moral high ground.'

There were a dozen questions she wanted to ask Sarah Nugent, but she waited a moment or two. Oonagh needed to tread carefully here. *Did you know your husband was abusing young boys?* couldn't be her opening gambit.

'Were you and Harry still sleeping together?'

'Just a fucking minute.' She slammed the glass down on the window sill. 'Don't think because I gave you that interview it gives you special privileges.' She was pointing now and Oonagh hoped she wasn't as handy with her fists as her brother had been.

'Don't come in here with your half-arsed theories and stupid fucking questions.'

'OK, I'm sorry. Please. Don't upset yourself. I didn't mean to offend you, Sarah, but we need to have some damage limitation here.' Oonagh had already decided on a follow up feature. It was now obvious that Harry Nugent was up to his neck in a lot more than some dodgy gambling racket and she needed this woman on board to uncover the truth. Sarah made to get out of the chair, but it was only when she staggered slightly that Oonagh realised just how drunk she was. That clearly hadn't been the first glass that morning.

'I'm sorry, Sarah, but you agreed to talk to me, so why not tell me the truth?'

'The truth, the truth? I don't know what the fucking truth is any more.' She was slurring her words and Oonagh was surprised at how easily she'd tipped over the edge. But then some drunks were like that. Seemingly able to handle their booze, then wham! Sarah wiped her nose with the back of her hand and staggered over to the window where the wine cooler sat on the floor.

Her brother poked his head through the door. 'You OK?'

She sniffed, nodded to him, then seemed to shoo him away with her hand. Telling him she was fine, telling him to beat it. He was clearly used to seeing his sister like this. In truth she looked far from fine. And this wasn't just the grieving widow routine. She knew a lot more than she was letting on. The cops would have asked her the usual questions; she hadn't been flagged up as a suspect. She had a cast-iron alibi and nothing to gain from Harry's death. Of course, there would be the insurance money. But she had more than a decent lifestyle and, as far as Oonagh could ascertain, Harry had pretty much left her to her own devices.

She waited until her heavyweight brother had closed the door then topped up her glass. 'You probably think I'm a total lush boozing at this time of the day?'

'No.' That bit was true. 'Not if it makes you feel better.' Oonagh felt a bit shitty, but the more inebriated Sarah became, the more likely she'd be to open up and spill the beans. 'After what you've been through.' That last sentence seemed to do the trick and she tipped the remainder of the bottle into her glass.

'The police were here earlier. Took Harry's laptop.'

'They likely to find anything on it, Sarah?'

'How the fuck should I know?' Whatever Sarah Nugent knew, she was keeping it to herself. 'Someone threw a brick through the window last night.'

Oonagh told her she was sorry and meant it. Admittedly, Oonagh hadn't exactly warmed to Sarah Nugent when they'd first met, but she didn't enjoy seeing her suffer either. The public would not take kindly to her. She waited until Sarah had fallen back into the soft leather armchair, legs crossed, sipping on her wine. 'Sarah.' Oonagh needed to think carefully on this one. 'Is there anything about Harry, anything about his past…?'

'What about his past?'

Oonagh wasn't sure just how drunk Sarah was, and how much she could get away with. 'Was there anything that would back up these rumours?'

'Like what?'

'I spoke to Jack Nesbit a few days ago.'

Sarah said nothing, which Oonagh took as the green light to keep going. 'He's also of the opinion that Harry was…' she looked at Sarah for a hint of recognition '… being, inappropriate, with some of the young boys he coached.' The high-gloss house seemed to lose its shine. 'Claimed that everyone on the board of the Boys' Club knew.'

Sarah Nugent looked at Oonagh, apparently waiting for her to continue. 'Sarah, you don't seem shocked, or even surprised, by that allegation?'

'Takes a lot to shock me, you know.'

'I spoke to George Alexander too.' Oonagh didn't elaborate; instead let Sarah make up her own mind about what he'd said. 'Is there *any* truth in this?'

Sarah didn't answer, preferring instead to get lost in the bottom of her glass. She dropped her head into her hands; everything was turning sour around her. Oonagh leaned forward, touched the arm of her chair. She looked up, her eyes still red. 'What is it you expect me to say?'

'Just tell me what you know.'

But the alcohol was taking its toll and Sarah Nugent slumped back in her chair. 'They knew,' her voice was slurred but Oonagh could still make it out. 'They all knew.' Barely a whisper now.

Oonagh's chest tightened. It was the same phrase Harry Nesbit had used. 'Who knew, Sarah? Who are *they?*'

Oonagh crouched down and held her by the shoulders. 'Who are you talking about, Sarah?' She shook her gently, tried to make her speak, but it was useless. Her slack mouth fell open as her chin dropped onto her chest and her words became lost in a drunken stupor.

14

Parking in the city was becoming a right pain the tonsils and Oonagh tugged at her bag, nestling the strap securely onto her shoulder as she walked through the park. It was easier to leave the car at home today. In truth she was glad of the fresh air and the chance to stretch her legs. Also it meant she could drop in somewhere on the way home and treat herself to some lunch with a glass of wine. She looked at her watch: barely 10 a.m. Had she been working from home she'd have already promised herself a wee drink as a pre-lunch treat in the next hour. This was the better option. She was sure of it.

Yesterday's meeting with Sarah Nugent hadn't gone as well she'd hoped. She'd been too drunk to give any more details about her dead husband's predilections, but Oonagh was convinced she knew more than she'd let on.

The sky threatened rain as she climbed the stone steps leading into the main entrance of the Mitchell Library. Oonagh never failed to get a feeling of comfort from its impressive interior; the domed building dominated Charing

Cross, and instilled in her a sense of civic pride. With over a million reference books, it was one of the largest libraries in Europe. That and the fact it had free WiFi, a café and newspaper archives going back over a century meant it was the perfect place to while away a morning.

The Glasgow Room housed most of the Scottish newspapers, thankfully now on microfiche. She wasn't sure what she was looking for, and guessed whatever Harry Nugent's secrets had been, it was highly unlikely that she'd find them splashed across the pages of a national newspaper. But still, she had to look and see what she could uncover.

She'd called ahead and they had the files waiting for her: everything featuring Harry Nugent. It was staggering how much was still not online. Sifting through them was no easy task. Her mind wandered constantly and she felt jittery. It was only when a guy on the seat next to her gave an exaggerated cough did she realise the loud rat-tat-tat noise was coming from her fingernails drumming on the desk. She mouthed an over-the-top *sorry* and went back to scanning the screen in front of her, desperately trying to concentrate in case she missed something.

There was loads that she already knew about – the big stories involving Harry and his good works both on and off the pitch – but there was nothing in print that indicated anything sinister. She scanned the records as far back as she could. There was very little from his early days, which was hardly surprising, given that he wasn't as famous then, and also the world wasn't as obsessed with celebrity.

His wedding had made page six of one of the local rags. A black and white snap of him and Sarah with a predictable caption underneath – *I'm just mad about Harry* – and a few lines about how the couple met during one of his many charity appearances at Breakmire Hospital. The hospital had been closed for the best part of two decades, but the press coverage of his appearances there was impressive. By the look of it Harry had used his contacts to ensure a steady stream of celebrities through the doors each week. Sporting heroes posing for pictures, singers, soap stars, you name it, they appeared to be a very welcome ray of sunshine in an otherwise dreary place. From what Oonagh could gather, everyone who'd turned up had brought the over-sized comedy cheque, a big bumper donation raised by Generous Harry, topped up or matched by whichever celeb was doing the rounds that week. Oonagh calculated that Nugent's business earnings and the fact the donations would have been tax deductible meant that the monies amounted to no more than pocket money to someone like him.

His holier-than-thou persona was getting harder to swallow, even without the rumours of him being a paedophile, abusing boys entrusted to his care. What Oonagh couldn't get her head around was why Nugent had singled out Breakmire as his charity of choice. He could have visited any number of hospitals in and around Glasgow, and higher profile ones at that. For someone as publicity hungry as him it didn't really make sense. The asylum had languished on the outskirts of the city and appeared to be no more than a holding ground for mental health patients. Oonagh knew he'd have got far more column inches had he attached himself to one of the children's hospitals, or a cancer care unit.

She cross-referenced her search to see if it threw up anything else about Breakmire, but there was nothing. A search of the trustees was less than impressive. Oonagh half expected to find at least a junior royal in there whose coat-tails Harry could have clung to, but they were the usual smattering of local council officials, a hospital consultant and an investment manager. It didn't do to speak ill of the dead, but it was obvious Nugent was getting more than the warm fuzzy feeling of being a do-gooder from his works there.

Oonagh sat back and rubbed her eyes with the heel of her hand. This was exhausting. She felt the tension crawl up her spine, settling in the base of her skull with the telltale ache that promised a cracker of a headache later. This was useless, like looking for a needle in a haystack. She'd only been there a couple of hours; it wasn't yet one o'clock, but she was tired, hungry and desperate for a drink. She was about to call it a day when she saw it. A tiny five line story, tucked away on page eight of *The Herald*.

> The body of a sixteen year old patient missing from Breakmire Asylum has been found in the hospital grounds. Hannah Gray was reported missing by staff on Thursday evening. A spokesperson from NHS Glasgow described the incident as regrettable, and said their thoughts are with Hannah's family.
>
> A report has been sent to the Procurator Fiscal, but there appear to be no suspicious circumstances surrounding Miss Gray's death.

Hannah Gray's death had been over twenty years ago, and, from what she could gather, just before Nugent's time at Breakmire, but for now it was the only thing Oonagh had to go on.

Getting a copy of Hannah Gray's death certificate had been easy enough. Anyone could walk into Martha Street Register Office and buy a birth, marriage or death certificate. It always astounded Oonagh that identify theft wasn't more common. The extract of the death certificate did indeed confirm that there was nothing suspicious about the cause of death: hypothermia. Oonagh's heart sank slightly. She wasn't sure what she'd expected, a scandal perhaps, something to build a story around? But this was hardly breaking news, and, from her experience over the years, sadly not that unusual with psychiatric patients.

The death had been registered by Hannah's dad, and the girl's birth certificate gave Oonagh enough information to at least make a stab of tracking down her parents, neither of whom were on the deceased register, so, unless they'd died in the last few weeks, Oonagh felt sure she'd be able to find at least one of them.

She stuffed the copies of the certificates into her bag, and knew she was clutching at straws. There was no real reason to speak to Hannah's parents, there was nothing to link her to Harry Nugent, but, as with most journalists, old habits died hard and Oonagh's mind was already racing ahead with possible theories. Hannah's death would not have shown Breakmire in a good light, contrary to the myth that there was no such thing as bad publicity. Perhaps a few celebrity visits with the incumbent charitable donations would have taken the heat off things for a while. Parachuting in Harry Nugent with his fake tan and even faker smile would have been a bit of decent PR for the hospital. Even had that been the case, it still didn't implicate Nugent in any way. But it was always something to squirrel away, another story for another day.

15

Tommy Gallagher 1983

The touchline was freezing, but he didn't care. Jumping from foot to foot, blowing on his hands, knowing he'd soon be on the pitch. It was just a training match. A few dads were on the sideline; his mum had wanted to come but he'd have got pelters from the other guys had his mammy turned up to watch him play. It was bad enough already. Harry's Boy, they called him. It was clear from the off he was Mr Nugent's favourite, or one of his favourites at least. His mum said he'd been picked out because he was the best, showed the most promise. He'd been mortified when his mum had come along to collect him that day, and insisted on hanging around to speak to Harry personally. She'd worn her best coat and those shoes that killed her feet. 'I want him to see you come from a good family, Tommy,' she'd said. What difference would that make? As long as he could kick a ball, that was all that mattered, and the one thing Tommy Gallagher had known what to do was kick a ball. The rest of his family joked he could take a header before he could walk.

He no longer felt the cold, instead his blood felt hot, his mouth dry; he was anxious to get on the pitch. Even on the touchline he hadn't taken his eye off the ball. That was for losers. That was what Harry had said. Most of the others had to call him Mr Nugent, but Tommy and a select few got to call him Harry. His heart swelled in his chest. Soon he'd be in the big league. Playing in the first division. Harry said his success was 'a given'. That was the way Harry spoke. Always knew his mind, spoke the truth with no time for losers.

He caught sight of Harry at the other side of the pitch, snapping his fingers high above his head, then pointing to the green telling Tommy to get on and play. This was his goal, this was his dream, this was his life.

'Well done, son.' Harry slapped him hard on the back as he waited in line for the showers.

'*Aye, well played, big man... Good on you, TG.*' The other guys elbowed him, nudged him, gave him high fives. It felt fantastic. He couldn't keep the grin from his face. But why shouldn't he smile? Why shouldn't he feel proud, happy?

'Can you just come here a wee...?' Harry looked worried as he ushered him to one side. 'You OK?'

'Aye, Harry, brand new.' His pulse throbbed in his neck. Something wasn't right.

'You got an injury you're not telling me about, son?' They were out of earshot now of the other boys, but he could still hear their banter echoing around the shower room.

Tommy shook his head; there was nothing wrong with him. He'd played like a demon, or so he thought. His gut shifted slightly and he licked his lips, his mouth suddenly parched.

'I don't want to worry you, son, but, the way you were landing on your left leg?'

This was news to him. He felt fine, but Harry's face told him otherwise. 'I'll level with you, Tommy, if it's a problem with your Achilles then…' Tommy's legs suddenly felt very weak and despite himself he could feel hot tears springing to his eyes. 'Hey.' Harry ruffled his hair. 'Let's not get ahead of ourselves here. It's probably nothing but…'

Tommy knew an Achilles injury spelled disaster for a player. This could kill his career before it got started. But he felt fine, not even a twinge. But Harry knew his stuff. Something must be wrong.

Harry dropped his voice slightly. 'We don't want to mention this to anyone else.' Tommy nodded, not trusting himself to speak. Whatever the problem was he just wanted it to go away. 'It's just that if the physio finds out, well, he'll want to tell your mum… She might not want you to play.' Harry didn't need to say anything else. But he did. 'We could be in big trouble if we let you play with such a serious problem. You could be out of the game for months.'

This wasn't happening. Tommy hugged his arms around his waist. Breathed slowly. This wasn't fair. He looked up at Harry.

'Listen, son, I'm no physio but I've seen this sort of thing before. It could be something simple like a thigh or groin problem.' He caught Tommy's look. 'Most knee and ankle problems come from the hip,' he explained.

'Can… can you fix it, Harry?'

'Let's just have a look and see what's wrong first, eh?' Harry knew what he was talking about; he was lucky to have him on his side. Tommy was led into Harry's office and the banter from the shower rooms became white noise before disappearing altogether.

16

Davies couldn't stomach any more and slammed the folder closed, pushing the pictures out of sight to the far end of his desk. He needed some air and struggled with the catch on the window, forcing it down with one hand as he slammed hard on the frame with the other. He'd reported it as faulty months ago, but as far as priorities went for Police Scotland this was far down the list of jobs marked urgent. Suddenly the window swung open and he heard the crack of glass as the aluminium pane banged against outside wall. That was all he fucking needed. He looked down at the car park two floors below, grateful to see that no one was lying flat out with a shard of glass piercing their skull. Despite the noise, the window had merely cracked and he eased it back slowly, locking it in place and deciding fresh air was an overhyped luxury he could do without.

'McVeigh,' where the hell was Jim when he needed him. 'McVeigh,' he yelled, louder now, leaning out of his office door, making sure his voice carried half way through the station.

'Sir?' He swung round to find McVeigh behind him. A mug of tea in each hand.

'In here now.' Davies took one of the mugs, making his way back behind his desk. 'What's the latest?' He nodded to the folder and struggled to keep the emotion from his voice. Desperately wishing he could un-see those pictures. 'How's Toria doing?' He added.

'Bearing up. She's a tough cookie, that one.' McVeigh tried to sound upbeat, positive, but failed miserably.

They'd seized as much as they could from Nugent's house once the allegations had come through. His widow had put up no resistance and had been glad to get it out of the house. It was Toria who'd found the images on his laptop. The ones that proved where his sexual preferences had lain.

'Get the tech guys onto it. See if we can trace the source. Did he share the images with anyone?' He caught the look on McVeigh's face. He knew they were already across this. He also knew what a shitty job it was trying to track down the source of some of these sites. 'Just see what they can do, eh?'

McVeigh nodded, 'I've passed everything on to the National Crime Agency, sir.' This might have been part of the investigation into Harry Nugent's murder, but the NCA handled the organised crime, including images of child sexual abuse. 'This is just the tip of the iceberg. They suspect up to ten thousand Scots use the internet to watch this type of stuff on a regular basis.'

'What the fuck is wrong with these people?' Davies was glad he only dealt with homicides, which to him was the lesser of the two evils.

'A lot of the stuff comes from Russia. It's a nightmare trying to track it down. Almost seven hundred people were charged last year in connection with viewing sexual images of children. It's big business, sir, and it's not going away.'

The sickness in his stomach was creeping up to his throat. 'Make sure you keep your eye on Toria, McVeigh. You two are pals. The help's there if she needs it. But for now, we need to find out just how far this fucker was operating.'

Crime was changing and Davies wasn't sure he still wanted to be on the side of the good guys. The guys who had to play by the rules. Sure, there had always been the sick and the twisted. Brady and Hindley, Fred and Rosemary, shit, some didn't even need their surnames. But with the Internet it was becoming easier for these sick bastards to find victims, easier for them to exchange images and easier for them to evade the law.

'Shit, McVeigh, there was time when Glasgow earned its reputation as *no mean* city. Yeah, it was a dark place, don't get me wrong. Gang warfare was rife and no hard-man was safe. But women and kids? Fuck's sake, they were left alone.'

Davies was aware McVeigh was looking at him. It was probably the most he'd spoken to his partner since they were thrown together.

'Boss, my dad grew up in the Gorbals. But he says you could leave your door open, kids were out till all hours, but you knew who to steer clear of and as long as you did you'd be fine.'

Davies nodded. 'You're making me feel old, McVeigh. You know Fred West got run out of town?'

McVeigh sat back, seemed to be enjoying the very slight relief the banter brought from the horror of Nugent. 'I'd heard that. Thought it might have been just folklore.'

'Absolutely not. West had an ice-cream run in the east end. Handy with his fists as long as it was a wife or kiddie at the other end of his knuckles.' It had been before Davies's time, but he knew the story well. 'Word got round that he'd been messing with a fourteen year old girl who served in his van. He was tipped the wink and fled before the local gangs arrived armed with cans of petrol, baseball bats and machetes. They'd planned to cut his head off.'

'Bloody hell. I never heard that.'

'It never made headline news as, well, no one knew who he was. He was just another creep.' West had scarpered, leaving his wife and child behind. 'Point is, McVeigh, this wasn't a city to harbour child abusers. Or at least it never used to.'

Davies got up and looked out of the cracked window. He got a decent view of the city from here, the jagged skyline a mess of modern abominations blotting out the grandeur of Victorian architecture. Somewhere out there was the killer of Harry Nugent. And also out there were men and boys who'd been abused by him. He knew who he wanted to track down first.

'You OK, boss? You look like shit.'

Davies let out a laugh, the first time he'd even come near to smiling since he'd seen Nugent hanging from his banister. 'Call it as you see it, Jim.' His partner meant no harm; it was obvious to anyone within spitting distance that Alec Davies was struggling with this case. Though not for the reasons some might think. There would be no happy ending here. No satisfaction at catching those responsible for these crimes. Davies and McVeigh both knew that there was every likelihood that this man had died at the hands of someone he had abused, a victim of a revenge attack and, try as he might, Davies couldn't actually put his hand up and say he wouldn't have done the same thing in their shoes.

'I think they're ready for us, boss.'

Davies ran his hand across his face; he'd left it too late to shave. 'Aye, OK.' He had little appetite for this. Fucking press conference. What was he supposed to say? The girl from Comms had briefed him, coached his response, his delivery. Told him how to answer those awkward questions that journalists had a habit of asking. Those questions that suggested Police Scotland was up to its eyes in the biggest fucking cover-up since Jack the Ripper.

He pushed his shoulders back and tugged at the lapels of his jacket as he made his way through the double doors to the briefing room. He recognised most of the faces, radio mics were already set up on the table, TV cameras pointing to the empty chair he would soon occupy, and the dying breed of print journalists poised, pens in hand. He didn't have to scan the room to find her. Oonagh O'Neil was sitting in the front row ready to take no prisoners.

17

Getting information on those who claimed to have been abused by Harry Nugent was no easy task. Alec imagined they were terrified it put them in the frame as a suspect, but this was no killer sitting in front of him. Then there would be the others who would no doubt follow. The nutters, the bampots, the attention seekers who hadn't even been in Glasgow during Nugent's reign. Those who fancied getting in on the act for a few moments of glory, or even a bit of compensation. And that wasn't counting the inevitable few who would wander through the door claiming they'd killed Nugent, either because they'd heard voices, or their dog had made them do it.

Three credible people had now come forward. Admittedly they had gone to the press first, and Alec had used the threat of a warrant to get the names from the tabloid journalist who ran the story. As it turned out, it wasn't needed. Joe McLeish had agreed to talk, and had arrived at the station bang on time. Normally with allegations of sexual abuse it was best practice to have a female officer present, but not this time. Joe McLeish had insisted that both officers were male.

An informal chat, they'd said, and Alec tried to keep his tone as light and as neutral as possible, but inside his gut was churning for this grown man sitting in his office. The press conference that morning had not been easy. Batting off questions about why allegations of sexual abuse had not been investigated by the then Strathclyde Police, then to go on to fudge round the issue of having no real leads in the investigation. But there was no doubt about it. Since the allegations of abuse, the heat from the public to find Nugent's killer had most certainly cooled off. This morning had been a tough one alright, but this was going to be tougher.

'Joe, I know this is hard, but can you just tell us in your own words what happened?' The basic details had been outlined in the newspaper article. Joe, or Boy X, claimed that Nugent would take him back to his flat in the south side of Glasgow and carry out the abuse. He'd been fourteen at the time, and had shown promise on and off the pitch. It had all happened over twenty years ago. Not the best circumstances to gather evidence in an historical abuse case linked to a murder investigation, but for now it was all they had to go on.

'He used to make me ask him for money.'

'What?'

'After I'd, like, after I'd touched him, or during… when it was happening. He made me ask him for money.'

Davies struggled to get his head round this one.

'Then he'd throw me a fiver, sometimes a tenner. Scrunched it up, threw it on the floor and made me pick it up.' Joe's voice cracked at the memory. Alec could only imagine it salved some sort of sick conscience and appealed to his twisted logic if he thought of his victims as rent boys. As though that made it OK.

'Was there ever anyone else there at the time, Joe?'

Joe worried his hands together then leaned his chin on the steeple of his fingers. 'Sometimes, but they never saw.' He spoke softly, taking deep breaths between each sentence. Only the very slight crack of emotion in his voice. 'I have a family. I don't want my kids…'

Davies leaned over and placed his hand on the man's shoulder. 'Joe, I promise, you'll be afforded the very same rights and considerations as every other victim of sexual abuse.' Shit, even as he said it he knew what a raw deal most women got. Being quizzed about their sexual history, what they were wearing, everything that pointed the finger to their door. 'You'll have the right to anonymity and, because of the nature of this case, it's unlikely to end up in court.' What Alec needed was to get a clearer of picture of what Nugent was really like. This holier-than-thou paragon of virtue, who apparently didn't have an enemy in the world until someone decided to mete out some rough justice and hang him.

'Who else was there when it happened? Were there any other adults involved?'

'Once a couple of the other lads were there.' Joe looked up, but Alec didn't interrupt with the obvious question, just let him continue. 'We were watching telly. They were lying on the floor – there were cartoons on, I think. I was sitting beside Harry on the settee and he held my wrist and forced me to touch him.' He pointed to his groin, to make sure Alec understood. 'Then he touched me.'

'And the others saw nothing.'

Joe shook his head and swallowed hard, rubbing the palm of his hand across his mouth.

'Take your time, Joe.' Alec gave him a tight smile. 'You're doing well.'

There wasn't much that sickened Alec Davies, but child abuse was one of the few crimes where he would gladly throw the guilty party to a baying mob with pitchforks.

'Can you give me the names of the other boys?'

Joe shook his head. 'I can't remember. It was all a long time ago.' That came as no surprise; Alec bet Joe knew exactly who these guys were. He'd remembered where they were sitting, what they were wearing, what they'd said at the time. But he'd refused to go as far as naming them. Alec would need to bide his time on this one.

'I hate to ask you this, Joe, but I have to.' He paused briefly. 'What were you wearing at the time?'

'Joggy bottoms. He'd always insisted that the boys wore joggies on and off the pitch.'

'It's just that...' Alec had felt the need to explain, but Joe McLeish held his hand out, telling him he understood.

'Listen, it's fine, honestly. It was only years later I realised that was to save him fumbling about with zips and tight jeans and stuff.'

The memory looked as though it was about to overwhelm him. 'I don't know why I didn't kick him or punch him or tell him to fuck off.' There were tears in his eyes now.

Alec stood up. 'Joe, please.' He'd seen it all too often. Victims blaming themselves. This wasn't what he'd joined the police for. 'You were a child. You looked up to Nugent, you trusted him and he abused you.' Joe had started to weep and Alec didn't have a clue what to do. 'These guys groom kids from the word go. They use and abuse their power to get what they want.'

Joe McLeish pressed his fingers tight against his eyes, then blew into his hankie. He'd never told anyone of the abuse, kept it hidden for all these years.

'Why've you come forward now, Joe?'

He licked his bottom lip, leaned his forehead on the back of his hand, his fist clenched. 'Because I can't fucking stand the way he was being hailed as a hero. That man ruined my fucking life. D'you know there's not a day, hardly an hour, that I don't think about him.'

Alec felt weary. More weary than he'd done for a long time. He wanted to tell this man in front of him how brave he'd been to come forward. That he knew how hard this all was, that he was doing the right thing. But he knew it would have sounded trite and condescending.

'I was a good footballer, you know. Might even have made the premier, but that last day when… I just ran home and I've never kicked a ball since.' Alec could hardly bear to look into Joe McLeish's eyes, they were so full of pain. 'I can't even have a kick-about with my kids. Can't bear it.'

For some poor buggers the pain never seemed to go away. He tried again. 'Can you give me any names, Joe? Names of other guys who…'

He shook his head, chewed at his bottom lip. 'This was over twenty years ago. I've tried to blot out as much of it as I can, but all I can see is his face. And feel his breath. I could taste it. He was disgusting.'

Alec nodded. 'I know. But, please, if you can think of anyone, if any names come to you.'

'I take it I'm free to go?'

'Aye, of course.' Joe McLeish was no killer. This wasn't a guy who'd meted out his revenge on Harry Nugent. Alec was sure of that. 'Listen, Joe, take care of yourself.' Alec shook his hand and, without thinking, gave him a hug.

18

The fact that Harry Nugent had been abusing boys in his care had opened up a big fat giant can of worms.

'This puts a whole new slant on things.' Alec Davies knew only too well the allegations of historical sex abuse were a nightmare to investigate. They would be dealt with by Police Scotland's National Child Abuse Investigation Unit, but they'd need to liaise closely with the team as there was every possibility they could uncover something that proved crucial in the murder investigation. On top of this, they'd need to be across the possibility that allegations against Nugent had been deliberately hidden.

'What it does is it gives us a possible motive for Nugent's murder. Up until now we've had very little to go on.' McVeigh and Toria sat in front of his desk at either side. Apparently hanging on his every word. He needed a small team around him. People he could trust.

'Are we ruling out the gangland connection now?' McVeigh was the first to address the elephant in the room.

'We really can't rule out anything yet, you know that.' Davies paused and then inclined his head. 'Toria.' He gave her the go-ahead to speak.

'OK.' She looked slightly nervous and Alec couldn't help but feel a tiny swell of pride. She looked like a kid but knew how to handle herself. 'We know at least three victims went to the police with allegations against Harry Nugent, but there's no record of any complaints.' She read the mood in the room like a pro. 'Sadly, this doesn't necessarily point to a cover-up. God. I wish it did.' Alec raised an eyebrow. 'Sir,' she said, 'at least if it was a cover-up it pointed to a few bad apples. What we're seeing here is worse,' she paused. 'In my opinion.' Alec couldn't quite grasp what exactly could be worse, but he let her continue.

'This,' she went on, 'sadly is indicative of how we handled abuse allegations in the past. And I don't just mean the dim and distant past. I've been looking into this. Have you any idea the number of witness statements lost, victims never being contacted again by the police, claims of abuse left un-investigated, and in many cases no action at all taken against potential abusers, not even an initial visit from the cops. It's disgraceful. And points the finger at all of us.'

Toria had worked in Rape Task Force for a time before being assigned to MITs. Davies wondered why she'd moved on – she knew her shit, make no mistake.

'I'm not saying there's *not* been some sort of cover-up on this. I'm just suggesting that the way abuse allegations have been handled by the police in the past – and this goes across the force – means it's hardly surprising. The fact the victims were male, the fact they were young working class kids, and the fact that Harry Nugent was a well known and well respected figure meant that it's par for the course that the boys weren't taken seriously.'

Harry Nugent had indeed been a shrewd promoter of his own image.

'It's now estimated one in six men will be the victim of sexual assault at some time in their lives, yet government resources, police training, victim support, they're all geared towards helping women. It's little wonder so few men come forward. They often feel there's nowhere to turn.'

'And the reason some feel the need to hand out their own form of rough justice?' McVeigh posed it as a question, but no one had the answer yet. 'Any more victims coming forward?'

Davies knew this could well open the floodgates. Not only would this encourage more victims to come forward, it would give the green light to every nutter who fancied getting their face in the paper for the most outrageous reasons. He was fucking furious that details of the case had had top billing on social media. They never did find out who blabbed that Nugent had had his tongue sliced off. The comms team had managed to trace the first posting of it to a girl in Renfrew, but she claimed she heard it from some guy in Asda. It was a fucking joke. He knew they were struggling to keep up with the changing technology, yet could do little about it.

'Right, gang, let's take a breather.' Davies decided to call time on today. He wanted them all fresh in the morning.

He sat alone in his office, knowing that they now had a potential list of thousands of men who'd had a grudge against Harry Nugent, and a serious grudge at that. That man had used his position to groom and abuse vulnerable kids in his care. By the look of things it had been an open secret; what Davies couldn't get his head round was the fact that no one seemed to stand up and be counted. This city, this country and its obsession with football made gods out of the most vile creatures and it sickened him.

He looked at the clock and decided he was off duty. There was cold beer in his fridge back home, but he couldn't go back to his flat just yet. He needed to decontaminate himself from the day and what it had thrown up. He rested against the back of his chair and closed his eyes. Just for a moment. The buzz from his phone woke him. Darkness had fallen and his office had grown cold.

Hey handsome, you free for a drink?

He grinned when he saw the text from Oonagh. He'd been deliberately keeping his distance from her and she was guessing something was wrong. But he was too old for this game. Too old to fancy someone out of his league. She'd made it obvious from the get-go that she saw him as nothing more than a pal, but tonight that was all he needed: a pal.

As long as you're buying…

But there was no such thing as a free drink. She'd be pressing him for info. He toyed with sticking a wee smiley face emoji on the end of his text. Just to show how pally he was, but decided against it. Shit, when did life get so fucking complicated that even sending a text was a social minefield?

They'd agreed to meet in the bar just off Bank Street, not far from his flat. That meant he could drive home and park up, leaving him free to get smashed. He didn't imagine it would take much to persuade Oonagh to have a skinful and he felt a smile tug at his lips.

19

The flat was tucked away in the affluent suburb of Newton Mearns. Art deco by design, the block would have stood out like a sore thumb in a street dominated by Victorian sandstone villas and post-war bungalows had it not been hidden away in what an estate agent would have described as a gated and tranquil landscaped garden.

The gates appeared to open automatically as Oonagh drove towards them and she drew up outside the main entrance, pulling into a space marked 'Visitor Parking'. She'd hardly had time to press the buzzer when a soft click told her the door was open. In a city obsessed by its art deco past, this was impressive. A central stairway dominated the communal entrance, curving its way up the main body of the building. Full length windows at either side flooded the entire space with light. She'd decided to ditch the lift and walk up the two flights of stairs admiring the view. Sarah Nugent opened the door before Oonagh had a chance to knock. She looked different somehow. Dressed very simply in a black polo neck and black jeans tucked into knee-high boots, her hair pulled back in a ponytail. It was only when she started to speak that Oonagh realised this was the first time she'd seen her sober.

'Nice place.'

Sarah looked around, but didn't bother feigning surprise; she knew this little pied-à-terre was far from humble. 'Harry had several properties,' she said. 'Bought them over the years. Couldn't resist them.' The way she said it was as though Harry had bought luxury flats the way other people bought designer shoes. 'This was the one he kept for himself.' Oonagh followed her into the lounge. 'I'd offer you coffee, but I'm out of milk.'

Oonagh guessed Sarah Nugent wasn't really in the coffee making mood and just wanted to get down to business. 'You're looking well,' she said. But Sarah sat forward, resting her elbows on her knees, nodding quickly for Oonagh to get to the point.

'So, how much did you know?' It was subtext for *did you know your husband was abusing young boys.*

'About what?' Either Sarah Nugent was taking the piss, or doing a remarkable job of playing the dumb blonde routine.

'About what?' Oonagh struggled to keep the sarcasm out of her voice. 'About your dead husband.' She needed to keep her temper in check, she had to keep this woman on her side. 'Bloody hell, Sarah, you'd hardly have invited me here just to go over the same ground as the other day.' It suddenly struck Oonagh that perhaps Sarah Nugent couldn't quite remember their last meeting with the same clarity that Oonagh did. After all, she'd been pretty smashed.

'Not as much as you think.' She paused. 'But I sort of guessed where his tastes lay.'

Oonagh's hand balled into a fist. Once again she wanted to scream, but kept as calm as she could and simply asked, 'Why didn't you go to the police?'

Sarah Nugent looked up and let out a laugh. 'The police? I thought it was just young men he liked.'

'What?'

'I didn't realise the boys were underage.'

Oonagh had no idea if she was telling the truth or not.

'You need to believe me.'

Oonagh was struggling with that.

'Sarah, whatever you tell me, it'll be in confidence. I swear nothing will get out unless you give me the go-ahead.' The woman didn't look convinced. Journalists weren't known for their honest reputation and Oonagh had a job on her hands. But she reckoned this woman wanted to talk. Otherwise she wouldn't have got this far.

'Harry had a lot to hide.'

Oonagh's eyes widened as she anticipated what was coming next, but Sarah didn't continue. It was obvious she'd need to push her along. 'More witnesses will come forward, Sarah. Was it just an open secret?'

Sarah shook her head. 'It's hard to explain. He was just this really popular nice guy on the outside and a fucking monster on the inside.'

'Why didn't you leave?' As soon as she said it Oonagh could have bitten her tongue off. Abuse came in many guises and it wasn't always easy to walk away.

'I tried. Once.'

'And?'

'What you need to understand is that Harry Nugent was more than just a guy. He was a brand. A product. The whole package, and that meant happily married family man, good PR, squeaky clean image. That image paved the way for him to ride roughshod over anyone he abused.'

'What I can't get my head round is how Harry managed to get away with it all for so long. Someone had to have had his back here.'

'Harry had a lot of friends, in a lot of places.' Sarah paused. 'A lot of dirt on a lot of very important people.'

'Very cryptic, Sarah, but I need a bit more than that. Please, this is your chance to set the story straight.'

This time she laughed, really laughed. 'You've got to be joking. If I come out with that, can you imagine the number of die-hard fans that would turn on me? They loved Harry. And those who didn't would turn on me for not handing him in in the first place. Either way I'd be put through the wringer and hung out to dry. Bloody hell, I'd be as well being on house arrest.'

Oonagh wasn't buying it, but guessed she'd best leave that line for now. Sarah had her back against the wall and didn't look as if she was ready to budge. 'I take it the police have taken a full statement now?'

She nodded. 'I've told them what I know. Which wasn't much really.'

'OK, you help me, and I'll help you.' Oonagh hated using this line but it was the only one she thought would work at this stage. 'You know this particular brand of shit will hit the fan. And when it does, if there's even a whiff that you knew then you'll be thrown to the wolves. People are going to point the finger whether you like it or not.' Oonagh wasn't bullshitting, she'd seen it before. A hundred times. It was too late for people to get their pound of flesh from

Harry Nugent, so they'd make do with his widow instead. She'd badgered Alec last night when they'd met for a drink. Pushed him to tell her if they'd found anything on Nugent's laptop. He was too long in the tooth to let anything slip, everything he *didn't* tell her was deliberate. But he left her in no doubt what they'd uncovered. It had sickened him to the core.

What kind of woman could share her bed every night with such a monster? That was what would be coming next, as soon as the police issued a press release. 'This isn't going to go away, Sarah. You need a way to manage this. Damage limitation.'

Sarah dropped her head into her hands; everything was turning sour around her. Oonagh leaned forward, touched the arm of her chair. 'I can't promise you'll come out smelling of roses, but hopefully you won't be stinking of the brown smelly stuff either.'

Sarah sniffed and tilted her head back slightly, mindful that her mascara was in danger of running if those tears spilled over.

'And I hate to say it, but in my opinion, given what they now know about your husband, the police won't be busting a gut to find his killer.' She couldn't be certain, but something that may have been relief flashed across Sarah's face.

Oonagh decided to change tack slightly. 'When you worked at Breakmire, did you know Hannah Gray?'

Sarah stopped chewing the skin around her thumb and stroked the back of her neck. 'No. I don't think so...'

'She was a patient there.' Oonagh filled her in on the basic details. 'Ran away, was found dead in the grounds.'

The penny seemed to drop. 'I do remember. Yeah. That happened a few weeks before I started. But people were talking about it. Why?'

'No reason. Her name came up when I was researching Breakmire.'

Sarah narrowed her eyes.

'I was trying to get a handle on why Harry was so keen to help out there. Let's face it, we now know he wasn't as altruistic as we'd all thought so—'

'Do journalists have to take some sort of... pledge, or an oath or something?' Sarah cut her off before she had the chance to finish. Oonagh wasn't quite sure if she was taking the piss, pretending to be more naïve than she actually was, but whatever her motive Oonagh guessed she was asking if she could keep a secret.

'It's complicated. If the police get a warrant for information they believe I have, then I have no option but to hand it over. But until then, whatever I uncover investigating a story is my business.'

'I can trust you, then?'

'To be honest, Sarah, I think right now I'm your best bet.'

20

Tommy Gallagher 1983

He lay perfectly still. Certain that his sister could hear his heart beating from across the room, loud against his chest, his shame washing over him like a blanket.

'You awake, Tommy?' He ignored her high pitched whisper, instead breathing deeply to let on he was asleep. 'I'm cold, can I come in beside you?' He didn't get the chance to say no, as her gentle footsteps ran softly across the lino and she slipped in under the covers, cuddling into his back. He closed his eyes tight, stemming the tears. If he cried, she'd feel it; Ellie would know something was wrong. She'd never seen her big brother cry. Even when Dad died he'd made sure he'd held it in, rocking her back and forth to sleep each night as she'd cried herself to sleep in his arms. He felt her cold feet on his legs through his pyjama trousers, and her wee hand clung onto his jacket, gripped at his chest as she cooried in for warmth.

Tommy patted his sister's hand, let her know he was awake, but not up to talking. Soon her breathing grew shallow and it wasn't long before he felt her body lean heavier against him as she drifted off into sleep. He tried to let his tears flow with the rhythm of his breathing in case he woke her. He wondered if Dad could see him. Wondered if he knew. His stomach lurched at the thought as he drifted in and out of fitful sleep.

21

The noise of the traffic on Great Western Road made its way through the open window of his third floor flat. When he'd first moved here it had seemed so peaceful, so tranquil, he'd hardly noticed any outside noise at all. It was the first place he could seriously call home since the divorce, and perhaps that was what had given him a sense of peace.

Alec looked down onto the street below; students filed their way along the pavement, meandering onto the road towards the university. He wondered which, if any, of them harboured secrets. That was often the case if he was at a crowded event – he'd scan the faces and try to guess how many criminals were out roaming the streets. How many undetected killers, rapists, abusers were free to go about their daily lives without even a hint of their misdemeanours. The same with victims; there must be thousands of people out there who'd suffered, and were still suffering, yet for whatever reason they felt they couldn't come forward. They were the ones the cops had failed. And if those victims were just kids then they'd been let down even more.

Trying to get his head round the fact that there were no recorded complaints against Harry Nugent from any of the forces sickened him. Even if Toria was right, and it pointed more to incompetence than corruption on the force, he wasn't letting this one go. Those poor kids, those boys who'd asked for help and were let down, they deserved better.

He sat on the window ledge drinking his coffee, the cold breeze catching the gap on his back between his T-shirt and jammie bottoms. He should really get dressed, he had a shitload of work to do, but needed just a few moments of peace here. He took his eyes from the street and looked around the living room. The flat was adopting a very unlived in look and didn't really seem like home any more; hardly surprising considering how little time he spent here. Everything had gone so fast: life, the job, his marriage. Twenty years ago he thought he had all the time in the world, then one day, you woke up and realised there were more years behind you than there were in front. He used to laugh when his dad had told him that. How everything would just pass by in a blur, *'so make the bloody most of it, son,'* he'd said. Still said it when he visited.

Loneliness wasn't a word that he ever felt applied to him – he enjoyed his own company, for the most part couldn't be arsed with other people – but sometimes, occasionally, it would be nice, he thought, to have someone to come home to. Someone to offload and share the day with. But that wasn't really an option for him. But someone to be there *occasionally* wasn't really an option either, and who the hell in their right mind would be willing to listen to what he had to offload at the end of a working day? A mind polluted with all the horrors that life had to give. But more and more recently he'd been aware of a gap in his life. Something was missing. Whether that gap was Oonagh O'Neil shaped was hard to tell. He pushed the thought to the back of his mind; there were a million reasons that one wouldn't work.

Alec swallowed the remainder of his coffee and walked over to the small kitchen tagged onto the edge of the living room and rinsed his cup, leaving it on the unit above the dishwasher he'd never used. Hardly seemed worth it for one cup and the occasional plate. No one had shared this space since he'd moved in five years ago, and the likelihood was that no one ever would. But that was cool. His wasn't a life suited to sharing. He was fine with that, and on a reasonable day could even be considered happy – well, as happy as a grumpy bastard with a recurring ulcer who hadn't had sex for eighteen months had a right to be.

He drove north, edging out of the city towards Possilpark. Saracen Street had changed so much since he was a kid. It was still the main shopping thoroughfare, but now it seemed little more than a ghost of its former self. Redevelopment had resulted in many of the old red sandstone tenements being destroyed and locals being rehoused elsewhere. The once thriving Saracen Foundry was long gone too, had been from before his time. The entire area had initially grown up around the foundry, which had been famous for manufacturing the best ornamental ironwork in Scotland. But within fifteen years of its closure, those with a more enterprising gene had spotted a gap in the market, and Possilpark had become the hub of one of the most thriving heroin markets in the country.

Alec remembered his time as a young copper there with little fondness. He'd spent much of his beat catching petty dealers and mopping up the mess left by users, knocking on doors of bewildered families to tell them their son wouldn't be coming home that night but would they mind identifying his body instead. All this while the big names behind the problem, the high-end dealers, the drug barons, got off scot-free. Glasgow's economic history seemed to be steeped in similar shame: tobacco lords trading from the money they made as slave traders, industrialists thriving off the labour of the slum dwellers, and now drug barons, too big and too anonymous for the cops to catch.

He took a left just past the health centre and pulled over, double-checking the address on his mobile before walking into the close. He'd considered bringing Toria with him, not quite as a family liaison officer, but he knew that the presence of a female officer could soften the atmosphere. But she was up to her eyes in it, as was the whole team; anyway, this was an informal chat and that would be enough for now.

Scott Pettigrew had been one of the boys who'd made a claim against Nugent back in the day, almost thirty years ago. But it wasn't Scott Alec had arranged this interview with, it was his mum.

'They must be right feart sending a big noise like you.' Wilma Pettigrew looked him up and down as he stood on the doorstep, then shuffled through the narrow hallway to the living room, expecting him to follow. She bore the hallmark trait of the Glaswegian Wifie: took no shit from no one.

Alec gave her a smile that was lost somewhere in the back of her cardigan. 'I'm hardly a big noise, but…' He knew what she meant. This woman was no fool and obviously realised that cops of Alec's rank didn't really do house calls to lonely old women unless they needed to make an impression.

It was hard to pin an age on Mrs Pettigrew. Alec reckoned she'd be close to sixty-five, given the age her son had been when he made the allegations, but she could easily have passed for twenty years older. It was just the way it was in some parts of this city. She'd contacted the station once the story about Nugent's abuse had reached the front page of her local paper.

'See this.' She wagged her index finger in his direction. 'I don't want any of this ending up in the papers.' She eased herself down onto the chair. Alec moved to help as she dropped the last few inches, but she swatted his arm away, and instead pointed towards the small kitchenette off the main living room, telling him to stick the kettle on. He did as he was told, pottering about the tiny kitchen, opening various cupboards until he'd found everything he needed. The place was spotless. He placed two mugs on the small tray alongside the sugar bowl and, judging by the number of milk jugs in the cupboard, Wilma Pettigrew was not a woman to tolerate a milk carton on the table, so he poured some into one of the jugs, and carried the tray through to the living room. She pointed to the nest of tables at the side of the settee. 'Just let it brew for a while, son, eh?' She smoothed a blanket across her knees, beneath which Alec could see her discoloured feet, the men's slippers she was wearing cut at either side to accommodate the obvious swelling.

'Mrs Pettigrew, I'd like to ask you a few questions about—'

'If you don't mind me saying, son…' she held his gaze '… you're a bit late.'

Alec poured the tea, more for something to do than anything else. She was right, and there were no excuses. 'We let your son down, Mrs Pettigrew.' He handed her the mug, careful to place the handle in her fingers. 'But if you give me the chance, I'll try to put it right.'

'My son's dead, Inspector Davidson.' Alec decided against correcting her. 'What is it you actually want to put right?'

Christ, this was a tough one. What the hell was he offering this poor woman? And how on earth could it ever be right for her again? Scott Pettigrew had been twenty-two years old when his body was found in a back close in Dalmarnock over twenty years ago; the needle had still been stuck between his toes. He'd been unemployed, with a history of drug abuse; his death had been one of a dozen such cases and had hardly caused as much as a ripple in the city. Certainly there was nothing to link his death to Harry Nugent, but his mother was in no doubt who was responsible.

'I blame myself, you know. I made him go to the polis. His dad?' She smoothed one hand over her knee; it seemed to give her some sort of comfort. 'He wouldn't even listen, screamed at him for not fighting back. Made him swear to tell nobody.'

Alec felt the warmth of the cup on his hands, then blew on the tea before taking a sip, enjoying the strong tangy taste on his lips. 'How did you find out? Did Scott tell you that Nugent had abused him?'

She shook her head, still rubbing her knee, which Alec guessed was as arthritic as her feet. 'No, not at first. But I'd hear him crying in his room. I knew something was wrong.' She pulled a worn tissue from her sleeve and blew hard, dabbing her eyes before stuffing it back inside her cardigan. 'I went down to the polis station, but they couldn't be arsed. Didn't care.'

'D'you remember who you spoke to at the time?' Alec held out little hope for this if she couldn't even get his name right and he'd only introduced himself ten minutes ago.

'Aye,' she said, coming back sharp as a tack. 'Aye, I do. Sergeant Gemmell at Partick. Big tall fella he was, shock of blond hair.'

'So…' Alec needed to know what had happened, why this was never properly investigated '… what did he do? Did he take a statement?'

'Once I told the chap at the desk what had happened, he called us in. Ignored *me* completely, mind you, then told Scott if he knew what the word perjury meant. Scott didn't have a clue, but I knew. Anyway, he told Scott that it was very serious to tell lies, and that if he went to court he could be in serious trouble for lying. Might even go to jail.'

Shit, this was getting worse. 'And that was it?' Alec struggled to keep the surprise out of his voice.

'More or less, aye. Told Scott to go home and think about what he'd done. Said he wouldn't take a statement as he'd never been in trouble before and didn't want him to end up with a record. Made out he was doing us a huge favour.'

'And you left it at that?' Alec hadn't meant the accusatory tone that had crept into his voice and could have kicked himself.

'Listen, son.' There weren't many people brave enough to get away with speaking to Alec Davies like that, but Wilma

Pettigrew had earned the right. 'A woman from Possil and her boy? We were no match against yous lot.'

'Mrs Pettigrew, I'm so, so sorry,' Alec said, and he meant it. 'We've let you down. You and Scott and...' He was desperately trying to find a way to make it up to her, find the words to say he'd sort it, but couldn't.

She rocked back and forth, trying to gain momentum to stand up. Alec reached over and held her arm until she managed to get up and steadied herself on her stick. 'He was just another junkie to you lot.' She took the photograph from the mantelpiece. 'Another bit of litter on the street.' She handed it to Alec. 'But he was my boy and he deserved better.'

Alec looked at the school photograph in the cheap gilt frame; the kid couldn't have been much more than six, perhaps seven at a push. A boy grinning at the camera, hair messed up, school tie to one side and a slight tear in the V-neck of his jumper. 'That jumper was brand new that morning. He was immaculate when I sent him off.' For the first time since Alec arrived he noticed a slight smile on the old woman's lips as she recalled the memory. 'He was always getting up to mischief.' She took back the picture and wiped the glass with her hand before placing it back on the mantelpiece. 'He was a good kid.'

She eased herself back down onto her chair, this time accepting Alec's arm as he guided her the last few inches, then tugged the blanket over her legs. The sheer effort caused her to pant for breath. Alec crouched beside her; he wasn't good at this sort of thing, but wasn't sure what else to do.

'Wilma...' he placed his hand on her arm '... I know we're too late to do right by you or Scott, but I can promise that I'll do all I can do to find out what went wrong.' Even as he was saying the words he knew they'd do little good. 'You deserved better, Mrs Pettigrew, you and Scott.'

The cold air caught the back of his throat as he stepped back outside. Wilma Pettigrew had said nothing as he'd left, his words meant nothing to her, and instead had sat worrying the fringes of her blanket between her fingers as he let himself out.

22

Alec pushed open the door. He did knock, but was already halfway over the threshold before he heard that it was OK for him to enter. 'We need to talk.' There was no need for introductions as he approached the desk.

'It's customary to use *sir* when addressing a senior officer.' No one had been more surprised than Alec when Mike Conroy had been promoted to DCC. They'd trained together at Tulliallan and Alec had always found him a bit on the slow side. He could never quite get used to him being his new boss. But then again, dead men's shoes were always filled.

He nodded to Alec to take a seat, and to his credit didn't look as pissed off as he could have been. 'What's your beef, then?'

Alec guessed he knew what the problem was but paid him the courtesy of going over it anyway. 'This case,' he said, 'it's a fucking shambles and I need more resources. Sir.' The last word came out like the afterthought it was.

'Listen, Alec, the first twenty-four hours are crucial in a murder investigation.' Davies hoped that Conroy hadn't just learned this vital fact about policing and nodded quickly in agreement, urging him to get to the point. 'Well, we're almost two weeks down the line and you're no closer to finding out who killed Nugent. Now…' he took a breath, lacing his fingers together as though he were about to turn Alec down for a mortgage '… throwing money at it is not the answer.'

There was a fleeting moment when he considered telling his superior officer to fuck off, but realised that might not be the best career move. 'I'm spending half my time chasing poor bloody sods who've been abused, listening to horror tales going back decades and trying to give them an answer as to why we didn't investigate it at the time.'

'Get one of your juniors to do that—'

'You're not fucking listening.' He slammed his hands on the desk. 'Sir.'

Conroy stood up, perched himself on the edge of the table. 'Alec, we go back a long way, but remember who you're talking to.'

'Mike, sir, this is a fucking car crash. We've got cases of kids being abused, young boys who had their whole lives ahead of them ending up on a slab; just another dead junkie because we let them down.' He swallowed hard, surprised to find his voice cracking slightly as the emotion pulled at his jaw line. He tightened his lips. 'I need a separate team to concentrate on the abuse victims.'

'Pass is on to the National Child Abuse Investigation Unit. That's what it was set up for. Fuck knows it's costing enough.'

'No. That's *not* enough here. I need a specially trained team working alongside us on this. Co-ordinating their findings with us.'

'You don't call the shots, Alec.'

Alec stood up. 'This whole thing stinks of a mass cover-up and it makes me sick to my stomach.'

'Things were different then…' Alec had been hoping Mike wouldn't resort to that line, but he had. 'You know that as well as I do. Look at the way we dealt with victims of rape or domestic violence.' He circled one hand in the air, as though trying to conjure up other similar crimes. He clearly meant the police force in general but Alec's stomach shifted slightly at the associated guilt. 'All abuse accusations were a fucking nightmare. They still are to an extent. But back then, well, we didn't have the right training, attitudes were different…' He trailed off, thinking that was a good enough answer. It wasn't.

'I'm not convinced it was just a few badly trained coppers, sir.' Alec was deliberately overusing the word sir until it lost any of the respect Mike thought it gave him. 'This to me looks more like a cover-up. These allegations were deliberately hidden. The witnesses discredited.' He opened his briefcase and placed the buff coloured envelope on the desk. Mike raised an eyebrow as Alec slid the documents out from inside. There were several pictures, all chronicling various awards and charity dinners over the years, some with senior public figures. But it was the copies of press clippings showing the then Chief Constable of Strathclyde Police shaking hands with Nugent and other board members of the Caledonian Boys' Club that he was most interested in.

'Threadgold's dead.' Mike ran his hand through his hair and sat back down. 'D'you want to completely discredit his name?'

'What? You don't think the press are going to have a field day with this anyway?'

The familiar stirring of anger rose in his gut. Chief Constable Gordon Threadgold had been his mentor at one point. Not quite a father figure, but Alec had looked up to him for most of his career. He'd died after an apparent accident whilst cleaning his shotgun. For Alec, the memory of that day was still very much alive. He'd been with the newly retired Chief Constable just moments beforehand. Had called to his house to challenge him about why he'd held back vital information on a cold case he was reviewing: a murder investigation from the seventies. The pathologist had estimated Threadgold's accidental death had happened just minutes after Alec had stormed out of his house. It wasn't a day he was likely to forget in a hurry. 'It's not just him, sir, there are high profile figures in each of those stories.'

'Fuck, Alec, that means nothing. These charity events are all the same. You know what it's like – you get dragged into every shitey cause going.' Alec knew what he was getting at, but he also knew that Nugent had friends in high places. Friends that meant allegations against him would be easily swept under the carpet or thrown straight in the bin.

'You know as well as I do, sir, that we had a legal, and not to mention moral, obligation to follow up every one of those accusations.' He paused, aware he was raising his voice. He took a breath and checked himself. 'There's not one single statement or allegation recorded.' The scenario wasn't that hard to imagine. Alec could understand the rank and file plods taking a statement and wondering how the hell they'd tell their boss that his golfing buddy was being accused of being a paedo. Easier if they just binned any that came in. But he also knew that he had to tread carefully here. 'I'm not saying Threadgold or any of the men pictured were involved in the abuse.'

'I'm glad to hear that, Alec. Some of these men are very well known. One went on to become a Cabinet Minister—' Conroy tugged at the lapels of his jacket. That gesture alone made Alec want to smash his face in.

'But what they did do was give Nugent a get-out-of-jail-free card. Having them on his side meant he was never going to be investigated the way he would have been had he been an ordinary Joe Soap.' He stood up to leave; he'd taken about as much as he could stomach.

'Just drop it, DI Davies.'

'No can do, sir.'

'You may have to.' Conroy's last statement was very matter-of-fact but it stopped Alec in his tracks. 'If this is regarded as a matter of national security, then you have no choice.'

Alec stuffed his hands deep into his pockets to stop them from shaking. 'National security? You're joking me, right?'

'Look at my face, Davies – do I look as though I'm fucking joking?' Conroy rocked back on his heels. Outside the faint drone of traffic made the world seem normal.

'Don't be so ridiculous. How d'you propose we make all this go away? The public will be baying for blood. Too late, Mike. It's already out there. Tough.'

'The public don't give a shit. Not really. As long as they've got their beer on a Friday, their football on a Saturday, they'll be happy.'

'You're wrong, Mike. People care, and those kids deserve justice and I for one plan to see they get it. This story will be splashed across every media outlet going. And I'm not going to stop it. So, as I said before, you're too late. Genie's out of the bottle, I'm afraid.'

'Really?' He gave a sarcastic laugh. 'Look at the balls-up of the investigation into the Westminster paedophile ring.'

'What's that got to do with—?'

'Papers are full of pictures of Margaret Fucking Thatcher schmoozing with Jimmy Savile. That Currie woman. The one with the eggs...'

'Edwina.' Alec knew where this was going.

'She more or less handed Savile the keys to Broadmoor and didn't even get so much as a slap on the wrist. The Home Office, the fucking Home Office—' he was shouting now '—lost more than a hundred files relating to that paedophile ring at Westminster. A hundred files, and you think anyone really gives a shit about a few boys in Glasgow? Get real, Alec. You've been told to drop it. Now drop it.'

'Whose fucking pocket are you in, Mike?'

'Close the door on your way out, Davies.' There was no mistaking the anger in Mike's voice. What Alec couldn't work out was whether that was anger or fear in his eyes.

23

Oonagh slipped the pen-drive into the side of her laptop and heard it whirr into life. She looked down the list of files. Sarah Nugent had taken a certain amount of twisted pride in her late husband's eye for detail. 'You can say what you like about him,' she'd said when she handed over the documents to Oonagh, 'but he was fastidious about his bookkeeping.'

Oonagh had felt somewhat sickened by the comment. 'A bit like Mussolini and the trains?' she'd replied, but the reference had been lost on Sarah. It was strange how such a minor detail could be heralded as a redeeming feature in an otherwise grotesque human being. Oonagh imagined the defence of serial killers asking for leniency because of their immaculate handwriting or impeccable table manners.

Harry Nugent had been no fool, and neither, it appeared, was his wife. For someone who did a sterling job of acting on the wrong side of bright, this woman was smarter than the average bimbo. She'd acted on the right side of dumb to keep enough tabs on Harry to have access to most of his secret records. Oonagh suspected Sarah Nugent had known about Harry's double-entry bookkeeping for quite some time. He'd kept most of his records here, in his luxury art deco pad. It was all here in black and white.

As Sarah had said, Harry had owned several flats around the country. Most of which he rented out and property that presumably would now belong to his widow. On paper the rents had been minimal by all accounts. But Oonagh knew there was serious money changing hands here. According to Sarah, most of Harry's businesses had been cash transactions. From what Oonagh could gather he'd had almost twenty bank accounts. All registered under various company names with money being squirrelled away each month.

According to Sarah, Harry's flats housed a string of upmarket brothels, catering to whatever tastes his low-level clientele desired. Underage mainly. A fair degree of rough stuff. Transsexuals too. Although from what Oonagh could gather these young boys were forced to dress up, act out and be whoever was paying for their company wanted that night. Child abuse dressed up as a business transaction.

Most of it was written in fairly crude code. With just his clients' initials alongside each payment. CW appeared a lot but Oonagh had no idea what it meant. There was nothing in the documents to identify where the properties were or indeed any of the clients who enjoyed the fruits of his labour. Whatever perk was being offered at each of these flats, it was more than was provided at your basic Airbnb.

Oonagh wasn't quite sure what she was looking for. Sarah had claimed not to know any of the working girls or boys, but had a rough idea where they came from. Kids plucked from care homes, groomed from an early age with no one to fight their corner. Runaways lured into taking drugs, then prepared to do anything to feed their habit. Kids who had no one to come looking when they went missing. Oonagh knew the more vulnerable the child was, the easier they'd be to abuse, and the less likely they'd be to go to the police. The thought of these kids being beaten and abused for a couple of quid made her sick.

The meteoric rise of Harry Nugent wasn't difficult to plot. What Oonagh struggled with was understanding it all. This guy had the Midas touch, make no mistake. Everything he came in contact with was pure gold. A promising young footballer, he'd been injured out of the game before he'd hit the big time. For most that meant fading into obscurity. But for Harry that had seemed to be the making of him. He'd started the Caledonian Boys' Club with little more than *'a dream to help other kids, and a burning ambition to stay in the game that was his life'*. The last sentence was part of his biography, the part, no doubt, he'd written himself.

There was no shortage of inspirational quotes from or about Nugent, but nothing quite summed up how he'd managed to achieve the astounding success. The CBC was only a fraction of his business interests; where he'd made his big money was Pitch Perfect. Despite her revulsion for this guy, Oonagh had to admit to being impressed.

He'd not only secured contracts to supply the strips for most of the clubs across Scotland, he'd also won a lucrative contract to supply almost every school in the Central Belt with their sports kits and uniforms. In an era where uniforms were falling out of fashion, Harry had somehow managed to clinch the deal to supply polo shirts, sweatshirts and anything else that needed a school emblem. This had been a multimillion pound operation, with Harry at the helm. No wonder Mrs Harry hadn't really cared if he preferred the away games.

What Oonagh couldn't get her head around was the fact there had seemed to be very little competition for Harry. It was a pretty standard operation, nothing high tech or specialised about the business. How complicated was churning out a few polo shirts with a bit of fancy embroidery on them? Oonagh had passed loads of stalls selling similar stuff at Christmas markets. How the hell had Harry managed to keep his grip on the contracts for so long?

Going through the paperwork was the stuff of nightmares, well, the stuff of Oonagh's nightmares. Her concentration refused to play ball when faced with reams and reams of paperwork, all with seemingly endless lists of names. She now had two sets of accounts. The official ones, and the ones Sarah had passed on.

Getting the official company accounts had been the easy bit. As far as Harry Nugent's business interests were concerned, everything was above board. This little piggy was squeaky clean. On paper at least. He'd won contracts for at least three local authorities, the biggest being the old Strathclyde region before it was disbanded in 1996. But in its day it had sprawled across the west of Scotland with a population of almost two and a half million people. Its administrative headquarters had been, as one would expect, in Glasgow. So Nugent netting this contract really had been back-of-the-net stuff as far as his business interests were concerned.

It was all on public record as a PLC. Pitch Perfect had been a fledgling company back in 1994 when Nugent had first tendered for the local authority contract. Oonagh couldn't see much competition and there was no record, as far as she was aware, of any other companies bidding for it. Even so, how did a relatively new company manage to secure a deal worth millions? A company that until that time had no track record.

The business accounts were getting worse. The main factory had started off at a small industrial unit in the south side. But prior to that Harry Nugent had had no premises. She couldn't get her head around it. The biggest region in the country had awarded a multimillion pound contract to a little known ex-footballer, with apparently no business experience and no premises. Oonagh was no expert, but she was sure this wasn't the normal way of things. The sea of documents was overwhelming. She didn't know just how to decipher all this, but she knew someone who could.

The call came through at about eleven. Oonagh had been in the office earlier than usual that morning. It wasn't that she was trying to make a good impression on Alan, although she let him think that, but they were digging up the road outside her house and her Internet was down.

'Hello, missus, how're you?'

In all the time Oonagh had known Ash, he'd always referred to her as missus. It had taken four years for him to confess he didn't know how the hell to pronounce Oonagh and by the time someone had put him right – he'd thought it was Yoon-Ig – he'd just stuck with the preferred moniker. They were at uni together, or rather he'd been a PhD student and had taken a few tutorials. He'd only seen her name on the attendance list so had never heard it said out loud.

'I'm great, Ash, long time no see. Thought you were dead and buried.' That wasn't strictly fair as it had been Oonagh who'd missed calling him on more than one occasion. He'd been kind enough to come to her dad's funeral and had called frequently to make sure she was OK. He was good that way, but Oonagh had been so wrapped up in her grief, preferring instead to lose herself in work rather than share her pain with one of the few friends she had. If she was truthful she'd felt a sense of shame in her grief. Something she'd never been able to fathom. But something she'd never been entirely able to shake off either. That feeling that grief was something that happened to someone else. Death was something that happened to other people's dads, not hers. Hers had been warm and funny and vibrant. Not the type to die. What she'd hated most at the time was the pity. It had taken her quite a few years to realise care and pity were two different things.

'Naw, they'll not bury me. I've left strict instructions that I'm to be cremated...'

A smile spread across her face. One of Ash's more endearing qualities was that he took everything that was said literally. In one of her happier moments as a student she was telling him about something really funny, and of how she almost died laughing, when he looked horrified and asked if it was actually possible to die from laughter. She missed her student days. Days when she'd thought she had all the time in the world and when the prospect of turning forty had seemed like a death sentence.

'Anyway, missus, what can I do you for?' Ash was one of the best number crunchers in the country. Forensic accountants were now in very high demand.

'Ash...' she hated saying it but needed to reassure herself '... I need you to look at something in the strictest confidence, yes?'

Oonagh struggled to make much sense from the accounts and documents that she'd got from Sarah Nugent. Other than to see Harry Nugent was loaded and owned a whack of upmarket properties, it didn't give her much to go on. And she only had Sarah's word that he was running them as brothels.

'Oh, I'm intrigued now. Nothing dodgy, though, eh?'

She gave Ash the brief details, assured him there was nothing illegal about any of the transactions. She kept her fingers crossed under her desk for good measure.

'Aye, OK.' She gave a little punch in the air, then felt the immediate burst of that particular bubble when he added, 'I'm booked solid for the next few weeks but—'

'Shit, Ash, I need this soon as.'

He paused for a moment. 'Since it's you.'

'Yess! You're a pal, Ash, I owe you.'

'Oh, you betcha.'

'You betcha' wasn't usually on Ash's list of preferred phrases and Oonagh guessed he had a new friend from out of town. Someone with whom 'you betcha' rested easier than it did with Ash.

Oonagh put the phone down and copied every single strand of information, then made another copy of the pen-drive and had them sent over to Ash by courier. She was about to pack up and head off for an early lunch when the email came through on her phone with a document attached. There was always a poor signal in the office and it seemed to take an age to download. She'd almost forgotten about this. She scanned her eyes across it, taking in the basic information, nothing earth-shattering, until she got to the crucial two lines at the bottom. 'Bloody hell.'

24

The police tape cordoned off the lane at either side, the white tent covering the crime. The night sky was devoid of stars and lit by the sodium glow of the street lights. Industrial-size bins, overspilling with bottles and card, lined part of the lane; a few doorways created an inky-black relief against the soot grey buildings. Back exits to more salubrious surroundings. Police cars, angled nose to nose so they looked more abandoned than parked, cut off the view from the street. An ambulance, back doors open, sat with its engine off, in no hurry. Inside, the paramedic gently patted her passenger on the shoulder. 'You're doing well.' He sat hunched with his elbows on his knees, a regulation grey blanket draped over him. He looked up, clearly unconvinced. The red rings around his eyes said he was doing far from well, that, coupled with his grey pallor. This guy looked like shit.

Closing time was bleeding into the clubbing hour and a few late night stragglers had gathered at the far end of the adjoining street, obligatory fish suppers or kebabs in hand, craning their necks to see what was going on; ushering them back gave the uniforms something to do.

Alec Davies eased his way through, breaking the crowd shoulder first, flashing his warrant card. 'So?' He wasn't much on small talk. Just wanted to know the details. All he had at this time was the body of a man found hanging in Bath Lane. Just off Hope Street. The irony of the street name wasn't lost on him. Uniform had confirmed that Forensics were on the scene. He tipped his head in the direction of the guy sitting in the back of the ambulance. 'Is that him?'

'Yes, sir. In a bit of a state...' Uniform was trying to big up his part, but Alec held up a hand to cut him off and made his way over to the waiting vehicle.

The paramedic smiled at him. 'Go easy on him, Davies, he's in shock.'

Up close Alec could see this was little more than a kid. Late teens, maybe twenty something at a push. It was a mild night but his teeth chattered. Alec sat opposite him. He didn't yet know the full facts, but this wasn't the face of a killer. This was a scared kid. 'What happened, son?'

The boy was called Peter, Pete to his pals. He'd left his friends at the taxi rank and nipped down Bath Lane for a pee. Alec noticed the stain on the front of his trousers – Peter or Pete to his pals had clearly been caught short before he'd managed the deed.

'I thought it was just part of the doorway or something...' His voice broke; a line of snot dripped from his nose and fell onto the blanket. 'I didn't know... I was just... I can't really...' He wasn't making much sense. Hardly surprising really – the kid had just found a body hanging from an iron bracket in a back lane in Glasgow's city centre and was scared. The old brackets were strong, previously used as a pulley system to hoist up goods and furniture and the like in days gone by. They'd hold the weight of a body, no problem at all.

'Take your time, Pete.' Alec would get a full statement later down at the station, but he knew these first few minutes were vital, before witnesses had a chance to distort the truth with what they thought they'd seen, or tried to blot out what they'd actually seen. 'Was there anyone else in the lane?'

Pete shook his head.

'You sure about that?'

Pete shook his head again.

'What? You're not sure about that or there was no one else in the lane?'

This time he nodded. Alec tried not to lose his patience but let out a sigh. Pete picked up on it. 'I don't think so. I didn't see anyone.'

'So tell me again, in your own words, what happened. What you saw.'

It was the same story. He'd nipped down Bath Lane for a pee, paid no attention to what he'd thought was part of the building, but as he was about to relieve himself the object next to him had given way and he'd stumbled and grabbed hold of it for balance. It had only been as his arms were fixed firmly round it that he'd realised he was holding onto a body which had been strung up and bound tightly with rope. Thick wetness had covered his hands and when he'd focused on the face he realised it was blood, drying now, but coming from the gaping wounds in the mutilated head.

'I pushed it away, it battered off the wall…' the lad struggled to swallow back the tears. 'I didn't know it was…'

Alec eyed Forensics coming out of the tent in the lane. He told Pete to give a full statement to Toria Law, who had just arrived at the scene, full of vim and vigour by the looks of it. She'd obviously been out on the razz, judging by her clothes. Alec initially thought her legs were just really cold, he had no idea they made tights that colour. There was some weird looking glitter on her hair and she pulled long silver earrings from her ears and slipped them in her pocket as she drew near.

'Where's McVeigh?' he asked. She shrugged her shoulders and looked slightly flushed, panicky almost, as though she were supposed to be responsible for his safe arrival and had let the side down. But he'd already turned his back on her, desperate to get more from Forensics. He felt instantly calmer when he saw the police surgeon. Rosemary was good. Shit-hot at her job.

'Alec.' She nodded in greeting as she peeled the plastic gloves from her hands, folded them together and stuffed them into the pocket on the front of her white paper suit. Alec waited for her verdict. 'We've a load of tests to run, but looks like asphyxiation.

'Time of death?'

She let out a laugh. 'This isn't *CSI*, Alec, it takes more than prodding the body with a thermometer to even make a rough estimate.' Alec knew better than to push her for too much at this stage – Rosemary was a stickler for protocol. Wouldn't make a call without the full evidence. But he'd give it a go anyway.

'Was he alive when they strung him up?' Alec didn't have to look around to see if there were CCTV cameras in the vicinity. This was Glasgow city centre. Impossible to fart without it going on camera.

Rosemary gave a non-committal shrug. 'Hard to tell, but probably.'

'And the injuries? Pre or post-mortem?'

She took a deep breath. 'Judging by the blood, the injuries are consistent with the victim being alive at the time.'

'What're we looking at here?'

'Sliced his ears off.'

Fuck. He couldn't fail to make the *hear no evil* connection, and with that the connection to Harry Nugent's murder. That was all he needed, some mad vigilante with a Stanley knife roaming the streets of Glasgow and stringing up their victims. He could see the press gathering at the far side of the lane. 'This goes no further, Rosemary. Yeah?'

She gave him a look. A look that told him he was questioning her integrity. 'Sorry,' he added. 'I'm just up to my neck in it right now.'

'You look as though you could do with taking your foot off the gas, Alec.'

He was sure she meant well. 'Any other bits of him missing?'

Rosemary shook her head, as though it was a routine job to her. 'No, seems to be otherwise intact. Oh, and we've found his ears, by the way.'

Alec raised his eyebrows. 'And?'

'Stuffed into his mouth. Think that's what choked him. The hanging was just a bit of street theatre.' She pulled off her paper cap. 'Tell you something, it was a clean cut.' Davies got the distinct impression Rosemary admired the handiwork of this particular maniac.

'Shit.' He was trying to process this information when he spotted his partner's red hair in the distance above the gathering crowd. Where the hell were these people coming from? Did they not have homes to go to?

'Boss.' McVeigh waved over to Davies as though he'd spotted him in Asda. *Christ, I wish he wouldn't do that,* he thought as McVeigh walked towards him, brushing what looked suspiciously like glitter from the shoulder of his jacket. It had better bloody not be. 'What've we got, then?' McVeigh rubbed his hands together, unaware of the potential trouble he was in. Alec filled him in on what Forensics had told him.

'Shit. Can you imagine dying with the taste of ear wax in your mouth.' They'd hardly noticed Toria coming up behind them. Davies had to admit she had a strange way of looking at things, but she was shaping up to be a good cop.

The adrenalin flooded through his body, which was just as well as he hadn't slept for the best part of twenty-four hours. He needed a decent sleep, a shower and a shave, in no particular order. None of which was likely given the fact there was a killer on the loose, casually roaming the city choking people with their own body parts. What kind of fucked-up world were they living in?

They needed to identify this victim, and fast. It didn't take his detective badge to make the connection with Harry Nugent. This was no random murder. This had all the markings of a gangland killing. A revenge attack on a rival drug dealer, or money-lender who'd pushed his luck once too often. Or maybe another paedophile. Perhaps he should have felt a slight pang of professional shame at the comfort that brought him – not because the victim had been served a particularly savage type of rough justice, but rather because it was unlikely that the killer was a danger to the general public at this immediate time. He'd bet his pension that he was unlikely to strike again any time soon.

His phone buzzed in his pocket and he answered it with his thumb as he pressed it to his ear. 'Fuck.'

He could see Rosemary get into her car; she looked as tired as he did. Poor soul. She'd be getting no sleep tonight either.

'We've got another one,' he said, making his way back to his car and expecting the others to follow.

25

It hadn't taken long to identify both victims; they'd had their driver's licences and credit cards on them and one had even had his Tesco Clubcard on his body when they'd been found. Clearly the killer didn't give a shit about the cops knowing who they were.

'Fuck.' Sometimes there was no other word for it. Graham Petrie, the unfortunate chap who died with the taste of ear wax in his mouth, was a fifty-two year old accountant. Recently divorced with two children and, until he was found swinging in Bath Lane, hadn't been known to the police. Andrew Cruickshank had a rather more picturesque setting to his demise. His body had been found hanging just off Kelvin Walkway with a lovely view of the river, which had been wasted on him as Toria had pointed out at the time: 'Shame he couldn't see it… what with his eyes being gouged out and stuffed down his throat.'

The mutilation, as Rosemary had confirmed, had been carried out whilst he was still alive. On the face of it he'd been an ordinary guy, twice married, former taxi driver and, apart from a drink-driving conviction over twenty years ago, was pretty much under the police radar with no obvious connection to either Nugent or Petrie.

The atmosphere had been tense that morning. Davies had already gone over the bare facts, which were scant to say the least, not that that stopped press speculation. Hardly surprising really.

This wasn't going to be easy and the Chief Constable would have his balls on a plate if he didn't shut this one down quick-style. This killer was targeting certain individuals for a reason and was unlikely to be a danger to the public at large. But anyone who could orchestrate the hanging of three middle-aged men and mutilate their faces had a core of steel running through them. They were waiting for the full post-mortem reports, but the initial findings were that the two latest victims had died within twelve hours of each other. This was vague to say the least. Davies knew that could mean anything up to twenty-four hours apart, or they might well have died simultaneously, meaning they were looking for not one, but two killers working together. That would be some fucking collective grudge. Perhaps Nugent's murder really had been a gangland execution and had nothing to do with his depravity.

'Right, guys, we need to establish what the two victims were doing in the twenty-four hours before they died. Was there anything that linked them? Were they known to each other? Did they drink at the same bars?' Davies knew there could be dozens of tenuous links, some might be significant, others meaningless. But they'd have no choice but to check every single one.

'Sir...' no matter how many times he'd told her otherwise, Toria fell back into the habit of raising her hand before speaking '... has there been a warrant to seize any laptops, computers, tablets...?'

She was one step ahead of him. 'As DC Law has alluded to, we need to investigate the possibility of a paedophile ring. But nothing to the families, right?' She looked desperate to get going but he needed to have a quick word at the end of the briefing and asked her to hang back for a few minutes.

'CCTV?' Davies gave Jim the nod to jump in. 'There're no cameras near the Kelvinbridge site,' he said. 'Nearest ones are Queen Margaret Drive. But we're checking every car that was in the vicinity in the previous twelve hours and cross referencing number plate recognition with those in and around Hope Street.'

Davies felt his heart sink further into his gut. Few criminals with the nouse to carry out these executions would be cruising around in the family hatchback. Beat-up vans, dodgy number plates, stolen cars. They knew how to cover their tracks. Once again, the press would be their best bet and it was more vital than ever to keep them all on-side.

'I'm assuming the cameras on Bath Street came up with something better?'

Jim stood up, passing him the stills from the CCTV, which he pinned on the wall behind him. He'd already picked out the ones he thought relevant: three drunks staggering up Douglas Street, arms round each other, holding each other steady. It was impossible to make out their faces but the one in the middle looked by far the worse for wear; he wasn't being helped along, he was being dragged, his feet trailing on the ground, head hanging. Alec checked the time on the picture: 23:43.

'Get me the tape for this.'

Jim was already on the case, knowing this might well be their victim, half dead, being dragged into the lane, too far gone to put up any sort of a fight. Crimes committed in plain sight were often the easiest to stage.

Closing up on the faces didn't make for easy identification – grainy pictures on a damp night, heads down, hoods up – but it gave them a probable time of death and at least something to go on. And Alec knew that, despite no clear facial recognition, it was often possible to make a rough guess as to the ages of those in the frame, and it was always surprising how many people were recognised by the way they walked, their mannerisms, their body language.

He looked at the picture again. It could be Petrie; there was no way of telling. 'Can we get our tech guys onto this?' Davies knew that software was becoming increasingly sophisticated and they might well be able to say if the guy being dragged along was the same height and build as their victim. 'Get this tape to every news outlet we know.' He addressed the uniforms at the back of the room. 'Check for any similar scenario with drunks being dragged down Byres Road.'

Davies cornered Toria before she left the briefing room. He'd sent her and McVeigh home just after 3 a.m. the previous night; not because he was getting soft, but he'd needed them fresh for the morning and, being the old fashioned type, he'd much rather his officers weren't wearing blue tights and covered in glitter.

'Sir?'

'I've assigned someone else to look through Petrie and Cruikshank's computers.'

She squared up to him. 'Is this because I'm a female officer, sir? I'm as capable as the next man of this investigation.'

He placed his hands on her shoulders; he wasn't the touchy feely type, but needed her to know he was on her side. 'Listen, Toria, there's not one *person* on this team capable of looking at such images without being affected. I'm handing it over to Vice.' She looked as though she was about to interrupt, but he held his hand up. 'They're specially trained in child abuse sites. You know as well as I do, they've got a hellish job. But they get the right training, and they get the right support. You're no use to me traumatised. I need you on your feet and part of this team.'

She nodded. 'Sir.' And walked away.

'They must have been up to their necks in some shit.' McVeigh handed him a coffee as they walked back to his office. 'Neither of them are on the sex offenders' register either.'

Davies was exhausted. He'd not been home in over two days, once again deciding to grab a few hours' shut-eye at the station last night. He was spending so little time at his flat now he wondered if he'd be better selling it and making his locker here a bit more homely.

He sipped his coffee, scalding his tongue slightly. He couldn't settle and had to get out of the station, needed to get back to the crime scene. He handed the mug back to McVeigh. 'Any chance you'll ever make a decent cup of coffee?'

The Scene of Crime Officers were still at the scene when they arrived at Bath Lane. Sometimes these things just took as long as they took, and that was that. A few reporters were still hanging about, drinking coffee from disposable cups, chatting together, enjoying the skive knowing full well they'd get little more out of the scene. A small crowd of almost uninterested bystanders remained huddled around the edges of the cordoned off area and Davies wondered how bad Sunday afternoon telly really was that some people preferred to stand on the periphery of a crime scene trying to catch a glimpse of gore. What they hoped to see was anyone's guess. Petrie's body had already been removed; Forensics now believed he'd been attacked and mutilated in a disused storeroom on the first floor, then pushed out of the window. Davies knew every piece of information he needed would be relayed back to him in the office. But old habits died hard and he just needed to get a feel for the crime scene.

'Choking someone with their own ears,' Jim said as they got back into the car. 'Now that's some seriously sick bastard at work.'

Davies shot him a look. He wasn't helping here.

26

'Whatever it is,' said McVeigh, 'they've pissed someone off big style.' Either he was getting soft or going daft in his old age or both, but McVeigh didn't irritate him quite as much as he used to. And on a good day he could be a bit of a laugh. Although that sort of thing was always subjective.

Nothing incriminating was found on any of the devices seized from either Petrie or Cruickshank's homes. Although that didn't rule them out of being part of a paedophile ring there was no evidence of that being the case. Usually that would have been good news for Davies but as it stood it just gave him a bigger headache than usual to deal with.

'I mean, slicing off someone's tongue and ears and...' McVeigh was on a roll now, clearly taking Davies's lack of response as permission to carry on. They stood on the doorstep, McVeigh stamping his feet as usual against the cold, his flimsy jacket flapping in the wind as Davies tugged the collar of his padded anorak tight around his neck. One of the best things he'd discovered about having McVeigh as a partner was his remarkable ability to hold an entire conversation single-handedly without expecting a reply. 'And Nugent.' He made that face usually reserved for alcohol-free beer. 'Must have been a nightmare for his wife.'

Davies pressed the doorbell again, gave it a few seconds before knocking loudly.

There was a car with a personalised number plate in the driveway; that and the fact every light in the house appeared to be on suggested that Frank Fitzgerald was at home. He owned the taxi company that Andrew Cruickshank had worked for and Graham Petrie had handled his accounts at one stage. It wasn't much of a link, but the only one the cops had so far to connect at least two of the victims. He'd already given a statement, had no real motive and boiler-plate alibi, not that that meant much. Fitzgerald wasn't the kind of man who did his own dirty work. A small-time gangster, he was well known to most of the low-level businessmen in Glasgow, and, of course, the cops.

'Can you imagine seeing that, him swinging there?' McVeigh was in full flow, describing Nugent's corpse in detail. 'I mean for fu… Oh, hello.'

The door was opened by a young girl pulling headphones from her ears. She looked barely out of her teens and thoroughly pissed off by the intrusion. She looked them up and down, clearly expecting them to make the first move.

'Is your dad in?' Davies couldn't be arsed being politic; he'd seen it too many times. Craggy old guys who'd made a few bob, snaring young girls and thinking that was some sort of status symbol.

She shrugged. 'No idea. Haven't seen him since I was six.' Davies suppressed a smile; this one was good.

'You his boyfriend, then?' she asked, clocking his smile.

'No, I don't like guys that shit on their families. Can we come in, then?' He pushed his foot against the door, expecting some resistance, but it opened wide.

'Be my guest – what's one more sad old pervert among friends?' She walked slowly through the hall towards the back of the house. It was all oak beams and white walls. The kitchen had a vaulted ceiling, a wood-burning stove on at full pelt and a wall of glass that opened up to a view that would have made Monet weep. How the hell did people afford to live like this?

'Wow.' McVeigh was turning around, his neck bent at almost a ninety degree angle, staring at the ceiling.

'I don't suppose you get to see the inside of civilisation very often on a copper's salary?'

Touché. This particular double-edged sword let them know she was smart *and* had recognised they were cops. But the fact she neither asked their names nor for ID suggested she had little loyalty to her benefactor.

'Nah, just wondering why the beams are using traditional pitch and rise fixings on a contemporary fold and slant construction.' McVeigh's frown looked seriously concerned. 'D'you get a problem with leaks at all?'

Davies disguised his snort as a sneeze, laughing into his hanky.

'What the fuck d'you want?' She was clearly more than a little pissed off now. Didn't seem to like being on the back foot.

'D'you want to tell Daddy Warbucks that he has a visitor?' Davies had stopped smiling and meant business.

'Some time today, preferably,' McVeigh added, making a pantomime of looking at his wrist, then tugging his sleeve down sharply when it was obvious he'd forgotten to put a watch on.

'Gentlemen, to what do I owe the pleasure?' Fitzgerald wandered into the kitchen, larger than life and twice as ugly. His dressing gown was tied low around his waist, under his gut. It had some sort of designer logo on the pocket and sleeve that Davies could neither read nor recognise. He stretched his arms out, yawning in a ridiculously theatrical manner to let them know he'd just woken up, before winking at his girlfriend, then cocking his head to one side and making a kind of clicking noise normally associated with guiding horses. It seemed to do the trick and the girlfriend trotted off, closing the door softly behind her. It was the modern day equivalent of, *'Oi, get yer knickers on and make us a cup of tea.'* Davies shot his partner a look. He felt as though they'd stumbled onto the set of *The Sweeney*. Why did these pricks do that? He'd heard that the junior league mafia in New Jersey spoke like every other kid on the block until *The Sopranos* was aired. After that they developed accents and characteristics that lived up to their on-screen stereotypes. Davies had noticed it here too. Small-time crooks acting like extras from *The Sweeney*, or swaggering about as though they were in *Taggart*. It was a fucking joke, or would be had it not been so sad.

'You're looking well, Fitzgerald.' Davies always preferred to be gracious to the host, who twitched his eyebrows in return.

'Not bad, eh?' He cocked his head towards the door, in apparent reference to the poor girl he was shagging. Obviously thought it gave him a bit of kudos. Thought Davies envied his lifestyle.

'Oh, I prefer mine when they're old enough to shave.' They both shot a look at McVeigh, who had somehow managed to drop a bombshell without even a flicker of emotion showing on his face.

'What?' Fitzgerald's nostrils flared as he stared at McVeigh for a response, but instead he leaned back against the worktop, looked around the kitchen and decided he had finished speaking.

Davies quickly picked up, couldn't afford to lose any ground. 'What was your involvement with Harry Nugent?'

'Harry who?'

Davies was getting tired of holding it all in. Tired of the modern ways, the anger management courses, the gender neutral toilets, the sharing, caring attitude that cops were now supposed to display; they were all getting on his tits. 'Listen.' He managed to button his lip and not call him a fat fucking slug; instead he sighed and folded his arms. 'Nugent? You know. The guy who was found hanging from the rafters, the guy who's been plastered all over the news this past week, the guy who's more well known in Glasgow than a Provvie Cheque?'

Fitzgerald licked his tongue over his bottom lip like a lizard. 'What about him?' he asked, gallus as fuck.

'He's dead and I want answers.' There was a very slight flicker of something – he couldn't quite tell what – in Fitzgerald's eyes. 'We know you have connections to Andrew Cruickshank and Graham Petrie—'

Fitzgerald let out a laugh. 'What, some bloke that taxied for me and an accountant that filled out my tax returns ten years ago get themselves killed and you think that puts me in the frame?' He stood up, opened the fridge and started slugging milk straight from the carton. 'Is that honestly the best you have just now? Fuck's sake, no wonder Glasgow's such a cesspit if we're relying on yous lot to keep us safe.'

Davies let out an exaggerated sigh. 'I'm not even going to ask you to play nice.' He stood up to leave. 'I'll come back, with a warrant.' Davies had to box clever with this one. He didn't actually have a reason to arrest or even hold Fitzgerald at this time. He just wanted to piss him off a bit.

They made their way to the door as Fitzgerald's whistle pierced through the house. As if by magic the girlfriend appeared and opened the hall door.

'You know, you don't need to stay with a creep like him.' McVeigh was better with people than Davies.

'Really?' She glanced back through to the kitchen. 'Being with that "creep" is paying for my PhD.' She thought for a moment. 'I can either work in Wetherspoon's for a year, or spend a few hours with him. He's a dead loss and can't get it up, so as far as I'm concerned it's easy money.'

McVeigh's mouth dropped a few centimetres before he checked himself. 'PhD? In what?'

'Consumerism and Eco Biodiversity.'

'Shit. Really?'

She rolled her eyes. 'No, I'm a fucking hooker, ya twat. Now piss off.'

She slammed the door, leaving both of them pondering that one as they got back into the car.

*

Oonagh stood on the doorstep and rattled the letter box. She'd managed to track down Hannah Gray's mum to an address in Milngavie, just north of Glasgow. By all accounts she was no longer with Hannah's dad but had kept her married name which had made her easier to trace. Oonagh's earlier attempts to speak to Vivienne Gray had been less than successful; she'd refused to speak to Oonagh and slammed the door in her face at the first mention of her daughter's name. But this time Oonagh had a greater sense of urgency.

She waited a few moments more. There was no car in the driveway but it might have been in the garage, which had been locked when Oonagh had tried the handle. There was a light on in the hall too, so she worked on the assumption that someone was home. She crouched down, peering through the letter box. 'Mrs Gray, please, I just want to have a few words with you…' Nothing. 'Mrs Gray? Five minutes is all I'm asking.' Oonagh dropped her card with her contact details through the door and felt like a total shit as she made her way back down the path to her car. What she had to say to Vivienne Gray couldn't be done over the phone.

27

'So tell me, Ash, what've you got for me?'

Oonagh had agreed to meet Ash in the little tea house off Otago Lane. No one ever really paid too much attention to anyone else there; disparate elements of society were left free to plan worker revolts, discuss indie referendums or look at vintage knitting patterns unhindered by judgement, prying eyes or earwigging. Also it was where Ash had suggested and it would have taken up too much brain space for her to think of somewhere else. She pulled up a chair, preferring to sit upright as Ash appeared to have been swallowed by an overstuffed beanbag masquerading as a sofa.

His laptop was open and fired up on the coffee table; Ash had the look of a hungry dog faced with a family-sized bag of biscuits. He licked his lips slightly; this really was meat and drink to him. Whoever would have guessed accountants had so much fun?

Ash ran through the basics. 'This guy is loaded, Oonagh, no mistaking that. And, I have to say, his bookkeeping is very impressive.' Oonagh was beginning to realise that even the most evil villains were looked upon favourably if they had a well-kept set of books.

From what Ash could see, Nugent had bought up a load of small, almost bankrupt, businesses over the last twenty years. Because they'd been in receivership he'd got them for peanuts, but they were the perfect front for his other business ventures, keeping his name out of it. With over twenty business accounts, he used the failing businesses to make full use of tax benefits and allowances, with a steady income streaming into each one each year. On their own they didn't amount to much, but lumped together they netted a hefty profit each year.

'You see this part.' Ash pointed to the screen. 'He just uses initials for each transaction. And there are properties for each once. Whoever this guy is, he's accumulating millions. Seriously, I'm impressed.'

This didn't really give Oonagh very much more to go on, other than the fact Harry Nugent was loaded. There was nothing to say what the businesses were.

'There's nothing dodgy here that I can see, Oonagh.' Her heart sank slightly; this wasn't quite what she was paying over the odds for. Initially Ash had offered his services for mates' rates as a favour, but Oonagh had insisted on paying over the odds to get the results quickly. She'd almost balked when she'd seen the email he'd sent with his prices on it. His hourly rate would have paid off the national debt of a small country and she doubted if she'd be able to bung that amount through on expenses. She'd hoped it was worth it, but now wasn't so sure.

'Right, the initial tender for the parent company, Pitch Perfect, had been granted almost a quarter of a century ago.' He raised his eyebrows over his glasses and waited for a nod before he continued. 'But, despite Strathclyde being disbanded as a region more than twenty years ago, Pitch Perfect's contract had been automatically renewed by the new Glasgow City Council ever since.'

Forensic accountant seemed so much more exciting than chartered and she was in awe of the way he seemed to be able to gnaw his way through figures and make sense of them all. 'I know, Ash, but can you humour me here? Where's the dodgy bit?' She needed to know what Nugent was up to.

'Oonagh, the accounts themselves are squeaky clean.'

Shit, she'd been hoping he'd at least been dodging taxes. Something, anything to pin some dirt on this creep.

'It's this part that gets more interesting.'

Oonagh stopped sipping her tea for a moment, anxious to hear more.

'From what I can see Pitch Perfect paid no business rates in the first year.'

'That's not unusual, is it?' Oonagh knew there were all sorts of incentives for new businesses.

'The premises were leased too.' Again, it wasn't exactly earth shattering information. Things that business analysts found fascinating didn't really do it for Oonagh, and neither did this tea that tasted like the inside of a sock drawer, but she let Ash continue. 'And this is where it gets interesting...'

Thank God.

'The only records in any of his accounts for rent or business rates were for a nominal amount.'

'Oh! Tell me more.' She didn't feel that excited but Ash seemed fired up so she knew this must be leading somewhere.

From what Ash could see, after the first gratis year, Pitch Perfect had paid a paltry twenty quid annually for business rates. The lease on its south side factory was even less, the ownership of the factory eventually passing over to Nugent for *grace and favour*. This was sounding more and more rotten. Oonagh wasn't exactly shocked at the suggestion that there were some dodgy business deals going on behind the closed doors of local authorities, but Harry Nugent was being handed success on a plate. They seemed to be greasing his palms, not the other way around.

'Do we know who signed off the initial tender, Ash?'

'Yip, the business licensing department. It was rubber stamped and looks kosher.'

'Is there a signature? Do we have a name?'

Ash ran his finger down the screen. 'You betcha, got that here. It was... Graham Petrie.' Ash sat back. 'He's the one you need to talk to.'

Oonagh agreed but, given that he was found swinging from a hook in Bath Lane less than three days ago, that would prove tricky.

28

The newsroom was buzzing. The discovery of two more bodies swinging in Glasgow's city centre minus parts of their faces had taken the investigation into Harry Nugent's murder on a completely different path. Now it was all systems go to establish a connection between the three men. And from what she could gather, Oonagh was the only one so far to connect two of them.

'I want this story.' Oonagh had gone over all the arguments in her head about why she, and not the senior crime correspondent, should be covering this; she needed to box clever here. There was no way she could let anyone know at this stage about Petrie's link to Nugent. 'I've already established a relationship with Nugent's widow…' She was champing at the bit, but careful not to let on just how much Sarah Nugent had told her.

Alan wasn't really interested. Instead he went for a bit of drama, rubbing his temple with his thumb and forefinger. 'Oonagh, you're actually the only person who can give me a headache before you come in the fucking door.'

'Nurofen's pretty good for that.'

'You're not the crime correspondent, Oonagh.' She held her hands out, palms upwards, saying, *so what?* What she really wanted to say was, *and the crime corr is so busy toadying up to Glasgow gangsters and taking backhanders that he's letting one of the biggest stories of the decade slip from his grasp*.

Alan looked up from his screen. 'I can't just hand over a story of this magnitude.' He stopped and caught her eye. 'You've got something else, haven't you?'

Shit. Her poker face was letting her down. She shook her head. Tried to act dumb.

'You know more than you're letting on, O'Neil.'

'Like what?' There was no way she was admitting to how deep she was into this at this stage. Not until she had a cast-iron guarantee it wouldn't be snatched from her.

'Oonagh, we need to work as a team here.' Alan was trying to appeal to her better nature. 'If you're sitting on something that could give us an exclusive…' he faltered slightly '… then it's your… your duty to pitch in here.' Unfortunately for Alan, Oonagh had left her better nature at home that day. She'd heard some nonsense in her time, but this was in a class of its own.

Oonagh was no stranger to how these things worked. 'No, Alan, honestly. Nothing more than a burning desire to do a good job.' One look told her he knew she was bullshitting him, but she stood her ground.

Alan tried to read her expression, then gave up and wafted his hand around, which generally said, *close the door on your way out*.

The red tops were scattered all over the news desk. Each

headline desperately trying to make a connection between Harry Nugent, Graham Petrie and Andrew Cruickshank. Whatever had happened, this was no small-time drugs deal or a petty gambling debt. That much was obvious. So far Andrew Cruickshank was the missing link. And why the hell Petrie had given Nugent the golden ticket was anyone's guess.

Oonagh was desperate to get the low-down from both families, but the police had put a lock down on them and banned the press from even approaching them. She wandered out of Alan's office, purposely leaving the door open just to annoy him, and pretended not to care as she picked up the phone and dialled.

The Ship's Bell was one of the oldest pubs in the west end. Its function in this instance wasn't just to serve a round of drinks, but it was quiet and dark and she knew they'd be pretty much left alone without too many people trying to earwig in on their conversation. It was also close enough to the studio that she could walk and get some much needed fresh air. The blackboard outside said that steak pie was today's special. That hadn't changed since the early nineties but they did fish and chips too. Oonagh noticed a new sign, freshly chalked, informing punters they now served cocktails. It had clearly changed since the last time she'd been.

Despite the foray into the brave new world of cocktails, the interior looked pretty much as it had done for the past twenty years. Scrubbed clean tables and several booths tucked in along the side of one wall, plush red velvet cushions long since worn flat by the countless bums that had frequented The Ship's Bell over the years. The place was half empty, or half full, depending on your demeanour and a quick scan told her Alec hadn't arrived yet. The barmaid's smile, which was as wide as the Clyde, owed more to a set of badly fitting dentures than a warm personality, but as Oonagh approached the counter the smile reached her eyes as she dried off a tray of glasses and asked her what she fancied. Oonagh had left her car at the studio so decided to throw caution to the wind. 'Oh, go on, I think I may try one of your cocktails.'

The barmaid continued to wipe the glasses. 'Margaret, the lassie that does them, is off sick today.'

'Wine?'

'Red or white?'

'Gin and tonic, please. Double.' She spotted Alec through the frosted glass of the front door. He was easy to recognise, being taller than your average Glaswegian, so she ordered him a sparkling water; he was a stickler for the rules and never drank on duty.

'I can't stay long, Oon. I'm up to my eyes in it.' This seemed to be Alec's default now every time they met. She leaned over to give him a kiss, but he moved his head awkwardly and Oonagh lost her balance and landed a kiss on his shoulder.

'Sorry,' she said, rubbing the lipstick from his jacket.

They sat in a booth, which was surprisingly comfy, and she was surprised to feel a very slight pang in her chest. Whether that was because she was ready for a session or she genuinely was sorry he couldn't stay, she wasn't quite sure herself.

'What a fucker of a day this is turning out to be.' Alec

gulped down his water, eyeing the impressive array of whisky along the entire length of the bar.

'So what's going down?' She hoped she sounded innocent enough. Alec seemed to have a built-in bullshit alert when it came to Oonagh and knew when she was hiding something.

'Oh, just work, you know.'

She stuck her tongue in her cheek, tried not to smile. 'You know what I mean, Alec, stop being coy. I'm talking about the case.'

He shrugged his shoulders. 'Your guess is as good as ours.'

The official line was that the inquiry was still at the initial stages; there was nothing at this stage to suggest the cases were linked. Which was cop-speak for *all three people were killed by the same person but we're not sure who*.

'Did you find anything dodgy on Petrie or Cruickshank?' She waited a moment, desperate to know if either were part of Nugent's network. 'I take it you seized their laptops and phones and stuff?'

'How the hell did you know about that?'

'Sarah Nugent. She told me you'd taken Harry's laptop.' She reassured herself that she hadn't broken any confidence. Alec knew she'd been talking to Nugent's widow. 'Come on, Alec, it hardly takes a criminal mastermind to think that might be the link.'

He shook his head, his shoulders slumped; he looked worn out. 'Nothing. Shit, it would almost have been easier if we had. At least that way…' He stopped himself, clearly didn't want to say the inevitable. That they'd have welcomed finding images of abuse if it'd meant cracking this case. 'Och, you know what I mean.'

'I know.' She touched his arm and he patted her hand, giving her a little smile. Oonagh was as certain as she could be that the police knew nothing about the link between Nugent and Petrie. She kept her own findings on Harry Nugent very much to herself. 'They'll have been up to their necks in something.' Keeping up the pretence.

'Oonagh, have you ever thought about joining the CID? We could really do with someone with your insight on the team.'

Alec never failed to make her laugh, even when he was being brutally sarcastic. 'Thanks, Alec, but I'm not sure I could go back to shift work.' He was getting harder and harder to get information out of this weather, and she told him so.

'We're in the very early stages of one of the biggest cases in the city's recent history and you've got a lip on because I won't start giving you clues?'

'I bet it was gambling.'

He nodded. 'Probably, or drugs, or human trafficking, or...' He was doing that sarcastic thing again.

'Listen, Alec, can you give me anything here?' One look at his face and she had her answer.

'Can we leave it, Oonagh?' She was about to interrupt, badger him, when she caught a look in his eye. 'I'm knackered, haven't been back at the flat for two nights and I just want an hour away from the office, and phones and questions and...' He downed the last of his water, then rubbed his eyes with his fingertips. 'I just want a breather.'

'That bad, eh?'

He nodded and, despite his reticence at giving her any inside information, Oonagh had that warm fuzzy feeling from the adrenalin rush of knowing that the shit was about to hit the fan.

29

The Aston was hidden underneath Glasgow's Central Station, formed from a subterranean warren of tunnels once used to store liquor and grain brought into the city. With its mood lighting and state-of-the-art décor, it had undergone an impressive transformation. Oonagh walked down the metal staircase leading to the main bar and caught her heel in a hole on the bottom one which sent her flying into the back of a waiter, who thankfully had an empty tray and, from what she could gather, lightning speed reflexes. He spun round and grabbed her under her arms.

'I'm getting good at this,' he said, making sure she was upright before moving on.

Oonagh looked round, cursing the stupid bloody interior designer who thought it was a good idea to install a perforated staircase in a Glasgow bar that specialised in gin.

She didn't recognise her at first; it was only when she tilted her head to one side and gave a very small nod that Oonagh made her way to the last booth.

'I like the new look.' Sarah Nugent's long shaggy blonde hair was gone, replaced by a copper-brown shiny new short cut, flicking out around her face. 'I almost didn't recognise you.' Oonagh waited to see if that was why she went for the change, to make it less likely people would recognise her, but she didn't offer any explanation. Just asked Oonagh what she fancied to drink, then gave the waiter the order.

'Have the police asked you about Graham Petrie?'

Sarah nodded. 'Him and the other chap who was killed.' At least she had the decency not to act completely clueless. 'But I couldn't tell them much. Didn't know them.'

'Did Harry know them?' Oonagh already knew the answer to that one, but was keen to hear Sarah's version of events.

'Not that I knew of.' For now, Oonagh had to believe her, and at this stage wasn't sure if the police had made the same connection she had between Petrie and Nugent.

'I've had a forensic accountant look over Harry's records, Sarah.' A look flashed across the other woman's face. 'Don't worry, it's in confidence, there's nothing to attach you to this.' Oonagh paused before dropping the bombshell; she wanted to gauge her reaction. 'Graham Petrie was the one who rubber stamped Harry's initial business tender back in '94.'

Judging by her expression, this was news to his widow.

'He headed up the council business licence department at the time.' Oonagh knew that it was this initial contract and its subsequent success that had given Harry the help he'd needed. Had secured the much coveted and very lucrative council contracts. What she couldn't work out was why.

'Have you any idea why Petrie would give Harry such a leg up, Sarah?'

She shook her head, her thoughts lost somewhere in the bottom of her glass.

It didn't make sense. There was no apparent connection between the men either before or afterwards. But all Oonagh did know was that at one time that pair had been as thick as thieves. 'I assume it's no secret to you that Harry was worth millions?'

Sarah let out a sigh, bit her bottom lip slightly and couldn't meet Oonagh's gaze. 'Yeah.'

From what Sarah had told her, Harry's luxury flats were a front for underage brothels that provided entertainment for high ranking public figures.

'Sarah, you need to tell me who these kids are. The ones in the brothels.' Nugent's clients had a taste for the twisted and perverse, and Harry had to ensure he had a steady stream of young boys and girls at their disposal. Sarah said nothing. 'These kids are still being abused. For fuck's sake. There's no such thing as underage brothels. It's child abuse. No other word for it.' The amount of money Nugent was being paid each month was staggering. And Oonagh guessed it was just the tip of the iceberg. She made to leave. 'I'll ask you once more. If you don't tell me, Sarah, then all bets are off and I'm going to the police.'

Sarah grabbed her wrist; there was no mistaking the look of fear in her eyes. 'Please.' She held onto Oonagh's arm. 'They'll kill me. And if you go to the cops...' She paused, shook her head. 'Let's just say I can't see them rushing to investigate this properly.'

Oonagh eased herself back down onto the chair. She wasn't quite buying Sarah's theory, but at this stage she knew she didn't have enough evidence to identify the brothels. 'OK. Who were his clients, Sarah?' What she needed now were hard facts. 'And addresses of the properties.' As far as she could tell most of it was written in code.

'I've given you as much as I can. That's as much as I know.'

Oonagh drummed her fingernails on the table. Any sympathy she once had for Sarah Nugent was wearing thin. This woman had enjoyed a lavish lifestyle off the back of human misery and Oonagh's patience was exhausting itself.

'I know what you think of me. That I'm trash, as bad as he was.' Sarah faltered for a moment, took a deep breath, the tip of her nose tinged with the red threat of tears. 'D'you think I'd ever have been allowed to speak out? He'd have killed me.'

'The police would have...'

'Oh, please...' She laughed in her face. 'D'you know how many high ranking officers and politicians use services like this?' Sarah sat back, folded her arms and shook her head, seemingly appalled by Oonagh's apparent naivety.

'You need to start naming names, Sarah. You've ridden on this gravy train for long enough.' Oonagh was getting pissed off now.

'The truth is I don't actually know.' Oonagh guessed Sarah Nugent and the truth weren't the most comfortable bedfellows. 'It's complicated,' she added.

'You don't say.' This was going nowhere and Oonagh needed to get her back on track. 'If I'm going to make a programme, a feature length documentary, then I need you to be as open with me as possible.' Oonagh was bluffing – slightly. She already had the makings of a good doc on her hands, but with the high profile names she could blow the lid on this one.

'I honestly don't know.' Sarah looked directly into Oonagh's eyes. 'I swear, I wouldn't have given you this much if my plan was to hold out on you.' Her voice cracked slightly. Oonagh reached her hand across the table, touching Sarah's arm.

'Oh, hello, love.' The voice was instantly recognisable and seemed to come from nowhere. Oonagh quickly pulled her hand away from Sarah's arm and sat upright. 'Mum. What are you doing here?'

Fran smiled and gave Oonagh what could only be described as a knowing look. 'Mum, I'm actually working, can you...?' Fran switched her smile and knowing look to Sarah, then walked off. Oonagh spotted Owen come out from the toilets; he waved and was on his way over when Fran intercepted him and bundled him out of the door.

'Look, I'm sorry about that, it's just...'

It broke the ice. Sarah gave a soft laugh. ''S OK.'

That sick feeling stirred in the pit of Oonagh's stomach. She no longer had the guts for this. She'd covered many stories over the years and liked to think of herself as hardened. The tainted blood scandal had nearly broken her at the time. Talking to victims of the biggest peace-time tragedy in the UK. But child abuse, this was killing her. Try as she might she couldn't shake the feeling that she was glad

Nugent had suffered at the end. Hoped it was as slow and painful as it sounded.

'When did you first know that Harry was, well, that his tastes lay elsewhere?'

Sarah looked off into the middle distance. 'Harry was never what you'd call a *pushy* boyfriend. It was quite nice at first, but after we'd been married for about a year it was obvious he wasn't interested in me. He made all sorts of excuses not to have sex with me until eventually he couldn't even look at me.'

Sarah claimed that she had initially thought Harry might have been gay, something that would never have been admitted by a sports personality twenty years ago. Even now it could toll the death knell of their career. For some professions, homophobia and toxic masculinity were a given. An acceptable part of the culture.

'And how did you feel about that, Sarah? Most young brides would want some sort of physical contact with their husbands.'

Sarah pulled her jacket from the seat beside her and draped it around her shoulders. 'We don't all want the same things. Let's just say Harry was different from the men I was used to, and that...' She let it trail off.

'When did you realise there was... more to it?' Oonagh was surprised at how much she struggled to vocalise what Harry Nugent had been, what he'd done to those boys, what he'd facilitated other men to do.

Sarah shrugged. 'It's strange; there was no one single moment. It was just something that became sort of obvious as time went on.'

Oonagh struggled to get her head round this. 'It's amazing what we can normalise.' She didn't really mean that. She hoped to God she'd never be in a position where that was the norm.

'I didn't look too much into Harry's business affairs in the early days, then, by the time I delved a little deeper, well, it was too late.'

'What about Breakmire? What was going on there?'

'What d'you mean?'

Oonagh recapped some of the obvious corruption she'd uncovered from Nugent's documents. 'It was a joke. The staff were either on the make, or someone was creaming off a whole load of expenses.'

'Harry got me out of there pretty quick. I gave up my job just weeks after meeting him.'

Oonagh's heart sank, but she tried not to show it. 'Come on, Sarah. You worked there. You must know something of what went on?'

Sarah looked down at the table between them. She did that thing she'd done when Oonagh had first met her – scratched away at an imaginary stain. 'All I know is that Harry pretty much seemed to have the run of the place.'

'And no one questioned this?'

'No, not really.'

'But part of it was a secure unit. How can that be?'

'I told you before, Harry had a lot of friends in high places. It was like he had an access-all-areas pass to whichever part of the hospital he liked. He'd come and go as he pleased, whatever time of the day or night.'

'And no one questioned that? Some failed footballer swans about a hospital with vulnerable patients and no one checks him?'

'You need to understand – one of Harry's main skills was spotting a weak link and exploiting it. I told you he had friends in high places. And when he realised some of the staff were on the make, he used that as a threat to get them sacked.'

'Why not just blow the whistle on any corruption?' The whole concept seemed ludicrous to Oonagh. Just how many latex gloves and plasters could one person blag? There didn't seem to be anything else worth nicking from a hospital.

For the first time Sarah smiled, almost let out a laugh. 'Are you kidding? Once Harry got wind of a few dodgy overtime claims, excessive food and drink orders that were never reaching the patient, well, that was like a gift from the gods. Harry liked to have one over on people. It was his way of staying in control.'

Sarah Nugent stood up to go. She had the worried look of someone who had said too much. 'I need to head off.' She slid from the booth and was making her way to the door before Oonagh had a chance to stop her.

She hurried after her, throwing a tip down on the bar, smiling at the waiter who'd saved her blushes on the way in. 'I hadn't even had a drink when I took that tumble.' She laughed.

'Don't worry, your secret's safe with me,' he said, passing to serve another table.

Oonagh trotted back up the stairs, which led to the main concourse of Central Station. As usual it was thronging with people, the noise of the tannoy system competing with the Salvation Army band singing Christmas carols.

Something had been scratching away at her, playing on her mind for days now. Harry Nugent. She'd had to fork out for a forensic accountant to decipher his books, which he'd kept hidden from prying eyes. That man was careful to cover his tracks, yet someone like him would drop the ball and leave his laptop at home full of dodgy images. It didn't make sense.

Oonagh turned to catch Sarah Nugent getting into a black cab on Gordon Street. She was struggling now to believe a word that woman said.

30

Jim McVeigh was sitting at the far end of the bar, the victim of yet another haircut. Oonagh walked over and ruffled his head affectionately. 'Nice one.'

He flushed slightly and ran his hands over the top of his head. 'D'you think? Not too short?'

Oonagh, who had long suppressed a desire to take a pair of clippers to Jim's hair and relieve it from active duty, decided to lie. 'No. That's a good cut. Precision.'

'That new Turkish barber at the bottom of Hyndland Road.' Jim was lapping up the praise. 'He's really good.'

'What is it about Turkish barbers, eh? They're popping up all over the place.' Oonagh tried to steer the conversation away from Jim's hair. She felt she'd gone as far as she could with this one.

'This one's actually from Uzbekistan...' he took a sip of his drink '... but he couldn't afford to have that put on the sign.'

Oonagh burst out laughing. 'Seriously?'

Jim raised an eyebrow, gave her a look and shook his head. 'What're you having?' He stood up and glanced at his watch. 'The boss'll be here in five minutes.'

'What's that you're drinking?' Oonagh nodded towards his glass, which had a slice of pink grapefruit bobbing about in it.

Turned out Jim's poison was rhubarb and ginger gin which he assured Oonagh was most refreshing and she just had to try it.

She could have done with staying in tonight, she'd planned on an early night and had been in her jammies when she'd texted Alec on arriving home from meeting Sarah Nugent. She needed to pick his brains about something and suggested lunch the next day. Truth be told she also wanted to see him. They'd been friends for a long time, but recently she felt something had changed between them. He'd turned down lunch, explaining that all leave was cancelled for the foreseeable future, but mentioned that he'd be grabbing a quick pint with Jim on the way home if she fancied joining them. It was a manky night but she'd pulled on some clothes and headed down to Byres Road before she had a chance to change her mind.

Alec came through the door while Jim stood at the bar. He tipped his head, apparently agreeing to whatever it was that Jim said, made his way towards the table and sat opposite Oonagh. There was something different about him. She couldn't quite put her finger on it. He'd also had a haircut and Oonagh wondered if the barber was doing a special two-for-one on local coppers. It wasn't that though – he seemed less tired, looked better. Maybe even a bit younger.

'You're a bit spruced up.' He looked pleased that she'd noticed and Oonagh's stomach shifted slightly as she wondered if the extra effort was for her.

Jim negotiated his way back to the table, the three drinks squeezed between his hands, and set them down. 'I was just saying your boss is looking very dapper.' She was fishing to find out why before she went in for the kill.

Jim was clearly delighted to be given the free rein by Oonagh to gossip about his boss. 'Think he might be trying to impress someone.'

Alec knitted his eyebrows, tightened his lips slightly, telling Jim to shut it. He did and Oonagh took this as her cue to change the subject – to the one thing she really wanted to know about.

'Right,' she said, 'come on, you guys, give me what you know.' They both looked at her, pretending not to have a clue what she was on about. She raised her eyebrows and folded her arms.

'There's nothing to tell.' Alec was holding out on her. She was sure of it.

'You must have some kind of lead.' Alec shook his head and Oonagh knew she was being stonewalled. 'It's gangland after all, isn't it?'

'Oonagh, bugger off. There's nothing to tell.' Alec sipped his pint, but it was obvious that somewhere along the line Harry Nugent had crossed the wrong person, and the cops knew it. Otherwise they'd be going mental to find his killer, not sitting in a bar sipping pink gin. Oonagh decided not to share this last hypothesis with them.

'Anyway,' Alec changed the subject, 'why're you not at work? You're getting almost as lazy as him.'

She looked at her watch. 'Because it's almost nine o'clock?'

'Shit. Is it?' Alec laughed and Jim got up to go to the loo. She waited until he was out of ear-shot. 'Alec, can you just tell me one thing?'

'That depends.'

'Those images on Nugent's laptop…'

'Christ, Oon. Not this again. Please, you really need to give it a rest.'

'Your tech guys should be able to trace when they were uploaded, yeah?'

'Who've you been speaking to?' He came back too quickly. It was obvious something didn't add up.

'I'm right, aren't I?'

'I've no idea what you're talking about.'

'Those images, they'd been uploaded recently. Just tell me.' Oonagh could tell by his face and the fact he refused to answer that she was on the right track. She ran her fingers through her hair and leaned back on the chair. Alec tipped his head, looking over her shoulder, Jim was making his way back to the table.

She opened her bag, looking for an excuse to change the subject. 'Right, I'm on the bell, same again?'

But Alec stood up. 'Not for me. I need to get off.'

'Oh?' Oonagh tried not to sound, or feel, disappointed. She'd somehow hoped they'd be making a night of it and couldn't tell whether he genuinely had to leave or she'd pissed him off with her questions.

She turned to Jim, who was giving her the thumbs up. 'I'm happy to get pissed on ginger gin and grapefruit.'

She was about to try to persuade Alec to stay a while longer when she saw him come through the door. Instead she tugged at Alec's jacket. 'Look,' she said, head tilted, chin tucked, but eyes pinned on the dark haired guy who'd pulled up a seat by the window.

'What?' Alec instinctively twisted round, as did Jim.

'Don't look,' said Oonagh. 'Well, don't stare. Don't make it obvious.'

'Make what obvious? And what the hell am I supposed to not be looking at?'

Jim shrugged, looked clueless. Oonagh was going to have to help them out.

'The guy who's just come in. Ian Rankin.' The guy in question sat near the window with his back to them and most of the other punters in the bar. Jim craned his neck slightly. Alec looked none the wiser.

'What, the Rebus guy? What's he doing in Glasgow?' Jim was bobbing his head about, trying to get a better look. Oonagh slapped the back of his hand. 'Stop making it so obvious.'

Oonagh was a huge fan, but had never met Rankin in person. She toyed with the idea of going over, but what if he thought she was a crazy fan-girl stalker, or didn't know who she was, or, worse, did recognise her and still thought she was a crazy fan-girl stalker?

'Go and say hello.'

'No! He'll think I'm really...' she thought for a second '... trivial, or thick. People always think newsreaders are thick.'

Alec was clearly losing patience. 'Fuck's sake.' He left

the table and wandered across the crowded bar, stopping to tap Mr Rankin on the shoulder. Oonagh saw them exchange a few words, Alec tipped his head in their direction a few times and she could see the crime writer twist round in his chair, but there were too many people to make out his face, so she couldn't tell if he looked pleased or hacked off about being disturbed. Alec strode back over to where she and Jim sat. 'Is he well known?' Clearly no lover of crime fiction, Alec looked decidedly unimpressed with it all.

Oonagh nodded. 'What did you say to him?' She didn't imagine Alec did a great line in introductions.

'Just said my friend really likes you, would you like to join us for a drink?'

Oonagh's mouth hung open. Oh, shit, it was one step away from the *'my friend fancies you'* line from school, and she suddenly noticed Rankin weaving his way through the room towards them. Probably to threaten her with a restraining order.

'I wasn't a fan before,' said Alec, making to leave for the second time, 'but, bloody hell, writing all those books and the poor bloke can hardly speak English.'

Oonagh was trying to digest this last piece of information when a total stranger, who just moments before had been masquerading as a famous Scottish crime writer, arrived at their table. He grinned at them with perfect teeth, nodding his head, before sliding onto the seat beside Oonagh. Pressing his thigh against hers. Shit. It was the wrong guy. He held out his hand; limp handshakes were never Oonagh's thing, but she felt she'd given him enough encouragement to offer anything more.

'Pleased to meet you,' he said in a very thick Mediterranean accent; either Italian or perhaps Spanish, she couldn't tell which.

'My name is Estaban.' Spanish, then, she decided. Estaban went on to say he was a professor at the university. He didn't say which university, and was rather vague about the faculty he taught in, but he seemed to be on a roll and his English appeared to be far better than when he was speaking to Alec. 'Your friend said you liked me?'

She was drawing Alec daggers, who still didn't have a clue what was going on. Jim was now snorting into his ginger gin, having sucked the life out of the pink grapefruit, and Estaban had the confident air of a man who'd just saved himself a month's subscription from Match dot com. This wasn't going to end well. Oonagh had to think on her feet, and quickly. 'Estaban, I'm delighted to meet you too, but I'm afraid you rather misunderstood.'

He raised one eyebrow, inviting her to explain. 'It's not me who likes you,' she took a sip of her drink to buy a few vital seconds. 'It's my lovely friend, Jim, here…'

She didn't have to say anything else. Estaban was up and off, taking his ample thighs with him, before Jim had a chance to choke on his drink.

'Perhaps he just doesn't like redheads,' she said, and turned round to see if Alec was laughing too, but he was already making his way out of the door.

31

This was crazy. No matter how many times she looked at this it just didn't make sense. Harry Nugent had been given the keys to one of the most secure hospitals in Scotland, and access to some of the country's most vulnerable people. There was no proof that Harry was up to anything sinister at Breakmire, but it didn't take a huge leap of faith to guess that he'd been abusing young patients. Somebody somewhere had made a major cock-up, but sadly she doubted they'd ever have to pay for it.

Nugent's initial access to the hospital had by all accounts been in the guise of his sporting achievements and charitable works. Oonagh had seen it time and time again. The *celebrity halo*. The cloak of invisibility that ensured the rich, the famous, the do-gooders could do no wrong. Blinded by the pervert's fame, society went weak at the knees, rolled over and had its tummy tickled whilst the abuse continued unchallenged. This wasn't just an oversight by some overworked NHS staff too knackered to see what was in front of them. This had been rubber stamped by authorities far higher up the food chain.

Despite Oonagh's revulsion of the man, Nugent was a shit-hot businessman and knew how to exploit an opportunity. He'd gained the confidence of the hospital trustees by outlining a plan to streamline the operation. Suggesting he could blow the whistle on staff who were on the make. Looking at the expenses sheet, Oonagh could see there had been at least six birthdays a week at Breakmire, with enough goodies to sink the *Titanic*. And Harry had kept copies of everything. Oonagh guessed whoever was signing off this amount of grub would have their Tesco Clubcard rendered redundant through lack of use.

Over and above this was the overriding threat of fraudulent use of hospital accommodation. There had been three separate cottages attached to Breakmire. Pretty basic in themselves, but they had allowed staff to sleep on the premises when necessary. Despite the lack of luxury in these cottages, it appeared that certain members of staff with certain privileges had either been living in them whilst renting their own gaffs out, or simply using them as boltholes to conduct their own affairs. Oonagh couldn't imagine how goddamned awful someone's home would need to be to prefer living in a magnolia box in the grounds of an asylum. It was like 'Butlins meets *One Flew Over the Cuckoo's Nest*.

But if it took a thief to catch a thief, then Harry Nugent knew the ropes better than anyone, and could spot gaps in the system big enough to drive a coach and horses through, bringing that certain wee gravy train to a standstill. Not that this was enough to reign supreme over the existing staff, but his approval by the board had lent him an unfair advantage, which he'd used to hang the threat of power over anyone who'd questioned his motives.

The press coverage of his good works was astounding. His contacts ensured that every week a fresh celebrity paid the hospital a visit, and with that came the obligatory photo opportunity. It was well worth it. It gave him the pass key he needed. The access-all-areas lanyard. His golden ticket to wherever the fuck he wanted to go.

Some of the pictures made her feel sick. Him grinning away good-style with a group of patients, Blessed Harry of the vulnerable. This was getting increasingly murkier, but still there was no concrete proof that he was a dodgy pervert abusing the vulnerable and getting a major slap on the back for his trouble.

She'd gathered as much information as she could, sifting through what records she could find. It astonished her how many had been destroyed. There had been a list of every member of staff at the hospital, but it didn't include agency nurses or locums, and of course there would have been frequent visitors as well as official visitors, similar to Harry Nugent but without the malicious intent. This would be a bugger to prove, but so far it was looking as though Nugent had used Breakmire as his own private pleasure palace, the pleasure having been distinctly one-sided.

Her back was starting to ache from leaning over the laptop. She'd been there for hours just scanning the names, trying to find something that would leap out and tell her exactly what Harry Nugent had been up to. If she was honest with herself, she wasn't that concerned who had actually carried out the deed, but no one carried out such an elaborate murder because they were a bit pissed off. The wife had been pretty much ruled out early on – that wasn't the punishment doled out for leaving the loo seat up.

Oonagh felt as though she were drowning in a sea of paperwork. Harry Nugent had had his fingers in so many pies it was a wonder he'd had time for anything else.

Sophie had agreed to come in and help her for a few hours. It was her evening off and Oonagh knew she'd only offered to make a good impression. She hated taking advantage of Sophie's good nature, but she was really struggling here and this would take hours on her own. Besides, Sophie was shit-hot at this kind of thing. Could rattle through reams of information, key in important dates, key events and people and come up with a pattern. Oonagh glanced at the clock: just gone seven-thirty. She heard Sophie panting as she ran towards her down the corridor into the newsroom.

'Hey, thanks for coming in.' Sophie's face looked redder than usual, more so than just being pink from her exertion. 'How's the face?'

'Oh.' Sophie rubbed her cheekbone, blushing more. The bruise bursting across her cheek had faded to a pale yellow tinged with green. 'Fine.' She faltered for a moment. 'Fine, it's just… it's almost…' She let the sentence fade into nothing as she pulled off her jacket and Oonagh noticed a fresh bruise on her wrist. Sophie caught the look and tugged her sleeve, grabbing it into the palm of her hand.

'Sophe?' She wasn't sure she had the right to ask. 'Are you sure everything's OK?'

Sophie nodded, gave her a grin, logged in and got to work. Oonagh was far from happy with her answer. She'd worked beside her on a temporary placement for less than three months, and during that time Oonagh noticed she'd had more than her fair share of minor injuries; enough to keep a small cottage hospital busy. The black eye being the most recent, if she didn't count this evening's wrist injury. Subtle things at first, small bruises on her arm, which, looking back now, could have been finger marks, a swollen lip that was put down to an abscess and dodgy dental treatment. Oonagh knew classic signs of abuse when she saw them.

'Thanks for helping out this evening, Sophie. I promise I won't keep you very long. An hour at the most.'

Sophie gave Oonagh a little smile that didn't quite reach her eyes.

'I hope I haven't got you into trouble with...' Shit, she couldn't remember her boyfriend's name.

'Charlie,' Sophie chipped in to save Oonagh's blushes.

'So, Charlie's OK with you working tonight?' Her head was telling her to shut it, butt out, but her mouth seemed to be working independently. If some creep boyfriend was knocking her about then Sophie needed to know that she had somewhere to turn to. But Sophie just nodded, giving very little away other than, 'It's fine. Really.'

Oonagh got up and stretched her back. 'Coffee?' she asked, making her way to the ridiculously futuristic machine in the corner of the office. She didn't wait for an answer, and set about making them both a cup. Normally it was the trainee getting the presenter a coffee, but Oonagh knew that Sophie was best employed knuckling down with the stats. Oonagh reached into the fridge and fished out the milk.

'Have you and Charlie been...?' She tried to sound casual, but wanted to delve slightly more into her private life, but the hissing from the machine swallowed up her voice and she decided it was best to just let Sophie get on with things. The girl hardly looked up when she placed the mug of steaming liquid beside her on the desk.

Oonagh left her to it, hunched over, eyes hardly leaving the screen. On her own desk she sifted through the growing list of people who might or might not have had a grudge against Harry Nugent. What she needed to establish was how he could have been left to carry out so much abuse without being challenged. An archive picture of him handing over yet another comic-sized charity cheque, this time with the captains of two rival football teams shaking hands with him in the middle. *Harry Kicks Scotland's Football Bigotry into Touch*. As headlines went it was hardly the most imaginative, but in a country where tribal and clan warfare was part of the collective DNA, religious bigotry was just another notch on that particular bedstead.

Sophie's phone rang, making Oonagh jump. 'Yeah. Just coming.' A slight pause as she glanced at the clock. 'No, I'll be right there.' An hour had passed and Sophie sounded as though she was being given a hard time from the other end. 'Right, I'll be right out.'

'Hey,' Oonagh shouted across the room, 'tell Charlie to come in.' She had no idea if this would be a good or a bad thing for Sophie, but reckoned the fact she looked as though she was getting seven shades of shit kicked out of her every couple of weeks meant she'd hardly be able to make it worse. Sophie swung round, the phone still pressed to her ear, giving Oonagh that stare usually reserved for parents which said *shut it*! 'No, please don't,' she pleaded into the mouthpiece. 'I'll be just a few…' She looked at the phone for a moment before pressing the red button.

'Charlie coming in?'

Sophie sighed and nodded as she made her way to the printer. Oonagh could almost see her eyes rolling from the back of her head. There was a slight pang of guilt for interfering, but she pushed it aside as Sophie passed her the list she'd made and pulled her coat on, clearly desperate to get out of the door before her boyfriend arrived.

'I've made a list of every staff member who worked at Breakmire during the five year period when Nugent was there. I've split them into permanent as well as locum or agency.'

'I didn't think the agency staff were listed?'

'Yeah,' Sophie pulled out the sheet of paper, putting it to the top of the list, 'It's not definitive, doesn't say exactly what shifts they worked. It's just the agency used and the staff registered with them. I had to do a bit of digging for that. I can't find a patient list, I'm afraid, and official visitors are pretty sketchy too.'

'Wow, thanks, Sophie,' and she meant it. The lists had all been cross-referenced by dates, to see who exactly had come into contact with Harry Nugent. 'I'll mention to Alan how invaluable you are to this newsroom.'

Sophie nodded, 'Thanks,' and made her way to the double doors to the corridor. Oonagh followed and caught up her step, realising that if she wanted to see the brave Charlie who seemed to be handy with his fists she'd need to venture to the reception desk. Sophie stuffed her hands into her pockets, and, despite the corridor being fairly narrow, Oonagh got the distinct impression that she was keeping as much distance between them as possible.

There was no sign of him at Reception. The security guard on duty was talking to a rather bored looking girl with chestnut hair piled high on her head. There was something odd about her mouth and it was only as they got closer that Oonagh realised she was wearing dark blue lipstick, which went perfectly with her spray on jeans and denim-blue Doc Martens. Sophie gave a slight wave, then turned, giving Oonagh a half-hearted 'cheerio' before going through the barrier. The girl with the blue lips and matching boots gave Oonagh a thunderous look before reaching down to give Sophie a very quick, but very definite, kiss on the lips. She draped a territorial arm around Sophie's shoulder, only separating as they took turns going through the revolving door. Admittedly Charlie hadn't quite been what Oonagh had pictured, but she tried not to look too shocked and waved in a way that suddenly made her feel very old and somewhat matronly.

Back in the office she bundled together the papers that Sophie had printed off. Sophie had already emailed her a copy, but Oonagh liked hard copies to look at too. She automatically let her eyes scan the lists as she slipped them into a polythene folder, suddenly she stopped at the last name and her heart skipped a beat. 'Bloody hell!' She looked at it again, taking it in, and thought she could just kiss Sophie in gratitude – had she not been scared of Charlie.

32

Oonagh had arrived early. At least thirty minutes before her allotted time, which afforded her a bit of time to collect her thoughts and once again rehearse in her head what she was going to say. There would be no recording equipment permitted inside, not even a mobile phone, and she was already prepared for her pencil and notebook to be confiscated at the front door. Didn't matter much, her shorthand was rotten. She'd toyed with the idea of wearing a hidden video-cam – a wire, as it was often referred to in movies and TV shows. She didn't know any journalists in real life who actually called it a wire, but then she didn't know any journalists who carried secret recording equipment full stop. She'd already driven through the main security gates, number plate recognition allowing her to pass through before the guard at the second set of gates had made a rudimentary search of her car. She couldn't have looked much of a threat, judging by the time he'd taken. She'd be searched again, no doubt, when she walked through the doors.

She'd taken more care than usual getting ready that morning. Normally she'd put in a bit of effort for a visit, but today was different. Purposely free from make-up, she'd scraped her hair back in a ponytail and, although she wasn't one for wearing much jewellery, had left her earrings at home. It wasn't the fear that they'd be stolen, but Oonagh knew they'd be the first things to be grabbed in the event of a personal attack. Her clothes too, had the hallmark of *nothing to see here.* Dark grey fleece, navy joggy bottoms and a pair of trainers, nothing flash; she'd bought them from Asda the day before and had walked round the park a few times trying to rid them of their new-shoe naffness.

Oonagh stood as directed, feet apart and arms outstretched. A prison guard ran a probe across her body, down each leg and over her arms confirming she wasn't wired – well, not in the way they'd meant. An overdose of coffee that morning had left her as high as a kite. Everyone around her seemed strangely happy. She hadn't been sure what to expect, but prison staff being this jolly unnerved her slightly. She'd been expecting a few grumpy buggers at least, but they appeared to be somewhat normal. It must be a nightmare working there – the only difference between the cons and the screws was that they needed to buy their own lunches and got to go home after eight hours, but then had to keep coming back until something better turned up or their mortgages were paid off.

Once through the initial barriers she was led past Reception and through a double set of security doors. A guard came out to meet her, hand outstretched, a smile as wide as the Clyde, and introduced herself as Nadine. 'Have you been briefed about what to expect?'

Oonagh nodded. 'I take it someone will be with us the entire time?' A flurry of butterflies stirred in her chest; she swallowed hard and was suddenly aware of a thin band of sweat along her top lip. She took a tissue from her pocket and made a huge play of blowing her nose, getting rid of the telltale sign of nerves at the same time.

'She'd prefer to meet you in her cell but the door will be unlocked and there'll be a guard on the floor the whole time.'

Oonagh wanted to ask how long it would take the guard to wade in if Scotland's most notorious serial killer took a dislike to her, but didn't want to sound as scared as she felt. Hazel Andrews had been jailed for life, with a recommendation she serve thirty years before being considered for parole, for the murder of at least five patients in her care. A senior ward sister, she'd gained the admiration of her colleagues by saving the lives of several patients who'd gone into cardiac arrest. It was only after this had happened three times in as many days that others became suspicious. There seemed to be an abnormally high number of incidents when she'd been on duty, and a subsequent investigation had revealed a higher than usual number of deaths too.

She'd worked on the rehabilitation ward of former service personnel. Wounded in the line of duty. Andrews had been convicted of five murders, but it was feared the number could well be double or even treble that. Patients dying in hospital wasn't that unusual an occurrence and that was why she'd managed to get away with it for so long. Turned out she'd been injecting her patients with epinephrine, a heart stimulant which was practically untraceable. The ones she'd liked she'd saved and got loads of glory; the others she'd let die. That seemed to be the only way that Oonagh could get her head round it.

She followed Nadine the Nice along the corridor. Her bag, along with her mobile phone, had already been taken from her and secured in a locker at the front reception desk. A locker that, Oonagh noted, she needed a pound coin to access. The most immediate thing that struck her was the noise. Or lack of it. She'd expected shouting, doors banging, the jangling of keys. But there was none of that. The soft carpet underfoot swallowed up the sound of their steps, and Oonagh thought the neutral grey wallpaper and matching border would look more in place at an old folks' home than a prison. Although there seemed to be little difference. She reckoned the food would be better in here. Couldn't imagine many hardened criminals putting up with the slop that was dished out to vulnerable pensioners.

Another set of double doors, locked of course, and Nadine the Nice was still smiling. Still chatting. 'We have a no shouting policy here,' she explained as someone on the other side punched the numbers into the keypad on the wall to allow them through. 'Not from the staff and not from the inmates,' she continued as the door eased open where another guard was waiting. Just a brief nod, then, 'We find it creates an altogether more peaceful and calming atmosphere and everyone benefits from that.'

Oonagh tipped her head in agreement, secretly wondering how the hell you convinced a ruthless killer not to raise her voice. Nadine the Nice certainly had hidden depths. Most of the women behind bars in Scotland were on remand. And most of those for drug related offences, non-payment of fines and prostitution. It didn't take a PhD in criminal psychology to see that they all stemmed from one thing. Poverty.

'Our new programme addresses many of the social problems that these women face.' Nadine the Nice was clearly a mind reader too. 'We're aiming to house them all in smaller units, make it more like a flat share than a prison. Prepare them for life back on the outside.' Another set of locked doors. 'We equip them with skills to find work, get them off the streets, encourage them back into education.' She stopped at the end of the corridor and waited at the final set of locked doors. Oonagh had to admit to being impressed. Nadine the Nice was like the Good Fairy of the prison service. One wave of her magic wand and all ills cured.

Oonagh could see two officers approaching them from the other side of the locked doors. They too, were rather smiley and Oonagh started to feel she was missing out on some brave new world behind bars. The female keyed in the security code from the other side, whilst the male officer used the keys to unlock first one set, then the other. She instinctively knew she'd reached the most secure section of the prison.

'Thank you, Nadine.' The female officer gave Nadine a little smile and a nod. 'You can go now.' And with that Nadine skipped off back down the corridor, giving them all a little wave.

'Nadine, is she the...?' Oonagh stopped before asking if Nadine was in charge. She already knew the answer.

'Nadine is one of our special turnkeys. She's earned a lot of privileges and we find her behaviour has indeed shown marked signs of improvement with the increased responsibility she's been given.' The female guard didn't let on, but it was obvious they knew Oonagh had been taken for a ride.

'And the no shouting policy?'

'Oh, that's real, all right,' the guy chipped in, 'but Nadine likes to tell people it was her idea.'

Shit, if she was being duped by some con with a dislike for loud noises, she'd be flipping slaughtered going in to visit a serial killer. But despite Nadine bigging up her part, most of what she'd told Oonagh was the truth. Apart from the bit about them having wine with lunch. That bit was made up, but the machinations of prison life were pretty much as Nadine had described. Oonagh was still sick with nerves at the thought of meeting Hazel Andrews.

'Don't worry, we'll be here and her door will remain open at all times.'

The open plan area was simply furnished, but clean and much more homely than she'd expected. There were only six inmates in this unit, with three members of staff; Oonagh hadn't decided yet if this was a good or a bad thing. The cells were situated around the edges of the main communal area, creating a hexagonal room.

Hazel Andrews was inside her cell, third room to the left of the security doors. The entrance to each cell, Oonagh noticed, was narrow, about half the width of a normal door. It immediately made her feel anxious, claustrophobic. Alistair – prison guard – guided her through, introducing her to Andrews.

She wasn't sure what she'd expected. Pictures of Andrews were easy enough to access online. Everything from her final year school picture, her happy, carefree twenty-first birthday celebrations to her police mugshot and the obligatory ones of her being led from the courts to the prison van with a blanket over her head after she'd been sentenced. The last picture had been taken over fifteen years ago. The soft brown hair was still cut short, greying slightly at the temples. She was taller than Oonagh had imagined, but then most people were tall compared to Oonagh, and she had a gentle way about her, walking softly the two or three steps it took to greet Oonagh at the doorway. She held out her hand, which Oonagh instinctively shook before taking the seat that had been placed just inside the door beside a table inside the cell. Andrews sat on the bed opposite, tucking her legs up underneath her.

'So, Oonagh O'Neil, what is it you so desperately want to chat to me about?'

'How well did you know Harry Nugent?'

33

It was dark by the time Oonagh arrived home. She didn't bother switching on the lamp in the hall – there was enough light from the street to guide her as she punched the number into the alarm keypad on the wall before making her way through to the kitchen. Instinctively she stepped over the two floorboards at the bottom of the stairs. The ones she'd stumbled and fallen upon all those years ago when she'd been attacked. The ones that had been cleaned and scraped and sanded to remove every last trace of that night. There was a time when she'd slept with every light in the house on; she was sure the local power station had installed a special generator just to deal with her house alone. Now, this evening, walking through the house with nothing but the sodium glow from the street and headlights from the cars on the main road felt like a mini-victory. Granted, it wasn't yet five o'clock, but this was Glasgow in November.

She slid her bag from her shoulder and dropped it onto the table. Just one drink tonight. Just enough to take the edge off this shitty day. She wasn't sure how much longer she could do this. She pulled a postcard from beneath the fridge magnet as she reached in for the bottle; Oonagh might have promised herself just one drink, but she never bargained what size the glass would be. The picture on the card made her laugh; it was a woman in a cinema with her dog sitting on the next seat laughing at the screen. *'I'm surprised,'* says the man behind her. *'Your dog actually seems to be enjoying the movie.' 'So am I,'* replies the woman, *'he hated the book.'* The message on the back simply said, 'miss you'. It was from her old friend, Tom. She'd known it would be from him as soon as it had dropped on the doorstep yesterday morning. He was the only person she knew who still sent little cards and letters with the frequency of a DFS sale. Judging by the stamp and the postmark, he had arrived in upstate Virginia, halfway through his US tour.

She glanced at the mini recorder now sitting on the table, the red light flashing to show there was at least one active file she hadn't yet listened back to, but she didn't know if she had the stomach for it. Not yet. Once had been enough today. With no recording equipment permitted in the prison, Oonagh had rushed outside after her meeting with Hazel Andrews and recited the conversation as far as she could remember. Like most journalists, Oonagh had a very good short-term memory for facts and had got most of the information on tape before it flitted out of her mind.

She placed the bottle back in the fridge. This wasn't a wine sort of night, she thought, and reached instead for the gin nestled on the shelf overhead. She poured herself as large a measure as the wine goblet would allow, leaving a tiny margin at the top to waft some tonic over.

Andrews had been an agency nurse around the time of Nugent's reign at Breakmire. Initially she'd acted dumb, made a play of looking up when Oonagh had asked her about him, as though she'd been trying to pluck a memory from the air. Oonagh's hand had balled into a fist, but she'd managed to remain calm, or at least as calm as her churning stomach would allow. The cell, with its narrow door and barred windows, had threatened to trigger a panic attack. Oonagh had been great recently. Almost six months since she'd been gripped by the overwhelming, irrational fear that at one time had reduced her to her knees in tears. An irrational fear that could take control, convince her she couldn't breathe, that she would die unless she ran away as fast as she could, yet at the same time crippled her physically, rooting her to the spot, leaving her terrified and helpless. Less than five minutes in the cell of that woman and the initial telltale signs of an attack had begun to scratch at her body. Oonagh hadn't been able to run, to just leave. This was way too important: she needed to know what this woman knew about Nugent. It had taken every ounce of strength to fight the onslaught of an attack using the technique she'd learned. Touch five things – not easy when her possessions had been taken from her at Reception; instead she'd leaned forward and stroked the sides of her trainers, pulled a strand of hair from her ponytail, felt the soft fabric of her sweatshirt as she'd tugged the collar with both hands and run her thumbnail down the zip of her pocket. All the while counting backwards from ten. Andrews had just looked at her. Oonagh had breathed deeply through her nostrils, not trusting herself to speak, feeling the thin trickle of sweat make its way down her back until at last the fear had begun to subside and she'd let out a final long slow breath through pursed lips. The whole episode had only lasted a minute, if that.

Several more seconds had ticked by until at last Andrews had said, 'What is it you want to know?' Oonagh had resisted the urge to heave a huge sigh of relief. Andrews had mistaken her silence as a stand-off.

'What was the attraction of Breakmire?' she'd asked. 'Why did he devote so much of his time to there?'

Hazel Andrews had said nothing, but a muscle twitching in her cheek had suppressed a smile. It had taken her a few seconds before she'd spoken. At first Oonagh had thought she was just going to give her a recap of what Sarah had told her. About Harry Nugent having the run of the place. But then she'd casually dropped into the conversation that, far from actually abusing the patients himself, Nugent had been peddling the most vulnerable, selling their services on to his friends in high places. Oonagh had tried not to react to this story, instead allowing Andrews to continue.

It appeared that Nugent had in fact busted the scam of certain members of staff using the cottages in the grounds of Breakmire for their own benefit. Instead, he'd used them to house some of the most vulnerable patients at night. Ensuring that when his clients had come to call, they too, had had unhindered access to the girls. The thought that Harry Nugent had been abusing girls and running a brothel out of a psychiatric hospital sickened Oonagh to the core. She'd listened as Andrews had recounted Nugent's reign there, devoid of emotion. Oonagh had gripped the edge of the chair she'd been sitting on, had felt the rounded metal frame cool on her fingers as she'd looked directly into the other woman's eyes. She was no expert, but she knew in her heart that this was what evil looked like.

Oonagh made her way through to the living room at the front of the house and nestled into the softness of the armchair, the huge bay window giving her an uninterrupted view of outside. Not that there was much to see. Even if it hadn't been dark, the front of the house was elevated without even a glimpse of the street below. From where Oonagh sat, even on a light night all she'd have seen was the top of the solid, red sandstone tenements of Hyndland in the distance. The steady thrum from the passing traffic was strangely soothing, the headlights catching the mirror on the far side of the room. She held the goblet in both hands and closed her eyes, trying not to think of Hazel Andrews, and what had gone on in that warped mind.

The buzz from her mobile jerked her awake, spilling the remainder of her drink over her sweatshirt. Shit. She jumped up, tugging the sodden material away from her skin as the phone landed on the floor. It landed screen side up and she grabbed it quickly and thumbed accept, taking her mum's call.

'Hi, darling, d'you want to meet us in the restaurant or…?'

Shit. Oonagh glanced at the clock: almost seven. She must have dozed off and once again she'd totally forgotten about meeting her mum. 'Yeah, Mum, that's cool. See you there.' She'd already begun pushing her trainers off from the heel with her toe. 'I'm running very slightly late,' she added, knowing that she was due there at seven-thirty. 'Just talk among yourselves until I get there.' She kept her voice upbeat and hung up before Fran had had a chance to reply, then bounded upstairs to get changed, taking the steps two at a time.

Oonagh got the taxi driver to drop her off on Queen Street. She fished a twenty pound note from her purse, the smallest change she had. The fare was just under eleven quid. The driver had been chatting to her the whole journey, recognised her from the telly, quizzed her about every famous person from Ant and Dec to Nelson Mandela, as though Oonagh's stint reading the news in Scotland gave her an access-all-areas card to celebrity-land. She hated this bit, the 'keep the change' bit, and made a mental note to carry as many small notes as possible. She'd look like a right tight arse if she waited for her change, yet hated the thought of coming across as flash. Working class shackles were hard to shake off. The taxi driver, clearly used to the dilemma of the common-made-good, gave her the thumbs up and drove off with his 93 per cent tip without even offering to open her door.

She tried to shake off the memory of her visit to Hazel Andrews, but that woman had got under her skin. There was something toxic about her. Images of those poor girls being abused flashed through her mind. Oonagh tried to clear the mental picture from her head as she made her way through the pedestrian precinct; the canopy of lights hanging over Royal Exchange Square lit the November sky. Every night was Christmas Eve here. She would deal with Harry Nugent again tomorrow. Tonight she needed a break.

The familiar red and cream sign for The Rogano was visible through the sandstone archway that framed the end of the square. Her mum's favourite restaurant; Oonagh knew some big announcement would be made tonight, and she'd been practising her *'I'm so delighted for you both'* face since she'd got the call. And she *was* delighted. She'd never want her mum not to be happy, it was just... Well, she wasn't really sure what it was exactly, but the thought of her mum marrying someone that wasn't her dad sent a wave of sadness through her body. A sadness that she couldn't ever see going away.

Despite it being a mild evening, she pulled the collar of her coat up tight around her neck, edged her way past a man puffing away on a ridiculously large cigar outside and made her way into the main restaurant.

Preserved in time like amber, the restaurant bore the hallmark of the finest art-deco design. Its 1930s ambience gave Oonagh a sense of comfort. Her mum and Owen were already seated and Owen stood up when he saw Oonagh walk through the bar to join them. He even had decent manners. Was there anything wrong with this man? As long as he didn't expect to be called Dad she'd maybe just get away with it. Fran was like an excited teenager – probably a bad example, as teenagers, from what Oonagh remembered, rarely displayed excitement. Oonagh glanced at her mum's hand: no ring. Yet. She'd feign surprise. Didn't want to steal their thunder.

She was about to sit down when the waiter took her by surprise and moved her chair towards her, bumping it against the backs of her thighs, forcing her down quicker than she'd intended. 'Thanks,' she said, glancing up at him, willing him to beat it.

'So?' She grinned and looked at her mum then to Owen, waiting for them to break the news. She hoped to God her smile was working and didn't look as sad as she felt. 'What's the big announcement, then?' She realised she was hamming it up slightly and pulled back. Gave her mum a chance to take the floor.

Fran reached across and laid her hand on Owen's. 'No *big* announcement, as such.' She gave Owen's hand a little squeeze as she looked at Oonagh. 'It's Owen's birthday next week and we're going away for the weekend, so I thought it'd be nice if we went somewhere special for dinner first.'

'Oh.' Oonagh felt somewhat crestfallen. 'I thought you said you had news for me?'

'Well, I do have some news too.' Fran gave Owen's hand another little squeeze.

'Which is?' Oonagh was trying not to lose her rag, but her mum wasn't half dragging this out. She already had a nightmare vision of being bridesmaid and forced to wear some hideous creation that made her look like Bette Davis in *Whatever Happened to Baby Jane?*

'I'm going back to university.'

The comment came from left field and caught Oonagh off guard somewhat. 'Whoa. Can we rewind here a second? You're what?' An uninvited pang of disappointment stung her chest, and suddenly she was mourning the loss of the pink organza bridesmaid dress that she'd now decided, in the right light, would look quite fetching.

'I'm going back to uni.' Fran was grinning like the Cheshire Cat; Owen wasn't much better; Oonagh was just confused, as she hadn't realised her mum had ever actually left uni in the first place, which was usually a pre-requisite for going back. But Fran was on a roll. 'I've been accepted to do my masters in creative writing and after that, well, who knows—?'

Oonagh cut in. 'You can do a masters in creative writing?' She struggled to keep the surprise and even a note of jealousy out of her voice. When she'd been a student the only courses available had been bog-standard boring old crap ones that she'd bunked off from so often she'd struggled to get a second-class honours.

'How's your book coming along, Oonagh?' There wasn't a trace of malice in Owen's voice, and he had no idea how much she dreaded that question.

'It's not, Owen. I decided to shelve that project for now.' Oonagh's foray into novel writing had ended before it began. To her eternal shame she'd paid back the rather paltry advance from the publishing house, citing all sorts of excuses as to why she needed to put this one on the back burner. Even she hadn't had the balls to say that she'd realised when she said she'd wanted to write a book she meant she wished she'd *written* a book. Two very different things. Owen gave what she took as a knowing smile, and thankfully dropped the subject. She'd arranged in advance for a bottle of champagne to be brought to the table, although this now seemed a bit over the top, she was glad of the distraction when the waiter laid out three fluted glasses.

'I should have told you to bring your friend along,' her mum said, holding her glass up.

'My who?' She wasn't sure to whom Fran was referring and held the stem of her glass as the waiter eased the cork from the bottle.

'That nice girl I saw you with at Central Station.'

Oh, dear God. Her mum thought Sarah Nugent was her girlfriend. 'Mum, I was on a story. I hardly know her.' Oonagh wasn't quite sure how to feel about her mum's assumption that *she* was gay, but had to admit to a feeling of pride that Fran would be cool about it.

'Well, I'm just saying,' Fran continued, holding her glass towards the waiter, 'if ever you do want to bring someone *special* home, then it's fine by me.'

Oonagh glanced at Owen to see if her apparent new-found status was the consensus of opinion, but he wasn't looking. Instead he put his hand over his champagne flute and gave a slight shake of his head to say no bubbly for him. Instead he raised his glass of sparkling water, 'Slange.'

'You the designated driver tonight?' Oonagh was glad to steer the conversation away from her imaginary lesbian love affair and onto safer ground.

'No, well, yes, I am driving, but, well…' he faltered very slightly '… I don't.'

Oonagh raised an eyebrow; despite her own habit, she liked the thought that her mum's boyfriend would never be drunk and incapable. 'Good for you,' she said, and meant it. Oonagh sipped on her drink, letting the bubbles smooth over her tongue. 'Have you ever drunk?' It was none of her business, she was just making conversation to stop her mum coming out with any more of her theories.

'I'm in recovery, Oonagh.' She was about to ask from what when the penny dropped. There wasn't a trace of shame in Owen's voice, and to give him his due he looked her straight in the eye. Fran gave his hand another squeeze, then stroked the side of his face. It was a small gesture, but so intimate that Oonagh felt a lump in her throat at the closeness between them.

'I had no idea.' Oonagh was genuinely shocked. She'd known Owen for the best part of two years now, but suddenly realised she knew very little about him.

'No reason why you should.' His eyes had a little sparkle. 'It's not like being a vegan. I don't need to keep going on about it.' He raised his glass and Oonagh laughed. She was warming to this man, and felt comfort in the fact there was still so much good in her world.

34

'Why did you do it?'

'Because I could.'

Hazel Andrews had requested another visit. Oonagh had met some right hard cases in her time but this one took the biscuit. Killing people entrusted to her care came as second nature to her. Oonagh was desperate to talk about Harry Nugent and his time at Breakmire, but Andrews had steered the conversation onto her killing spree. As though she was proud of her record. Oonagh went with it, hoping to gain a bit of ground, then move in with her own agenda.

'There are lots of things we can do, but we don't all act on them.' Oonagh had to keep focused here. 'Something must have triggered your… your actions.'

Andrews stood and up and wandered over to the window – didn't take her more than two strides. Her room was comfortable enough but could hardly be described as spacious. Bijou was probably the term used by the Scottish Prison Service. The tabloids were full of stories about cons having flat-screen televisions, access to the Internet and the life of Riley. Despite the attempt at giving them some sort of home comforts that tiny wee door to the cells was locked shut at night and Oonagh felt sick at the thought of being trapped here.

'You ever saved a life?' Andrews was leaning against the wall, craning her head slightly to look through the small window at head height.

'Can't say I have. No.' Oonagh thought back to the time at Pollokshields East railway station when a young guy had looked dangerously close to the edge. It looked as though he'd been crying. Couldn't have been more than twenty. It had been a winter's morning, still dark, they'd been the only two there and he'd walked down to the end of the platform just as the train had come into view. He'd gone too far and would have had to walk back to reach the train doors. Oonagh felt the panic in her gut as the train thundered down the tracks. This one wouldn't stop here and was going at full pelt. She ran towards the guy and grabbed him round the waist and they both fell backwards as the train thundered past. She cracked her elbow on the ground; he was heavier than he'd looked. Turned out he'd just been going to the edge of the platform for a quick smoke, and the red eyes had been down to a bad cold that he couldn't shift. Oonagh had been mortified.

'It's the best feeling in the world,' Hazel added, unaware Oonagh's mind had wandered. 'Better than drugs, better than sex.' For the first time Oonagh detected a note of sadness. 'Better than anything.' Hazel folded her arms; there were none of the clichéd characteristics that one might expect from a convicted killer. Hazel wasn't coarse, there was no harshness in her voice and no haunted look as she recounted her past. From here Hazel Andrews looked like an ordinary, everyday person. The type of woman one could easily pass on the street without a second glance. The person who maybe lived next door, or who exchanged a bit of idle chit-chat with fellow passengers on the train each morning. Or she would have been had she not been banged up.

'Ever tried drugs?' Her question came from left field and caught Oonagh unawares. She shook her head.

'Coke? Weed?'

'Nope.'

'You liar.' Andrews smiled; as usual it didn't quite reach her eyes, and she kept her voice soft. 'Posh girl not like being caught out, eh?' She was either really good at reading people, or Oonagh was a lousy liar. She did get it wrong about her being posh though.

'Well,' she said, reaching for a cloth and wiping a leaf on the plant on the window sill, 'it's a bit like getting high.'

It took a few moments to register that she was talking about the thrill of saving a life.

'So that's why you did it, then? The feel-good factor?' Oonagh was aware that last comment sounded as though she was trying to excuse Hazel's killer instinct.

A smile played on the other woman's lips. 'That's what the social workers liked to think.' The smile was now a full-blown grin. Oonagh couldn't work out if she was taking the piss or not. She stood up, tugged the bottom of her sweatshirt and made to leave. 'Listen, love.' She was getting pissed off with this woman. 'I don't have time for this. If you're lonely and need a visitor I suggest you contact the Women's Institute.'

'What's wrong? Can't you take a joke?' Hazel let out a laugh, but it had a hollow ring to it.

'I'm not known for my sense of humour. Not when innocent men have been killed. No.'

Hazel Andrews had a back story that read like a Ted Bundy biography. She'd been in and out of care homes from the age of eight. Her dad died in a road accident when she was six and her mum gave Hazel up two years later saying she couldn't cope. It was assumed she meant after the death of her husband, but it had transpired that the whole family had struggled with Hazel from the get-go. According to court reports, she'd never felt the need to belong the way other kids did, and didn't seem to care that she had no pals. Social workers noted too that she barely shed a tear for her dad. A series of foster families inevitably ended up with Hazel being dumped back at the care home. When she was twelve, she'd attacked a boy in the care home with the leg of a chair and he'd lost an eye; she'd claimed it was in self defence and that the boy had struck the first blow. How the hell she'd ever got into nursing beggared belief. But she did and that was when her reign of terror really began.

'You know your problem?' Oonagh had many problems, but was interested to hear Hazel Andrews narrow it down to just one. 'Everything's black and white to you. Everything's all cosy in your world and you don't understand how the real world works.'

Oonagh let out a sigh, stifled the need to laugh, wishing that truly were the extent of her problems. 'Very astute of you, Hazel.'

Hazel sat back down on the bed, assuming Oonagh would stay. 'Them boys, they were thick.'

'They were patients, Hazel. Vulnerable people in your care.' Oonagh sat back down; at least they were back on track.

Hazel Andrews scratched the cover of her duvet. The gesture seemed oddly familiar. She chewed on a loose piece of skin around her thumb and spat it out. 'I was just a kid myself.'

Oonagh struggled to see that this woman had ever been a kid. To her it seemed as though she'd been born rotten; a murderous psychopath in a child's skin just waiting to grow up and unleash herself on the world.

'So, Breakmire?' Oonagh was almost scared to ask the question. 'What was your role in Nugent's empire?

Andrews crossed her legs, mimicked Oonagh's pose slightly, looked her up and down, dropped her eyes. She was trying to flirt with her.

This was beginning to wear Oonagh out.

'Nugent was an idiot. Would do anything for a wank.' Hazel genuinely looked disgusted. 'So is it true?'

Oonagh said nothing.

'Did they really find him with his balls cut off and stuffed into his mouth?'

It clearly hadn't taken long for the rumour mill to be working overtime on this one. Not bad enough that his tongue was sliced off, the gore-mongers wanted a different pound of flesh.

'Hazel, this is a chance for you to at least do some good.' Appealing to this woman's better nature might not be

Oonagh's smartest move, but she had nowhere else to go with this one. 'You mentioned the last time that Nugent was abusing some of the patients there. Passing them around his friends. Can you name any of the men involved?'

'Those girls were well taken care of.'

'What's that supposed to mean?'

'None of them were forced to do anything they didn't want to do.'

'They were vulnerable young women in a psychiatric unit. How the hell can you even justify this? Or make out they were happy with the situation?'

'Your wee world is just so cosy, Oonagh O'Neil, isn't it? You've no fucking idea how desperate these girls were for a bit of love. Friendship. Affection.'

'Passing them around a bunch of abusive creeps like the last pint before closing time doesn't constitute love, friendship or affection.'

'They were well rewarded.'

'Please, just tell me what the hell went on there. How the hell did Harry Nugent manage to run this brothel without anyone blowing the whistle?'

'You really are a stupid bitch.'

'Yes, Hazel, we've established that, love. But let's face it, I'm a stupid bitch that's had the good sense never to have been banged up.'

'It had been carrying on from before Nugent came on the scene. But it was small scale. He'd caught one of the volunteer porters touching up one of the girls, and came in one night and discovered him letting a few friends in to shag the girls who were up for it.'

'You mean rape mentally ill girls.'

'You say potato. It was no big deal. He'd take the girls down to the basement, and then... anyway, once Nugent knew what was on offer, he wanted in on the act, but cranked the whole operation up a few notches. It didn't take him long to realise the cottages attached to the hospital could be put to better use. And it was as though he'd already had his own clientele. Fuck's sake. The place was going like a fair within a fortnight.'

'Where did you fit in with all this?'

'Me? Don't know what you mean.'

'You were clearly across the whole operation. What was your role? Did you cover for him?'

'How did you manage to get such a good job when you're such a dummy?'

'Let's just say I got lucky, Hazel. Now, when you're done firing insults in my direction, d'you want to cut me some slack and tell me who the hell was working with him?'

'I'm not doing your research for you. This is all so you can get your wee story together and look good. And what do I get out of it?'

'Nothing, Hazel. I have nothing to offer you. I don't suppose you can remember the name of this porter?' Oonagh guessed that even if Andrews did remember, she'd be unlikely to share the information with Oonagh.

The silence between them was deafening and Hazel picked up a copy of *Take A Break* that was lying on the bed, flicking through the pages. The gesture told Oonagh the meeting was over.

Oonagh stood up. 'I'm done here, Hazel,' she said, trying

to sound as though it had been her decision to call this to a close as she walked towards the door.

'Petrie.'

Oonagh stopped dead. What felt like a bolt of electricity crackled through her body. 'What?' Unsure at first if she'd heard correctly. 'Hazel, please. What did you just say?' She fought the rush of adrenalin, desperately trying to conceal her exhilaration. Refusing to let Andrews know how important this information was in the chain of events. If Petrie was the volunteer porter at the asylum, that would explain exactly the hold Nugent had over him.

'What?' Hazel Andrews pinched her brows together, shrugged her shoulders as though she didn't know what Oonagh was talking about.

Oonagh wanted to grab this woman by the throat and throttle her and kiss her at the same time. But given they were in a prison with a team of guards in the next room she thought better of it, that and the fact Hazel Andrews was a crazed killer with at least three stone on Oonagh. She lingered for a few moments more, but Andrews was lost in the tacky magazine.

35

He'd agreed to meet her in a café out near Helensburgh. That wasn't always a good sign – public places usually indicated a reluctance to open up – but at least he'd agreed to meet and that was more than she'd had from any other leads so far.

Oonagh drove north on the Erskine Bridge, one of the country's most notorious suicide spots, flanked either side now with preventative barriers in a bid to stop those poor unfortunates jumping off. Then headed west onto the A82, passing the snow topped Kilpatrick Hills, before taking the left fork in the road. The Firth of Clyde opening out and bleeding into the mouth of Gareloch always left her breathless. She was familiar with Helensburgh; she'd often take a drive out just to sit looking out at the water. But today was different.

The café was modern but mocked up to look as if it were fresh from the fifties, intimate booths, chrome edged counters and low hung lights. As usual she was slightly early. That suited her as she'd prefer to be sitting ready, given that she had no way of recognising who she was supposed to be meeting. She stirred the insipid tea, already wired from too many early morning coffees. Yesterday had been her first full day without alcohol in as long as she could remember, but it meant she hadn't slept well and was desperate not to come across as jittery. She knew him as soon as he came through the door. Oonagh wondered if it was because she found it easy to recognise another damaged soul. He nodded and slipped into the booth, sitting opposite her. He looked younger than she'd imagined, not much more than sixty.

'So, what is it you want to speak to me about?' Peter Gray folded his arms across his chest. Oonagh wasn't quite sure where to start.

'Your daughter, Peter. Hannah.' He dipped his eyes, fidgeting with the sugar sachets bunched in the small bowl on the table. 'And her time at Breakmire.'

'What about it?' It was hard not to notice the grief and pain in this man; it was etched on his face, wept from his eyes, forced heavily down on his shoulders. She'd ordered him a coffee, and they both paused momentarily as the waitress placed the steaming mug on the table in front of him.

'I'm looking into the deaths of otherwise healthy mental health patients in Scotland and...' Oonagh had already rehearsed her story. There was no way she could dive straight into this one. He gave her a slight nod, enough to let her know to continue.

'It must have been a terrible shock. Hannah dying like that. Can you tell me, Peter, why was your daughter in Breakmire?'

'She was anorexic.' He said it as though that explained it. He seemed to read Oonagh's mind. 'That's why she was committed,' he added, then took just a slight pause. 'Oh, the treatment was very different in those days. We thought she was going to starve to death. It was… it was just horrible to see her so thin and in so much pain.' He took off his watch, smoothed down the leather strap and worried it between his fingers.

Oonagh didn't bother to ask what Hannah Gray's clinical treatment would have been. 'That must have been awful for you.'

He folded his arms tight across his chest and breathed heavily through his nostrils. 'She didn't seem to be getting better. Oh, she was putting on weight, but she was just turning into a different person before my eyes.'

'In what way?'

'She was delusional, hallucinating. Talking crazy stuff.'

'Did you speak to anyone, talk to anyone about your concerns?'

'Doctors, you believe them, don't you?' Oonagh nodded; she knew exactly what he meant. 'And it was always a different doctor I spoke to and they just said the same thing. She was putting on weight so that was good, but her increasing paranoia and erratic behaviour meant she couldn't come home.'

Peter Gray painted a pretty bleak picture of his daughter's time at Breakmire, a picture Oonagh knew was all too familiar. A family struggling to understand their daughter's illness, desperate for her to get better, the reluctant acquiescence to unknown medication. 'Trying to get an appointment to see her consultant was a nightmare. I don't think I ever spoke to the same doctor twice.'

'When you say she was hallucinating, what kind of stuff was she…?'

'Said monsters, demons, were coming into her room at night. She was scared to go to sleep and the night time terrified her.' He wiped the back of his hand across his mouth.

'What kind of monsters? Did she describe them?'

He looked at Oonagh in disbelief. 'What? She was losing her mind. There were no monsters. At one point she even thought the devil had visited her.'

'I'm so sorry, Peter.' From what Oonagh could gather, Breakmire was nothing more than a brothel run in one of the country's most secure hospitals for vulnerable patients. What Hannah Gray had been describing was most probably men visiting her at night; the systematic abuse of her and other patients. With her history of delusional behaviour no one believed her, so instead they upped her meds to shut her up. Oonagh was sick to her stomach with this one.

'Was there anyone she was close to there? Any friends she'd made during her stay?' Oonagh was aware she was referring to Hannah Gray's incarceration as though she'd been on holiday.

He shook his head. 'Not that I know of. All I know now is that she needed help and I let her down.'

'Peter, please.' Oonagh laid her hand on top of his, unable to shake off the knowledge that she was going to make his day a whole lot worse. 'You did all you could. You entrusted your daughter's care to the professionals. You trusted them.'

He let out a sarcastic laugh. 'There wasn't even a fatal accident inquiry.' He stirred the dregs of his coffee with Oonagh's teaspoon. 'The last words she ever said to me?'

He'd posed it as a question, but wasn't expecting an answer. '"Dad," she said, "can you take me home?" And I didn't. D'you know how that makes me feel?' Oonagh had no idea how he felt. Couldn't even begin to imagine the horrors that filled his nightmares each night.

'Peter, I know this must be so difficult for you.' Oonagh hated that line and wished she could think of something different to say, something comforting, something real, something that said *I want to make this go away for you*, but she never did.

'Her mum had wanted to wrap her up in a blanket and put her in the back of the car, but I stopped her.' His chin quivered slightly; he rubbed his hand across his mouth, but it wouldn't take the pain away. 'Said the doctors knew what they were doing. All I could see was that she was getting heavier so that was a good thing. She was like a skeleton when she first went in, her bones were sticking out, and I was just happy that she was starting to look normal again.' He swallowed hard, the tip of his nose tinged pink as the memory threatened to spill over into tears. Peter had split from Hannah's mum not long after their daughter died. Oonagh guessed the grief had been just too much for them to bear.

'Is it possible Hannah was telling the truth?' Oonagh caught the look on his face, then quickly corrected herself. 'Not monsters, well, not as such, but I'm investigating the possibility of some…' Oonagh wasn't quite sure what words to use; she felt ill equipped to be handing out this type of bad news to a stranger '… some sort of abuse at Breakmire.'

'What the hell's going on here? Why're you so interested in my daughter?'

She detected a note of anger in his voice. 'Peter…' Oonagh

took a deep breath and swallowed hard; there was no sugaring this pill '... did you see Hannah's death certificate?'

He nodded. 'Of course. Exposure, hypothermia.'

Part of her wanted to walk away now. This poor man had suffered enough. 'And the post-mortem examination?' He didn't seem to be grasping what she was saying. 'Did you actually see the post-mortem report?'

He shook his head. 'No, I don't think so.' He thought for a second. 'No. No, I didn't. Why?'

That was hardly surprising. Few families, if any, got to see the official post-mortem report as a matter of course, and at the time of Hannah's death it would have been unheard of.

'Are you saying my daughter didn't die from hypothermia?'

Oonagh took the buff coloured envelope from her laptop bag and slid it across the table, her heart thumping in her chest, her throat tightening; she had no idea if she was doing the right thing, but knew she had no choice. From the moment that email had dropped in her inbox she knew what she had to do. Peter Gray opened the envelope and took out the document, only two pages in total; it was the full autopsy report.

'Peter, the post-mortem examination does indeed have hypothermia as the cause of death.'

It didn't take him long to read the most relevant details: sixteen year old girl, superficial scratches on her arms, legs, hands and feet, which would be no great surprise as she'd run off in the dark dressed only in a thin nightdress. There had been a lesion or bruise across her forehead, possibly a friction burn, but, like the scratches, it was deemed superficial. Toxicology report showed that she'd had benzodiazepine in her system; again this would have been consistent with the prescribed medication. Cause of death; hypothermia. Hannah had crawled under a bush and by all accounts just gone to sleep. Such a tragic end to such a short life.

Peter Gray's eyes scanned the rest of the document. A muscle in the side of his jaw twitched as he read the basic details of Hannah's height, weight, date of birth and physical description, before reaching the vital information at the bottom.

'Fuck.' He held the document in both hands, his eyes darting across the page.

'I'm so sorry, Peter,' Oonagh said, and meant it. She had just added to this man's nightmare.

'How long have you had this for?' He was still clutching the A4 envelope in one hand as they walked along the seafront. He'd barged out of the café under the pretence of getting some fresh air, but Oonagh could see the salty tears stinging Peter Gray's eyes, and the biting wind along the shore gave him plenty of opportunity to wipe his eyes.

'Just over a week. I called you as soon as I saw it.' Peter Gray took the four steps down onto the shore and Oonagh struggled to keep up, her heels disappearing into the sand. 'I'm so sorry.' She'd apologised a lot this morning and she wasn't sure why. She'd opened up a Pandora's box and so many people were going to be hurt by this.

'Has her mum seen it?'

Oonagh shook her head. 'Your ex-wife won't speak to me. I tried but…'

'She won't speak to me either.' He stopped suddenly. 'So how the hell did you get a hold of it?'

Oonagh hesitated and worried about telling him that she'd paid a contact in the NHS for the report. It wasn't strictly legal, well, it wasn't legal at all, but she'd decided it was for the greater good. 'I have my contacts,' was all she offered.

'What can I do?' Oonagh wasn't quite sure what he meant. 'Who the fuck do I speak to about this? Who's going to fucking pay for what they did?'

Hannah Gray had been three months pregnant when she died. This was turning into a real shitty day. This wasn't the movies where a miscarriage of justice was uncovered and the forces of good prevailed against evil. This couldn't be wrapped in a neat package, with a few sound bites and a Twitter feed with #justiceforhannah making everything OK. The nightmare Peter Gray had been living since his daughter's death was about to get a whole lot worse.

'I'm not going to lie to you, Peter, this is going to be tough.'

That was probably the most understated thing Oonagh had ever said. Proving institutionalised abuse was a nightmare at the best of times, historical abuse was even harder. Throw into the mix the fact that the patient had been dead for twenty years and the said hospital was now lying derelict just added to the problems. There would be an inquiry, it would take years and the conclusion would be that our most vulnerable people had been failed and lessons would be learned – and safeguards would be put in place to ensure it never happened again. Oonagh could already smell the bullshit.

'I'm not sure if this will be a comfort to you, but I believe the men responsible are dead.' He stopped and looked at her. 'And their deaths weren't pleasant.' Peter Gray dropped his head, allowing just the briefest glimpse of satisfaction to cross his face.

36

Tommy Gallagher 1983

There was no room to lie on the floor with the other guys. As usual they seemed to have it sussed, laughing at some crap on telly. The music was blaring but all Tommy could hear was the sound of his own heart, thumping in his chest, and the deafening sound of blood whooshing through his ears. The other two lay on their stomachs, eating wine gums, propped on their elbows, legs stretched back, the odd foot swaying about. Not a care in the world. Not a fucking care. What the hell was happening?

Tommy felt the bile rise slightly in his throat as his stomach heaved. He was going to be sick. He was going to vomit, then they'd laugh. The others would laugh and call him names. He could feel his face scarlet-red; he reached to stroke his cheek, wiping the tears away. Quickly. Before anyone noticed.

He stood up – perhaps he could squeeze in between them on the floor – but the hand gripping his wrist yanked him back and he fell back down onto the sofa. He knew what was coming. That thing. He wanted to scream at the others to turn round, see what was going on. What was wrong with them? What was so fucking great about *The Banana Splits*? It was shite. Even in colour.

Derek flicked a wine gum and it hit Mic on the ear. A perfect shot. In return Mic elbowed him in the ribs and they wrestled about for a few seconds, just moments, yelling and swearing, but it was just kid-on. Tommy could see that. Tommy thought that would put him off, but it seemed to make him more eager. Tommy wanted to retch, and yet still the others didn't see.

If Tommy cried they'd all think he was a total prick. A right twat. They'd know he'd never done it. They'd all done it loads of times. Not with any of the lassies from school though. All lassies he'd never heard of, but Derek and Mic, and even Stewart. Stew, for fuck's sake. How did he know what to do? They'd all said they'd done it. The shame burnt Tommy's face and he tugged his sleeve down over his free hand to wipe his nose.

Derek and Mic settled back down, back to the programme. Cartoons now. They were laughing and yelling at the telly as though it could hear them. Oblivious to what was happening just a few feet behind them.

Tommy's wrist started to burn beneath the grip. He stared straight ahead, but knew his abuser's eyes were fixed on the other two on the floor. And then it happened. That sound. The sound he'd grown to hate. It was louder than anything, louder than the telly, louder than the blood rushing through his head. His stomach heaved once more and he managed to pull his hand free just as Derek and Mic jumped up. You'd think they'd never seen ice cream before. The van was right outside the window of the flat. 'Pop Goes the Weasel'.

Tommy's dad used to sing that to him when he was wee, and pull his finger from his mouth to make that popping sound. Used to make him laugh. But this was horrible, it was clangy and noisy, it was cheap and nasty and made him feel even more sick. Derek was dancing from foot to foot, waiting for the money. Mic was at the window, pulling back the net curtain. 'Hurry up, there's hardly anyone there. It'll be gone.' Derek snatched the fiver from the outstretched hand and swaggered out of the door, as if he was used to carrying that amount of cash. Mic was running on ahead; they could hear him outside the window, desperate to make sure the van didn't drive off before they got there.

'Ask me for money.'

'What?' Tommy didn't have a clue what he was talking about. 'Ask me for money.' His voice was low and he was gasping. He sounded angry. Tommy's wrist ached as the fingers dug deep into his skin.

'Ask me for money.' He sounded really pissed off now.

Tommy was desperate for it to finish, terrified he was going to pee himself. 'Can I have some money?' he said, hoping he would stop.

'Say it again.'

Tommy tried to speak but the words caught in the back of his throat and instead he started crying. Like a wean. The snot dripped off Tommy's nose and landed on his hand.

Derek and Mic were coming back up the stairs. Their voices echoing through the close. The van was clearly on its way as 'Pop Goes the Weasel' got fainter and fainter in the distance. 'You're a stupid prick.' He pushed Tommy out of the way and wiped the snot from his hand across the leg of Tommy's joggers. 'Can you do nothing right?'

Derek and Mic burst into the living room and Tommy jumped up, running to the toilet. But it was too late and he peed himself before he reached the lavvy. He could hear them through the door. Laughing and carrying on as though nothing were wrong. He was desperate to be one of them. Part of their gang. Instead he took off his jumper and wrapped it round his waist. Hiding the wet patch below. It didn't look too bad; he'd managed to pull down his joggers before they got too wet. He'd already taken off his pants. They were soaking. He tried to stuff them behind the toilet, out of sight, but you could still see them. There was a wee bit of wood boxing around the sink. It was loose and he pushed his hand in it to shoogle it a bit. He could stuff them behind there. The wood was only thin; it pushed in easily. There was a pile of pictures stuffed behind it. They were those Polaroid ones. His pal Frannie's dad had one. They didn't need to get them developed. You could see the pictures right away. It took Tommy a couple of seconds to work out what he was looking at. They weren't very clear. He couldn't make out faces. That looked like a leg, or maybe someone's elbow. Then he saw it. Clearly. He didn't know who the boys were as their heads were cut out of the photo. But he knew Harry. He recognised Harry Nugent. And other men too.

'Hurry up, ya prick. I'm bursting.' Derek battered on the door and he stuffed the pictures back where he'd found them. His hand shaking as he tugged the flimsy piece of wood back in place. Instead he stuffed the soaking Y-fronts into his pocket and tried to look casual as he unlocked the door.

'I left your ice cream in the kitchen.' Derek barged past,

unzipping his flies before he'd reached the pan. 'Harry gave us enough for double nougats.'

Tommy ran out of the bathroom, straight into Harry. He was smiling. The way he always did when he had an audience. He held him by the shoulders, digging his fingers in just a bit too hard. He knew Tommy had seen the pictures. It was written all over his face. He rubbed the back of Tommy's head. As if he was his favourite. The front door was open and Tommy made a run for it. Belting down the stairs, out of the close. He'd always been a fast runner. But now he ran so fast he feared he was going to be sick. He ran and didn't stop running until he reached home. By the time he got inside his lungs were burning, his chest was heaving and his legs felt like jelly. The smell of dinner coming from the kitchen hit the back of his throat and he retched. He retched and couldn't stop. He was sick all over the hall floor, on the new lino. His mum came running through from the kitchen. She placed her hand on his forehead and walked him through to the bathroom, holding his head over the pan, rubbing her hand in circles on his back.

'You're burning up,' she told him. Told him he was sweating and shaking like a leaf. She told him it must be flu.

Later she checked in on him; he pretended to be asleep and she kissed his head. He wanted to stay there. Forever. Where it was safe. But he knew he couldn't.

37

It was a nightmare trying to piece everything together, but at least Oonagh had made a connection. She could have kicked herself for missing it the first time round. To the outside world Graham Petrie had very little dirt on him. He was squeaky clean. After Hazel Andrews had revealed that he'd been working as a volunteer porter at Breakmire the penny had dropped.

She went back to the Mitchell Library and looked again at the asylum's board of trustees. There it was in black and white. Graham Petrie. No wonder he'd been able to get away with so much for so long. Oonagh had seen it the first time she checked over the document, but that had been before he'd been murdered, and none of the names had rung a bell at the time. Petrie had used his volunteering to gain trust and access to the hospital without rousing too much suspicion.

Nugent must have thought he'd won the lottery when he'd caught that little shite with his dick out. This sickened her. These women were supposed to be cared for and instead had been exposed to the most brutal regime imaginable.

The thought of going back to that woman again was making her skin crawl but she had little choice. She was the only one who could give her answers.

'Hazel, what can you tell me about Hannah Gray?'

Hazel Andrews smiled; she clearly liked being the centre of attention and holding the cards. 'I only agree to see you because I'm bored, you know.'

Oonagh nodded. 'Well, that's very good of you. I'll try to be as scintillating as I can. Now. Hannah Gray. You must remember her.' She posed it more as a statement than a question. She was done playing games.

Andrews put down her book, carefully placing a bookmark inside, before closing it over. 'She was nothing but trouble, that one.'

'Is that why she was killed?'

'She wasn't killed. She ran away. Daft bitch. I'd told her to just play the game.'

'So, she was one of the—'

'Comfort women,' Andrews jumped in before she'd had a chance to finish.

'Comfort women?' Oonagh was familiar with the term; the female prisoners of war enslaved into brothels, forced to work as sex slaves for the Japanese soldiers. Comfort women was a much more palatable name than victims of rape and slavery. The penny just dropped. 'Bloody hell. Is that what CW stands for?'

Andrews shrugged. 'Don't know.' And she was probably telling the truth. She'd have had no access to Nugent's records, so would have been unaware that he'd have abbreviated the term. 'It's what we called the girls who liked working with the men. It's such a nice term, isn't it?'

Andrews made this all sound rather nice. A million miles away from the reality of it all. The reality of girls being abused and forced into prostitution. 'People are stupid, you know that?' Once again, Oonagh got the distinct impression Hazel Andrews was directing this particular insult firmly in her direction, but didn't retaliate. It would do little good to rile her now. The important thing was to get as much information as possible. 'Things go on right under their noses,' she continued, 'and they don't bat an eyelid.' She ran her hands down her sweatshirt, lightly caressing her breasts. Oonagh guessed this was also for her benefit, trying to shock her. Coming from a woman who'd killed five patients in her care, watching her squeeze her own tits wasn't exactly sending Oonagh into a tailspin.

'It's not as though they weren't cared for.' Andrews shook her head, rolled her eyes. 'They had the best of stuff and most of them enjoyed it.' She gave a slight conspiratorial laugh. As though she was the only one in on the joke.

'Enjoyed it? *It* meaning being systematically raped?' This woman was one sick bitch and Oonagh was struggling not to spit in her face.

'You say potato.'

'You've tried that line, Hazel, and I didn't laugh the first time.'

'Give it a rest. Get off your moral high horse. Everyone does something wrong now and again.'

Hazel Andrews was clearly mental. Totally off her bloody rocker and Oonagh struggled to believe a word she said.

'Listen, we had a decent set-up. Those girls were well up for it.'

'So what was your role in it all?'

Hazel shrugged, started making her bed, paying particular attention to the hospital corners, which Oonagh had to admit were impressive. 'Are you quite finished, Hazel?'

'Hate mess. Always have done.' She moved to a pile of cards and letters on the table under the window. Oonagh gave her some breathing space to continue. 'Have you seen my fan mail?' Hazel nodded to the stack. 'Get them from all over the world.' She handed one to Oonagh, who only intended to quickly glance over it, but when she caught out one or two words she was transfixed. This was a fan letter to a killer, seriously. Oonagh wanted to heave. The address at the top said Missouri and was signed by some woman called Fiona. Oonagh tried not to let her mouth hang open as Hazel took it from her grip. 'I get dozens every week.'

'All from Americans?' Oonagh had no idea what else to say. She thought voting for Trump was bad, but this was a whole new ball game.

'Yip, they sure are.' Hazel mocked a Yankee accent and slapped her thigh. 'Those mother-fuckers are as mad as a three legged toad in summer.'

Dear God, this was getting worse. It was obvious Hazel was putting on a bit of an act for her benefit, but those letters really did show that there were a lot of very strange people out there. It made Oonagh's alcohol abuse, insomnia and low level psychosis seem rather mild in comparison. She was out of her depth here.

'As impressed as I am by your hospital corners and crazy-girl fan mail, can we get back to the point, Hazel?' Oonagh knew she'd need more to corroborate this than the word of Hazel Andrews, but, with Sarah Nugent on board and the accounts going back years, she'd be able to make a pretty decent fist of putting a case together.

She now knew there had been a brothel in the grounds of Breakmire and Harry Nugent had a client list that read like a who's who from *Hello*. The sedatives and drugs the girls had been plied with ensured they'd all been compliant, and the fact they were being treated for a wide range of mental illnesses ensured that it was unlikely they'd have been believed if they'd complained.

'This doesn't exactly tie in with Nugent's MO, though, Hazel. He was more into young boys, from what I gather.'

'Listen. He might have been a creep, but he was a fucking clever one. He very quickly realised what was going on. Once he'd caught that wee snotter, Petrie, with one of the girls, he had enough dirt on him to get what he wanted. Also meant he had the run of the place.'

This hadn't been just an amateur operation. According to Hazel, once Nugent was on board he'd decided to ratch it up a few notches. He'd made sure the girls were well groomed, had hairdressers visiting most weeks, they had their nails done, had been checked for venereal disease and only the youngest and prettiest had been targeted. It had ensured that Harry Nugent could appeal to some of his well known friends. The ones he'd known who would pay over the odds for this. Oonagh felt sick. This had the hallmark of a high-end business.

'So what happened?'

'One of the johns...' She paused to make sure Oonagh was keeping up. 'That's what they call punters, you know. Anyway, one of the johns went too far one night and a girl died.'

'What d'you mean?'

'He just used too much force.' Hazel looked quite indignant. 'It's easy done, you know,' she added, as though he'd accidentally killed a spider while getting out of the bath.

This horror was growing arms and legs. 'Who was this guy? A pal of Nugent's?'

Hazel pulled her shoulders up high against her ears. 'Dunno. Big noise, I think, though. He was always very well dressed. They're the worst, you know. They're the ones who like to knock the girls about.'

Sadly, Oonagh could well believe it.

'But we were very strict about that kind of thing. No bruising. No damaged goods. Fuck's sake, we were running a business. Couldn't have the merchandise looking like a pun o' mince.'

Oonagh struggled not to retch. Fought not to be sick at the inhumanity of it all.

'So, who was this girl?'

'Can't remember her name. I think it might have been Rachael, or Ruth, or something.'

'How the hell could you have covered that up?'

'We didn't. As far as I know they disposed of the body. It's not actually that hard, you know.' She waited to see if Oonagh was taking all this in. 'Hospital incinerators are pretty lethal.'

Oonagh wasn't buying this. 'What about her family? Someone must have missed her?'

Hazel shook her head. 'She was just another runaway. There are hundreds each year.'

Oonagh was almost scared to ask. 'And Hannah Gray, was she killed too? Tell me the truth.'

This time Hazel shook her head. 'No, I've already told you. That was an accident. She'd run away and no one noticed until the next day. Shame really. She was a nice looking girl.'

'That's horrific.'

She nodded. 'I tell you, Harry seemed really broken up about it. I think he'd taken a shine to her.'

That last sentence struck Oonagh. 'I thought that was before his time there?'

Hazel shook her head. 'Nope. He'd been hanging around for a few weeks. I remember it.'

Oonagh's mind was racing. All the press clippings she'd seen suggested that Harry's charity work had started six months after Hannah Gray had died, but it was possible that he might have been going there prior to any official visits.

'Hazel, have you told the police about this? You need to make a statement.'

'You're really annoying, you know that?'

'The girls.' Oonagh thought for a moment. 'I want to talk to one of them. Are any of them still alive?'

'How the fuck should I know?'

And with that the meeting ended.

38

Byres Road was busier than usual. The run up to Christmas seemed to get earlier each year; the Halloween pumpkins hardly had time to rot before the shops had cleared the ghosts and ghouls and fake spiders' webs from their display, replacing them instead with sparkly reindeer, fairy dust and enough glitter to choke a drag queen. The muzak had taken a decidedly cheesy turn too; Slade belting out 'Merry Christmas' and good old Shaky driving everyone nuts with his cheesy yuletide classic, which ensured he'd be enjoying the royalties for many years to come.

Oonagh needed time to think. The revelation that Harry Nugent had indeed been at Breakmire around the same time that Hannah Gray had died didn't really amount to much more than she already knew. Hannah was just another poor victim in a long line of people abused by that monster. Oonagh wasn't sure if she could back up Hazel Andrews' claims, and she would certainly pass them on to the police, but not just yet.

It was strangely mild for November and a slight haze

hung low in the air. Not exactly what you would describe as balmy, but the street was thronging with jacketless natives, and the odd rolled up sleeve. Glasgow could be cold and damp at the best of times – fifty shades of grey whatever the season – and it took near Baltic conditions for a Glaswegian to succumb to the frivolity of an actual buttoned up coat. Oonagh quickened her step, hoping Christmas would come and go in a blur. As a kid she'd loved every tinsel clad moment of it. But now… Now it was just another chance to get blind drunk and feel like shit the next day. A reminder of how lonely she was.

The windows of the café were steamed up, but she spotted Sophie's partner, Charlie, perched on a high stool, hands wrapped round a mug, sipping her drink at the counter that ran the entire length of the shop.

'Hey, fancy seeing you here.' Oonagh brazened it out as Charlie started, choking slightly on her drink. 'Mind if I join you?' She slipped her jacket off and grabbed a stool before Charlie had a chance to refuse. 'Sophe not with you?' Charlie didn't answer and Oonagh attempted a casual tone as she looked at the blackboard high above the front counter. 'What you having?' She leaned over and peered into Charlie's mug.

'Hot chocolate, and Sophie's in the loo.' There was no mistaking the hostility in her voice. It just made Oonagh all the more determined to tell her what she thought of her, but she tried to remain civil. 'Before Sophie comes out,' she said, 'I want a word with you.' Charlie had a good three inches on her but they were the same height sitting down and anyway, she guessed, like most bullies, Charlie only picked on people who were scared of her and wouldn't speak out.

'No.' Charlie slammed her mug down on the table. 'I want a fucking word with you.' She kept her voice low but deliberate and Oonagh reckoned this was not her first rodeo. This girl had form. 'I don't like the way you make Sophie work late and keep her out until all hours.'

'All hours? All hours? Did you really just say that?' What a flipping cheek. 'Sophie's actually *working*. I'm not asking her to go out clubbing with me.'

Charlie gave a low snort. 'I'm sure your clubbing days are long behind you.' That hurt. 'Listen, love, you're taking advantage and I don't like it.' This girl was one hard ticket; she clearly didn't like anyone having any influence on Sophie. If this was a guy Oonagh would be staging an intervention right now. Offering Sophie a safe place to stay, telling the guy to sling his hook or else.

Oonagh caught sight of Sophie coming out of the disabled loo. She was wheeling a pushchair with a young boy in it. It was difficult to guess his age: he was too old for the pushchair, but clearly in no fit state to walk on his own. She stopped in her tracks when she caught Oonagh with Charlie, who was by now squeezing past the tables to give her a hand.

Sophie smiled as she grew closer, but had that exhausted look of too little sleep and too much responsibility.

'This is Jake. Jake, say hello.' Sophie bent to pick up his beanie hat that he'd thrown on the floor.

'Hello, Jake. I'm Oonagh.' The boy grinned, then looked up at Sophie.

'He's my little brother. Doesn't talk much.'

'How old are you, Jake?' Oonagh made to take his hand

but he pulled it away. She wasn't much use at talking to children and knew she was coming across as a tit.

'Jake's eight, aren't you, Jake?' Sophie's voice elicited another huge grin as he bent his neck to see his sister's face.

'We'd better get going.' Sophie pulled the beanie hat back on his head and pushed the pushchair towards the door.

'Can I just…?' Oonagh laid her hand on Sophie's shoulder. Charlie could fuck right off. This wouldn't wait. Sophie nodded to Charlie, who took the pushchair and pushed Jake towards the door.

'I'll just be a few seconds.' Oonagh wasn't sure if Sophie was reassuring Charlie or telling Oonagh to get to the point.

'Sophie, you know if you have a problem you can talk to me.'

'I'm fine.' She held her hand up in a stop sign to tell Oonagh the conversation was over and walked out of the door.

Oonagh wandered back to her coffee just in time to see the waitress clear away her almost full cup when her phone rang. She didn't recognise the number and pressed her thumb down to take the call.

'You wanted to talk to me?'

Oonagh not only didn't recognise the number, she didn't recognise the voice either. 'I'm erm… sorry, who is this?'

'It's Vivienne Gray. If you want to talk to me you've got five minutes to say your piece, then I never want to see or speak to you again.'

*

Oonagh ordered a coffee to go, then hailed a black cab out on Byres Road. She had a load of stuff to do, but reckoned Hannah Gray's mum wouldn't be offering any second chances for this meeting. She gave the driver the address, a little bistro on the edge of Milngavie, a few blocks from where Vivienne Gray lived. Clearly the woman had no intention of inviting Oonagh into her home. She told Oonagh to be there at twenty past; that gave her less than fifteen minutes. The traffic was a nightmare and they got caught at every red light. Oonagh was sure if she was even a second late then Vivienne would scarper and never speak to her again.

She rehearsed what she was going to say in the cab, jotting down a few notes. It would probably be best at this point not to go into too many details, find out what Hannah's mum had to say first.

The bistro was just off the main road, and had a smattering of customers. A woman sitting at a table near the window stood up as she arrived and moved to shake Oonagh's hand. 'I'm impressed.' She glanced at her watch. 'Did you promise the taxi driver a bumper tip to get you here on time?'

Oonagh smiled as she sat down. Vivienne Gray was warmer than she'd been expecting. Not quite friendly, but not spitting nails either. 'I was in the west end, didn't take too long.' She could already feel the seconds ticking by and was desperate for the whole meeting not to be dominated by the traffic on the A81. 'Thanks for agreeing to see me, Mrs Gray. Can I ask, why the change of mind?'

'I spoke to Hannah's dad yesterday.' She got right down to business. 'He told me you gave him a post-mortem report?'

'Yes, I'm sorry, it probably brought up a lot of painful memories and—'

Vivienne cut in. 'I want you to respect my family's privacy, OK?'

'Of course, it's just that—'

'This has been hard enough. The death of a child never goes away, and your revelations are doing nothing more than bringing back nightmares and piling on the guilt.'

'Mrs Gray, there's a chance your daughter was being abused at Breakmire.'

Vivienne held up her index finger, indicating that she wanted Oonagh to stop speaking. 'Listen to me, we'll deal with this. We'll go through the correct channels and contact the relevant authorities.'

'Vivienne, I understand your—'

'No, you don't. I have no doubt this would make for a pretty good feature. I know who you are, Oonagh O'Neil. I know what you do. But this is our daughter's life you're talking about. I'm not having her plastered all over television. Face in the newspapers. People pointing the finger because we let her down.'

Oonagh had to tread very carefully with this one. She didn't want to cross the line. 'Mrs Gray, Vivienne, please. I've uncovered some more… information… I think…'

The other woman placed her hand on the table. 'You have a document which I strongly suspect you obtained illegally. Now you drop this whole thing or I'm going to the police.'

Oonagh weighed up what she'd be charged with. Hospital records were forever turning up on landfill sites, or sensitive documents getting left on trains. It wouldn't take too much imagination to invent how the report had come into her hands. But that wasn't the point. She had no desire to intrude on this woman's grief any more than she had already. 'OK.' She was deflated, but nodded quickly, before she had a chance to change her mind. 'But...'

'But what?' The initial relief that had passed by Vivienne Gray's face quickly faded now that Oonagh was about to insert a caveat into the proceedings.

'But I've uncovered the very strong possibility of an illegal brothel being run from Breakmire.' She held up her hand, aware that Vivienne Gray was about to interrupt. 'I'll keep your daughter's name out of things. You can rest assured of that. But you need to appreciate that I can't sit on this story. I can't make it go away. And to be honest I don't want to. This needs to be exposed.' Oonagh had enough to cover this with or without mentioning Hannah Gray. After all, her death had been an accident. The fact she'd been pregnant would indeed have strongly indicated that she'd been abused whilst under the care of the hospital, but it neither proved nor disproved that Nugent or Petrie had been involved.

The heartache once more flooded through Vivienne Gray's face and she clasped her hand over her mouth to stifle the gasp that escaped from her lips. 'We let her down, you know that?' She immediately seemed to soften, using the same term that her ex-husband had used.

'You did what you truly believed to be the best for your daughter, Vivienne.'

Vivienne Gray glanced at her watch. The five minutes were well and truly up. 'I can trust you, can't I?'

Oonagh nodded. 'Of course you can, Vivienne.' She took

a brief pause. 'But, please, don't let this one go. Don't give up without a fight.'

Vivienne Gray stood up and nodded, but Oonagh wasn't convinced. She walked out of the door, looking for all the world like a woman with the last ounce of fight squeezed from her.

39

Tommy Gallagher 1983

'Ya bandit.' The bus pulled from the stop just as he came round the corner. They were few and far between in this neck of the woods, so he decided to walk. The nerves, now a familiar feature in his belly, had started as soon as he'd woken this morning. They'd never fully gone away if truth be told. The shame too. He wore that like a blanket, sure everyone could see through it. See into his soul. He'd skipped out of the house, shouting his goodbyes from behind the door as it'd slammed behind him. He couldn't bear to see his mum's face. Couldn't bear the look of pride that would inevitably have been in her eyes. She thought he was a superstar. Boasted to her friends, told everyone on the block how talented he was. Even Auntie Ina. Auntie Ina whom he'd known since he was a baby. Even she got the full 'look at my Tommy, I'm so proud of him' routine. His throat tightened and tears stung the backs of his eyes so he was glad of the cold biting wind. It gave him an excuse to wipe his face.

Did they know? The other guys in the changing room? Did they know? He changed into his kit, wishing he could fall into place with the rest of the guys. The way he used to before. Before this.

'Oi, TG.' Frannie flicked a towel across his legs.

'Beat it, eh?' He grabbed the towel and threw it on the floor as he tied his laces. He just didn't have the stomach for merry banter.

'Fucking superstar, eh?' Frannie picked up his towel and walked away, joining the other guys for a bit of a laugh.

A few deep breaths and he'd be fine. Bouncing from foot to foot in time with his breathing, looking out at the pitch. 'The grass will be greener than any grass you've ever seen, son,' he'd said. 'And no matter what the weather, that sky will be cornflower blue. When you step out, wait for a moment. Just a moment, mind, and savour it, that moment before the noise of the crowd hits you.' His dad had played in junior league; dreamed of hitting the premier, but it wasn't for everyone. Tommy knew that. He'd passed that burning ambition onto his boy. Other kids got bedtime stories. Tommy would be treated instead to memories and dreams of his dad's short time on the pitch. His dad was gone now, but his words still rang true. Only for Tommy, this dream was turning into a nightmare.

It was still junior league, but this was the first step. Rumour had it that a talent scout would be here today. And that same rumour mill said that Tommy Gallagher was the one to watch. He walked out of the dressing room straight into Harry Nugent's hand, which pushed firm against his chest. 'Where you going, son?'

Tommy looked around, not quite sure of the question. 'I'm eh… I'm going out onto the pitch.' Where the hell else would he be going? His right leg trembled and he could feel those nerves grip his stomach. Harry's hand felt hot, even through the thickness of his jersey.

'Not today, son.' Tommy felt his throat tighten and Nugent didn't budge. Not an inch.

'Am I on the sub bench, Harry?' His voice cracked; he could feel the muscle twitch in his cheek as he tried to swallow the dryness coating his mouth.

'It's Mr Nugent, son. And you knew the rules.'

Tommy couldn't look him in the eye. 'Listen, Mr Nugent.' He looked at the ground, the sickness rising in his stomach as he begged his legs not to let him down. 'I just want to play…'

'No, you listen, son; you're not playing today, or any other day.'

He could feel his breath on his cheek. 'Harry… Mr Nugent, there's a scout out there. All I want to do is play football.'

Nugent dropped his hand, took a step back. 'Be my guest.' He gestured towards the mouth of the dugout.' Tommy waited for the catch. There was clearly a catch. 'Boys like you are ten a penny, Gallagher. Scouts have their pick of the bunch. They'd be hard pushed to go after someone with a drug problem.'

Tommy staggered back against the wall. The studs of his boots scraping off the concrete. A ball of anger formed in the pit of his stomach, but it gave way to fear. 'I've never taken drugs. You fucking know that. Never.'

Nugent raised his eyebrows. 'Zat right? Well, be sure to let him know.' He walked away towards the daylight.

'This isn't fair. This isn't fucking fair.'

Harry turned round, forcing his forearm up under Tommy's chin, pressing hard against his throat. 'Life isn't fucking fair, son. Get over it.' Tommy craned his head back, gasping for breath. Nugent released his grip, wiped his hand across his mouth and brushed himself down. 'Now.' This time he kept his voice low, but left Tommy in no doubt as to the sentiment of his words. 'I want you to get your things, get the fuck out of my face and never come near me again.'

Tommy nodded. A mixture of fear, revulsion and self-loathing propelled him back into the changing room as he grabbed his kit and ran. He wanted to scream; he should have torn this guy's face off. That was what the other guys would have done. That was what his dad would have done. They'd have been brave. They'd have acted like men. But instead he ran and didn't stop running until he reached home.

40

The asylum had long since been abandoned, but still the stench of decay hung heavy in the air. Broken glass lined the long corridors, smashed chairs, upturned cabinets and even discarded medical notes were strewn across the floor. Oonagh picked her way through the debris, mindful of the glass cracking beneath each step. She'd expected at least some resistance to entering Breakmire. Imagined there would be some sort of security at the derelict building. But there was none. Just the broken Heras fencing, which had been easy to breach.

She kept her phone clasped tightly in her left hand, 999 already keyed in, ready to press call should the need arise. There was very little light in this part of the building, despite the gaping holes where the windows once were. The thick metal bars were still in place. Through the corridor the abandoned wards still had metal framed beds in place. A pair of old slippers, tartan ones from a bygone age, sat neatly under one bed. To Oonagh that was the saddest sight she'd seen. She remembered when her dad had died and it had been up to her to collect his belongings from the hospital. A white plastic bag with a few meagre things he'd had with him on the ward: pyjamas, his soap bag with his shaving kit – her mum had insisted he was shaved each morning, despite the fact he'd never regained consciousness after the stroke – and his slippers. His wee slippers. They'd looked so pathetic. Her mum had known he'd have little use for them on the ward, but she'd tucked them under his bed nonetheless. Like so many patients. Slippers were one of the few possessions that gave them a sense of personal identity.

She wasn't quite sure what she was looking for, or exactly where in the building she was supposed to be. Andrews had alluded to Petrie using the basement initially to abuse the patients. The hairs on the back of her neck stood up and she felt the telltale tightening on her scalp. Her earlier bravery was subsiding; her legs felt heavy and she gave an involuntary shiver. She looked down at her phone: two bars. The staircase at the far end of the corridor presumably went down to the bowels of the asylum, which she guessed would cut her signal even further.

Oonagh took a deep breath. This place gave her the creeps. She clung to the banister as she walked down the stairs, the metal treads clanging with every step. She faltered at a half landing, resting her hand on the recessed shelf that had once been a window but was now bricked over. There was no air in this place. Her throat tightened and she took a few moments to adjust her eyes to the changing light that faded the deeper she went.

The dust was making her itch and she felt the slight flurry of falling masonry on the back of her hand. Instinctively she brushed it off and looked down to see a huge black rat nuzzling into her sleeve. Screaming loud enough to make her throat ache, she batted her hand against the wall, scraping off a layer of skin. Suddenly the decision on whether or not to go into the basement was taken from her as she belted down the stairs, trying to create as much distance as possible between herself and the overly affectionate rodent. It was only when she reached the bottom and danced about, trying to shake off the feeling of tiny claws running up and down her spine that she realised that rats very rarely walked alone.

'Oh, shit, shit, shit, why rats?' Mice she could deal with, spiders she could pick up with her bare hands without a thought, but rats. She hugged her arms tight against her body, her breath coming out in short sharp bursts and, despite it being a really stupid thing to do, kept her eyes closed tight. This was just not something she could deal with right now.

'They're more scared of you than you are of them.' Her dad's soothing words had done little to calm her down when she'd seen two rats running through the back close during the bin strikes in the seventies. He'd been holding her in his arms; she'd been just a toddler. *'Here,'* he'd said, picking up a stick, *'this'll do it.'* She'd thought at the time the stick was a makeshift weapon. A special rat killing stick, one designed by her dad. But instead he'd cracked it against the wall, and the noise sent the rats scurrying away as she buried her head into his neck. Refusing to open her eyes until they were safely indoors again. She'd had no idea until that moment that she was terrified of them. The mere sight of them causing her heart to thump in her chest, her breath to come out in convulsions and that petrifying feeling of her spine turning ice cold, being unable to move.

And now here she was, that same panic engulfing her. The tingling in her scalp encased her whole body. They were everywhere. Tiny claws scratching all over her. Pinpricks of pain, leaving her numb and unable to move. Rooted to the spot. She squeezed her arms tighter around her body, eyes still squeezed shut. Despite her dad's reassurance all those years ago, Oonagh doubted that any rodent would be feeling as shit scared as she was right now, but his advice as always had been right. *Make a noise. Scare them away.* She could hear them round about. No idea how many. In her head there were dozens, scurrying across her feet, darting out from behind the skirting boards, their fat tails whipping her ankles as they passed. But in reality she knew there were only a few, and by the noise guessed they were running along the edge of the room.

Blood rushing through her ears made it almost impossible to tell. She felt sick. Her legs like lead, the nausea was growing in her stomach. Slowly she picked up one foot and tried to slam it down. Pathetic. She tried again. It was a bit louder this time. Once more, then she screamed again, making it as loud as she could, and stamped her feet, trying to make as much noise as possible, cursing those bloody Asda trainers with their thick soles that absorbed the noise. All the while trying to ignore the sensation that gripped her entire body; a room full of rats, scratching up her legs, clawing their way up her spine and burying themselves deep into her neck and hair. The noise seemed to do the trick and sent them off in the other direction.

Slowly she opened her eyes. Peering through her fingers. One at a time. One hand clasped over her mouth as she struggled not to retch and instead concentrated on controlling her breathing. Oonagh fumbled with her phone, aware her hands were trembling. If she dropped it she might not have the nerve to bend down and fish it from the debris at her feet. She flicked on the torch; the light wasn't brilliant, but it was better than nothing. And as her eyes adjusted, the light slowly filtered down the stairwell from the floor above and bit by bit she managed to make out the room.

The basement was large, with several half sized windows at one end boarded over. The bottom half of the walls was tiled, as was the floor. The rest of the walls were decayed with peeling paint and stains that she had no desire to know the origin of. Shallow sinks lined one side of the room, the taps long since broken with only pipes jutting out from the walls remaining. In the middle of the room a slab. Oonagh initially assumed it was for post-mortems, but the leather head and limb restraints suggested something far more sinister. In the corner an ECT machine, its primitive knobs and dials still and benign.

Three doors at one side. She had no idea where they led, but guessed by the layout they were cupboards. It was unlikely they were further rooms. The telltale scratching to her left told her that bloody rat who refused to give up was still sniffing about. Rubble and masonry scattered the floor. She bent down and picked up a lump. 'Bugger off, you little fucker.' She was a good aim but it had scarpered; her scream scared it off long before the missile reached its target.

She picked up another rock, large enough this time to do some damage, and fired it at another one of the doors. More stones, more bits of rubble – she hit the doors as hard as she could. She wasn't taking any chances. If noise *did* scare them away, then she wanted to give them a head start and create as much distance between them and her as possible.

The first cupboard was little more than a glorified filing cabinet: shelves holding notes and paperwork. The second held disused bottles, jars, bandages, nothing out of the ordinary. Nothing to prove what she'd come here for. It was only when she opened the third she let out a cry of despair. Oonagh dropped her head into her hand, almost unable to look. She had no idea if it had originally been designed for the poor souls who'd been incarcerated in this asylum or if it had been installed by the sick bastards who'd preyed on the vulnerable. The tiled floor had a drain, above which were the remains of an ancient shower head. The sides of the cupboard were stained with what she hoped wasn't blood; a wooden baton and what looked like a metal cattle prod were propped up in the corner. Leather restraints were bolted onto the walls at ankle, wrist and waist height. Another one designed to be secured around the patient's head matched the strap-like bruise across Hannah Gray's forehead which had been mentioned in the post-mortem report. Oonagh struggled not to picture this poor girl, and countless others who had been locked in here as punishment if they hadn't complied. She wanted out of there. She'd seen enough but knew she needed some pictures. The basement on its own proved diddly-squat, only that Hazel Andrews had been telling the truth. It was exactly as she'd described.

41

Alec walked along Saltmarket. The city was changing, but somehow this street seemed to remain the same. Trapped in time. Soot stained tenements lined the street, blotting out any chance of the occasional bit of sunshine. Overhead, gulls screamed and swooped down to devour discarded chip wrappers. A pawn shop, one of the few remaining in the city centre, enticed passers-by. Cash paid for Rolexes. Any condition, it promised, suggesting no questions asked. Alec ran his fingers over his own watch just to make sure it was still there.

Behind him was the city's High Court, ahead the Tollbooth at Glasgow Cross where public hangings had taken place in a bygone age. An age even more brutal than the present. It passed as entertainment for some, before television, before *The X Factor* and other programmes more painful than watching someone being put to death. If social historians were to be believed, the hangings proved very popular among well-to-do ladies, who would dress up in their maids' clothes to get close to the action without being recognised.

He'd just come from the city mortuary. Hated that building, always had done. Despite the white protective overalls they gave him, the stench of death would cling to his clothes for weeks after each visit. Maybe that was just his imagination. At least today he hadn't had to actually look at anything gruesome. Just check on the cause of death of some poor old biddy who'd lain undiscovered in her Ibrox flat for months. It wasn't his remit, but he'd promised to pop in as he was passing anyway. As suspected, it was natural causes, and no relatives, or even a friend, had come forward. Eighty-seven years on this planet and not one living soul to be remembered by. How the hell did that happen? Did some people just outlive their own lives? Outlive their relationships, lovers, families? As usual with such cases the authorities were alerted because of the smell. Sometimes the utility companies came to break the door down because the lecky hadn't been paid in a year. Or the factor sending threatening red-letter reminders to tenants far too dead to care any more.

He was becoming more squeamish as time wore on and had lost what little appetite he might have had for the blood and gore so often associated with police work. The mere thought of it caused a slight turn of his stomach, which quickly rose up his chest and into his throat. The smell of death was worse than anything he could have visualised. That smell. He quickly cupped his hand over his mouth, grabbing at the dry retch that threatened to give the game away. A cobbled lane to his right steered a new smell in his direction. Fish. For fuck's sake. All he wanted to do was walk into town without vomiting on his own shoes. Was that too much to ask? A queue of women, bags of shopping at their feet, snaked down the lane, waiting their turn to buy fish, which the sandwich board at the mouth of the lane assured them was as fresh as they'd find this side of dry land.

Alec crossed the road, picking up speed the last few steps as the bus careering along London Road showed no sign of slowing down for him. He'd no desire to end his days under the wheels of the number seventy-eight and imagined Jim McVeigh identifying his body in the same red-brick building he'd left just minutes before. *'Aye, that's him all right. Grumpy bastard he was too.'*

It was uncharacteristically warm for this time of year, muggy even, but an old tramp huddled in the doorway of a tenement close on High Street tugged at the collar of his matted coat. Pulling it tightly round his emaciated throat. A single sheet of cardboard served as a bed. Next door was a bed shop. The picture windows showing sumptuous looking beds with designer covers. Loads of them. All empty. The irony was not lost on Alec and he fished in his pocket for some loose change, giving a quick glance round to make sure no uniformed coppers were about. It didn't do for Strathclyde's finest to be seen encouraging beggars. But the poor old guy looked desperate. What the hell was wrong with a world where this was the only option for some? He glanced at the change in his hand. Only a few coins, not even a pound. He pulled a fiver from his wallet and slipped it into the old man's hand as he passed. Offering one of those awkward looks between a smile and a 'you're welcome'.

The old man nodded in return. His yellow rheumy eyes brimmed over with gratitude, which made Alec feel worse and he quickened his step.

'Thanks, Alec.' His voice was coarse and gravelly. It stopped Alec in his tracks. He turned quickly.

'What did you say?' Whatever look he gave seemed to scare the old boy.

He faltered. 'Nothin'. Just thanks.' He stuffed the fiver into his pocket, perhaps fearful it would be taken back. Alec realised he was scaring him and softened. Slightly. 'No, after that. What did you say after that?'

The old man's chin trembled; his eyes shifted from side to side. He was clearly scared. Alec was in plain clothes but knew to folk on the street he had 'copper' written all over him. He reached out his hand, but stopped short of touching the man's greasy sleeve, stained with God knew what. 'D'you know me?'

Just the hint of a smile pulled at the corner of his mouth, and up close Alec could see he maybe wasn't as old as he'd first thought. 'Aye, Alec,' he said, seemingly grateful for the crumbs of normality this bit of chit-chat offered. 'I'd recognise you anywhere.'

Alec felt like a shit, didn't have a clue who this guy was. It was unlikely to be an informer or an ex-con calling him by his first name.

The old boy helped him out. 'It's me.' His voice quieter now. 'Tommy.'

'Oh, fuck.' Alec slumped back against the shop window; something inside him seemed to drain and the shock caused a wave of nerves through his legs. 'Tommy? Tommy Gallagher?'

Tommy grinned as though he'd been given the best news of the day. 'Aye. Big TG. Ye mind me now, don't ye?'

'Tommy, I'm so sorry. But…' there was no way of dressing this up '… what the fuck happened to you?'

The chippy had a sit down area at the back. Formica tables familiar from both their childhoods nestled into booths with padded plastic backed benches. Alec tried not to breathe in the smell from Tommy. Tried instead to remember his old pal.

They'd been part of the same crowd at school. Even shared a paper round back in the day. Tommy had been a good looking kid. Maybe not quite the school heartthrob, but the type of guy who'd been popular with the girls. He'd been good at football and had made them laugh. A winning combination for any teenage boy. Alec had envied him. Envied his easy going manner, the way he'd known just what to say when they'd passed a group of third year girls in the corridor.

He looked at this old man across from him. Shit, Tommy wasn't yet fifty and could easily have passed for seventy. The waitress plonked down the fish supper in front of Tommy, just a coffee for Alec. She hadn't used a plate, instead left it in the bright yellow polystyrene box. Tommy didn't seem to notice. Alec guessed she wouldn't have served Tommy at all had he not been with him. Tommy licked his lips as the smell of the food wafted into his face.

'Can I have a fork, please, hen?' The waitress pointed to the metal container with paper napkins and cutlery poking out of the top. Tommy's hands shook as he cut the fish with his knife and fork. The steam belching out from underneath the golden batter.

'Your mum never let us eat chips with our fingers, remember?' The memory brought a lump to Alec's throat.

'We had a laugh, though, eh?' Tommy recounted the past without a trace of bitterness.

'Aye, you were a good looking sod. Never short of a girlfriend.' Alec was paying lip service to this trip down memory lane. In truth it broke his heart to even think about the kid who'd turned into this old man who was grateful that Alec remembered him. He wanted the small talk over, but gave Tommy the chance to get some hot food inside him.

'Tommy, what happened?'

Tommy wiped his face with the paper napkin, cleaning the last trace of the fish supper from the corners of his mouth. There was a dignity in that gesture that humbled Alec.

'Och, just life, Alec. Life happened.'

Alec wasn't convinced. Life could have a way of throwing some curve balls and letting you down, but life had kicked the shit out of Tommy Gallagher and by the looks of it had kept on kicking. Alec eyed the waitress who brought over a mug of tea for Tommy and a plate of bread and butter. She must have softened slightly because it was a plain white mug. A chipped plain white mug, but at least she didn't humiliate Tommy by making him drink out of a disposable cup.

'Had a run of bad luck, that's all.'

Alec sat back, didn't push him. The smell of the salty chips coming from the front counter was driving him insane, but he'd already claimed he wasn't hungry and didn't want to embarrass Tommy further. It was bad enough that the poor sod was sitting here, life laid bare, no chance to big up his part. He waited for him to continue.

'Once my marriage broke up, I...' Tommy scratched at the rim of his chipped mug, trying to join the dots of being a married man to being a down-and-out sleeping in shop doorways.

'Hit you hard, did it?'

Tommy nodded, but Alec guessed there was more to it than that. Otherwise it would be standing room only on skid row if every soured marriage ended up with someone on the streets.

'My own fault, hit the bottle, lost my job, couldn't pay my rent...' Alec nodded. He knew this only too well. Hostels were littered with such stories. It was a terrifying thought how many people out there were only one month's salary away from destitution.

Alec looked at his watch, stood up to go. 'Tommy, listen, I'm sorry but...'

He smiled back at him. 'That's all right, Alec. It was decent of you to take the time. You didnae need to do that. I appreciate it. Thanks, pal.'

The past gripped Alec's throat; he was hardly able to speak. Opening his wallet, he took out what cash he had. Thirty quid. 'Tommy, if you need anything.'

Tommy reached out and accepted the notes. 'You can see I'm in no position to turn this down.'

Alec grabbed a napkin and scribbled his name and number on it. 'I meant what I said, Tommy.'

Tommy looked at the napkin and folded it neatly, placing it carefully deep inside his coat. 'Thanks, pal.' He shuffled out of the door and Alec watched him make his way towards Trongate, crossing at the lights, before being swallowed by the city.

42

Oonagh woke with the now familiar sickening pain creeping up her spine. Her T-shirt clung to her back, sticky with sweat, and the palpitations in her chest caught her breath. It wasn't yet light outside, but she was scared to go back to sleep in case she had another nightmare: terrifying dreams full of screaming children. The tablets were doing nothing; if anything they made her dreams all the more vivid. She leaned across and took a sip of the water from the glass on her bedside table, noticing her hand trembling very slightly, but she felt marginally better knowing that last night, at least, she'd gone to bed after managing an entire day without any alcohol. The second time in less than a month. She pondered making a wee wall chart, giving herself a gold star for every booze free day.

She got up and padded downstairs, it was almost seven and she had a shedload of work to do, so even without the threat of nightmares there was no point in trying to get back to sleep.

Trying to piece everything together was sucking her

further and further down a very dark and seedy wormhole. The coffee tasted bitter on the back of her throat, but was strong enough to ease the jitters that had threatened to engulf her earlier. There was no point in going in to the office; she could easily work from home and had everything she needed here.

A huge whiteboard hung beside her desk. On it was scribbled as much information as she had. She'd scanned and copied everything onto two separate pen drives, with no hard copies of any of the documents; she'd given them back to Sarah Nugent.

There was now a link between Harry Nugent and Graham Petrie: Petrie had signed off the council business warrants, which had enabled Nugent to launch Pitch Perfect with minimal business capital and even less experience. He'd also guaranteed his tender to supply most of the schools in the west coast of Scotland, which had soon amounted to a multimillion pound business. Petrie had clearly used his position at Breakmire to abuse the most vulnerable patients, who hadn't had a voice. Oonagh knew the care of mental health patients was sketchy but this was criminal. As far as she knew the police hadn't established the connection yet, but it would only be a matter of time. However, far from leading her to whoever killed them, it just opened the inquiry out further. This was all starting to make her feel sick and she was glad of the excuse to get out of the house, but guessed today's meeting would do little to make her feel better.

She'd asked a lot of Hannah's dad to sit on the information

just now. This stank of a huge cover-up, but she needed more before they went in with guns blazing. The last time she'd seen Peter Gray had been on the seafront at Helensburgh; she'd left him that day a broken man. And today he looked no better. If he'd felt he'd failed his dead daughter for all these years, Oonagh could only guess at what was going through his mind right now.

'I want someone to pay for this. I want them to fucking suffer the way I've suffered.' Peter Gray paced the floor. She'd initially worried he wouldn't want to see her again. That she'd be the bearer of yet more bad news, but it had been him who'd contacted Oonagh, and asked her to come to his house. Hannah had been an only child, yet there wasn't one picture of her that Oonagh could see in the house. It was as though Peter Gray was trying to obliterate the memory of his daughter.

'This is driving me crazy. I'm actually out of my mind now.'

'D'you have anything to help you sleep?'

He shook his head. 'Nothing works. I let her down. She told me all along this was happening and I didn't believe her. Animals. Fucking monsters.'

'Peter, I'll make a programme on this. It'll be part of a wider case of abuse at Breakmire, but you need a really good legal team on your side too.' Oonagh knew that the programme would raise more questions than it answered. 'But I want to leave Hannah's name out of things.'

He knotted his brows together.

'I spoke with Hannah's mum a few days ago...'

'She spoke to you?'

Oonagh nodded. 'But only to say she doesn't want to go public with this. I need to respect her wishes.'

'What about what I want?'

'Peter, you're angry, and, believe me, I'm desperate to get this on air, but we can do it without using Hannah's name.'

He looked defeated and crossed his arms, hugging them tight across his body. 'Aye. OK.'

Hannah had been in Breakmire for less than a year. According to Peter she'd never had a boyfriend and had rarely gone out with her friends. She'd been too ill. But she'd been pregnant when she died. What Oonagh couldn't work out was how the hell the Fiscal's office had let that one go. A young, emotionally unstable girl got pregnant whilst in the care of the NHS and there wasn't even an internal inquiry at the hospital.

'Did you manage to get Hannah's medical records at all? Or…' Oonagh knew the answer before she even asked the question.

'Not a chance. They've all been destroyed.'

'You sure they're not just not handing them over? After all, the post-mortem report was there.'

He bit down on his lip, looked reluctant to say too much.

'What?'

'Hannah's mum, we don't talk much, but she's a clinical psychologist.'

Oonagh didn't want to rush him but needed to know what was going on here.

'She's been doing some work for the NHS recently and I asked her to check. Nothing. There's nothing there that even suggests our beautiful daughter ever existed.'

'Hardly surprising, Peter.' It appeared the only documents pertaining to Breakmire were the records kept by Harry Nugent.

'Did Hannah get any other visitors when she was there? Perhaps someone else she could have confided in?'

'No. No one. Just us.'

'This doesn't mean we can't do something, Peter.' There was too much going on here. That familiar feeling of panic was starting to rise in Oonagh's chest. 'If you can trust me…' Peter instinctively nodded his head. 'I need to try to find someone, anyone, who was there. If we go in guns blazing, then it'll be harder. They'll close ranks. We'll get nothing.' It looked for now that Oonagh was his best bet to get answers as to what had really happened to his daughter.

Oonagh got home around seven. It had been dark since four and she was starting to feel that underlying melancholy that Scottish winters could bring. The never ending feeling of darkness. She didn't have a clue where she was going with this, and didn't know if she had enough left in her to cope. She thought of calling Alec. She needed someone to talk to, but he'd be the last person she'd be able to confide in about this. Alec was a copper first and a friend second. And anyway, he'd been decidedly 'off' with her the last few times they'd met. She also knew that if he got wind of what she knew, he'd issue a warrant to obtain all the information she had. The cops would be all over this and there would be an injunction on any programme. For now she'd just need to ride solo with this.

There were too many people, too many cover-ups and it made her feel sick. She was exhausted with it all. She felt like throwing the towel in, concentrating instead on stories about lost cats being reunited with their owners after seven years. She had enough misery of her own to cope with other people's.

She hadn't had a drink all day, and felt very slightly smug as she poured the cold white wine, stopping short of half filling the glass. She glanced at it; half empty or half full, there was always room for more.

43

'We found your name and number scribbled on a piece of paper.'

Davies looked at the napkin and nodded. It was his handwriting all right. He'd given it to Tommy Gallagher the day he'd met him in Saltmarket. Told him to call if ever he needed him. The assistant led Davies through the corridor to the room at the back. That smell again. No matter how many extractor fans and high-tech ventilation systems they installed, mortuaries had the pervading stench of death. Davies felt his heart grow heavy as he followed the assistant through the double doors. He'd told him his name, but was buggered if he could remember – he hadn't really been listening, if truth be told. Was thinking about Tommy. The laughs they'd had together as kids. The carry-on of ring-bang-skoosh. Davies wasn't sure if this version of kick the door and run away was particular to Glasgow, or if it was a pretty much universal practice to ring the bell, bang the door, then spit on the doorstep before running like blazes before the owner answered and gave you a thick ear.

He should have done more for his old pal. Maybe could have tried harder. He'd got him a fresh set of clothes, and another to change into, packed them into a new wee rucksack and made sure he'd got a bed for the night at the city mission hostel. He'd given the guy at the door a bung, made sure that Tommy would have a bed for the night for at least the next few months. The guy had eyed the cash, but had changed his tune when Davies had flashed his warrant card and explained what would happen if Tommy didn't have credit at that particular hotel. Davies felt his throat tightening when he remembered the gratitude in his old pal's eyes, then once more the guilt washed over him and he felt like a shit for not doing more.

The city mission was clean and basic. Homeless men and women could bunk for the night and at least get shelter from the bitter cold. And it was safe. Well, at least as safe as it could be. The guy at the door looked rough, knew how to handle himself, and Davies guessed he was no stranger to wading in when things took a turn for the worse. But they had a strict no-booze policy. From what Davies had gathered Tommy had stayed on the wagon for almost a week before turning up drunk. They'd kicked him out. The guy at the door had had the decency to give Davies a call to let him know. They were probably terrified not to, in case he thought they'd kept his money. Davies had told them to keep it, and make sure they had a bed for Tommy when he sobered up. That was three weeks ago.

The room was stark, clinical, wall to wall stainless steel. One wall had a bank of drawers; each one held what it was designed to hold. A dead body. The mortuary assistant pulled at the metal handle of one of the drawers and it slid open. Effortlessly, as if he'd done it a million times before. The white rubberised sheet over Tommy's body was fresh and clean and at this precise moment that was important to Davies.

'Ready?' It was a rhetorical question really. The guy was helpful enough, but probably assumed that Davies, as a seasoned cop, was well used to seeing dead bodies. He'd have no way of knowing just how stomach churning this was to him. How his growing nausea was eating away at his gut. It was getting worse. When he'd first started on the job it was no big deal. But with the passing of time he'd noticed he was becoming decidedly squeamish.

The sheet was pulled from Tommy's face and Davies flinched. His wounds had been cleaned, but what looked like the mark of a heel was clearly visible on his forehead. The flesh under his right eye was split and raw looking. Yellow and blue bruises burst across his chin and under his jaw line.

'What was the cause of death?' Davies held out his hand, waiting for the guy to give him the necessary paperwork. He read down the list; Tommy had had liver failure, ruptured spleen, some old fractures to his ribs and had clearly been set about in the days before his death. But it was pneumonia that got him in the end.

'You sure about this?'

The guy nodded. 'I can get the pathologist to have a word with you?' He phrased it as a question. 'He's tied up at the minute, but…'

Davies nodded. 'Aye, get him to call me when he's done.'

Davies rested his hand lightly on Tommy's cheek before the sheet was pulled back over his face. Poor soul.

Apparently getting beaten up was a daily hazard when you were homeless. The mortuary assistant was very matter-of-fact when he explained how commonplace such injuries were. And so many homeless were ending up on slabs, he dreaded the winter and the extra workload it would bring.

Davies thought he knew most of what went on in these streets. Thought he was hardened. Had that tough outer shell. But some poor old homeless guy getting kicked for sport by a few yobs on the way home was more than he could bear. Students pissing on him as part of a freshers' week dare. Having beer poured over his head while they laughed as he tried to lap up a few drops falling onto his face, desperate to get his fix for the night as they laughed at how pathetic the 'old alky' was. What kind of fucking world did we live in? What the fuck kind of homes were people being brought up in? The sickness in the pit of his gut gave way to anger. His fists clenched and he ground his teeth as he wished the nice guy would bugger off and let him punch the wall, punch the door, punch anything just to get rid of this anger. But instead he nodded and wandered out through the corridor into the street, with the smell of Tommy's body clinging to his hair.

44

Either Oonagh was losing her skills as an investigative journalist or someone was telling porkies. But whatever was happening, this just didn't add up.

They'd agreed to meet at the café in the park. Oonagh thought it best not to spend too much time at Sarah Nugent's home in case it aroused suspicion. Alec was already asking too many questions and she knew he was on to her; it would only be a matter of time before he issued a warrant for her research notes. But until he did she was grabbing the ball and running with this.

'You're looking well, Sarah.' Oonagh pushed the condiments to the side of the table to let the waitress settle the tray between them. A few mothers with pushchairs took up most of the other tables; soft leather sofas were dotted around the edge of the café underneath signs telling nursing mums they were welcome to feed their babies here.

'Thanks.' Sarah Nugent sipped her coffee. There wasn't a hint of the trauma that she'd been through. Two weeks after the death of her husband and the police appeared to be no nearer to finding his killer, or that of Graham Petrie or Andrew Cruickshank. But there had been no other mutilated bodies found swinging from lampposts in Glasgow, so that was one less headache to deal with. What Oonagh had uncovered was getting murkier by the day; she was also aware that as soon as the programme was aired the police would be on her for as much information as possible, and it could also mean the end of her friendship with Alec.

'Ever considered going back to nursing, Sarah?' A very slight hint of something, perhaps awareness, perhaps a knowingness, flashed across her eyes. They both knew it was a ridiculous question. According to Sarah Nugent, she'd left the profession almost twenty years ago, and the woman was loaded. There wasn't a whole lot of incentive for her to roll her sleeves up and wash bedpans.

'Oh, I've been tempted, of course...' There was no mistaking the sarcasm in her voice, but she looked directly into Oonagh's eyes, daring her to say more. This was one tough cookie. Oonagh allowed herself a brief smile. She couldn't believe she'd missed it first time round. Sifting through the records, desperate to compile names of staff who'd worked at Breakmire, and make the connection with Harry Nugent. She'd been so anxious to find names, she'd overlooked the obvious. The one name that was missing.

'Tell me, Sarah, how long were you a nurse for?'

'A year, maybe eighteen months. Listen, I really can't remember.' She looked at her watch. 'I thought you said you had some important information.'

Oonagh leaned forward. 'Sarah, I've checked and double-checked. You never worked at Breakmire. And as far as I can see you've never been a nurse either.'

The colour rose on Sarah's cheeks, making the rest of her face seem unnaturally pale. 'It was a long time ago… I never really completed my training. As I said, Harry stopped me working as soon as we started going out together.'

'I'm about to put this fucking programme together. Featuring one of the most high profile murders that Glasgow's seen for a long time. Has it not occurred to you that someone could actually put two and two together? Someone may recognise you?'

Sarah shrugged her shoulders, looked shocked by the apparent accusation. Perhaps she'd lived the lie so long she'd forgotten what the truth actually was.

'Sarah, come clean. There's no shame. You were never a nurse at Breakmire.'

She drummed her nails on the table, the beat getting faster. 'I was… I told you, that's where I met Harry.'

'You better stop bullshitting me, love. You were never a nurse. Never have been. I've checked – there's no record of you ever being a nurse anywhere in Scotland.' A crying baby in the background gave them some cover to the fact their conversation was getting heated. 'You might have met Harry at Breakmire, but you weren't a nurse, Sarah, you were a patient.'

She let that linger between them. Refusing to say any more, letting Sarah speak first.

'Are you going to tell anyone?'

'Well, unless you've actually been donning your Nurse Nancy uniform and performing clandestine enemas to unsuspecting patients in the west end, you've not done anything illegal.' Oonagh thought for a few seconds. 'Well, you've lied to me, and probably the police, but unless they can prove you did it with criminal intent they're unlikely to do much about it.'

'How did you know?'

Oonagh thought that was pretty bloody obvious, but humoured her nonetheless. She explained how she'd been scanning the list of people who'd worked at Breakmire when she'd suddenly realised Sarah Walker, as she'd been then, was conspicuous by her absence.

'It was Harry – he sort of re-invented how we met and I just went along with it.'

'So, what was the truth, then?'

Sarah had been in and out of care as a kid. Staying with various foster families; often split from her brother and sister. 'Mum was on her own, couldn't really cope, so we used to get farmed out every so often.' As a teenager she'd shown signs of depression, then went on to self-harm. 'I even tried to kill myself once. To be honest, I'd no idea if I actually wanted to die, but I'd taken an overdose and after that I got admitted to Breakmire.'

'And that's where you met Harry?'

She nodded.

'Were you one of the comfort women, Sarah?' Again she nodded.

'Guys would come in.' Her eyes dropped. 'We thought we were special at first. Enjoyed the attention.'

Oonagh touched the side of her arm. 'It's OK, Sarah, that's how these grooming rings work. Make their victims think they're getting better treatment than everyone else.'

What Oonagh needed now were facts, names, dates.

'I wasn't a kid, though. I was nineteen.'

'Sarah, please, you were a vulnerable adult. You were

supposed to be getting cared for. Not being raped by some creep that thought if he threw money at you it made it all OK.'

"Suppose. Harry singled me out and we actually started dating. She made little air quotation marks with her fingers. That usually annoyed the hell out of Oonagh but she reckoned under the circumstances she'd let this one go.

'So what was all the pretence of you being a nurse?'

'Harry didn't want people prying into my background or judging me. So he just told me to say I'd worked at Breakmire.'

Oonagh guessed that was a better back story for him than the fact he'd abused a vulnerable patient with a history of self-harm, plucked her from the ward and decided to dress her up as a bride. This guy really was despicable.

'Did you have much contact with Hazel Andrews?' Again, Sarah nodded. 'And?'

'Honestly? She was actually really nice.'

'You have lovely hair, you know that?' Sarah turned and looked up, but Nurse Andrews just smiled and gently eased her shoulder back round to the front to face the mirror and continued brushing. She placed the brush on the dressing table and took a tiny silver locket from the uniform of her pocket. 'Here,' she said, pulling back Sarah's hair and fastening the clasp around her throat, 'just a wee present...'

Sarah fingered the locket between her fingers, feeling the smoothness of the little heart in her grip. Thank you Nurse Andr—'

'It's Hazel, remember? We're friends, after all.' Hazel switched off the main light as she stood by the door. The bedside lamp cast soft shadows around the room. Sarah had it all to herself, a reward, Hazel had said, for doing so well. It was so much nicer than the ward she'd been in when she'd first arrived. That was stark and cold and the sheets had scratched her bare feet at night.

'You look lovely, Sarah. So pretty.' Sarah felt the warmth of that remark flood through her body, feeding every part of her. She smiled as the emotion reached her face, causing a blush across her cheeks.

'You up for receiving a visitor this evening?' Hazel must have caught a look from Sarah. 'Oh, sweetheart, you don't have to. I was only trying to—'

'No,' she said, offering a little smile. 'It's fine. Yes, yes, of course, Hazel.'

'Well, get yourself dressed and ready, sweetheart.' And with that she closed the door.

'She'd given every one of us one of those cheap little lockets.' Sarah had shown little emotion as she'd recounted her time at Breakmire and her relationship with Hazel Andrews. 'It probably seems odd to you that I wanted to please her, but she was just so nice to me.' Sarah's relationship with Hazel Andrews had been one of classic victim grooming, but even now Sarah couldn't quite see it like that. 'I was nineteen. I was an adult. I knew what I was doing.'

*

She tugged at the hem of her dress tunic, which was too short and too tight and kept creeping up her thighs. Hazel had said she looked nice, but she felt stupid wearing this – she was too old for a school uniform, and it made her look like a kid again. Sarah smoothed her hair down as she glanced at the clock on the wall, but that had stopped a long time ago; now it was forever six-fifteen in her room. He'd be here shortly though, and she'd need to be ready. They didn't like to be kept waiting; besides, she didn't want to upset Hazel.

'At the time I thought she was being nice to me because she liked me. She was always ready for a laugh.'

This didn't surprise Oonagh. Things were never as black and white as they seemed, and neither were people. Even killers, as it turned out, enjoyed a bit of banter at work.

'So she was behind the brothel?'

'Don't judge me here. All I know is she was nice to me.' Sarah caught the waitress's eye, and she came over. 'You licensed?'

'Sure. Just wine though – is that OK?'

'Yeah, large glass of house white.'

The waitress looked at Oonagh who faltered for a moment, then, 'Oh, on you go, I'll have the same.' Her car was parked just a short walk away in a residential street, but stuff it, she'd take a taxi.

'So?' Oonagh was desperate to get back to Hazel Andrews and her part in all this. 'I'm still not getting the link with Andrew Cruickshank.' As much as Oonagh had delved into the background, there was no mention of Cruickshank, but he must have been involved. His was no random murder.

'The taxi driver.' Oonagh initially thought Sarah had posed that as a question, then realised she just had that strange upward inflection at the end of her sentence. 'He was used as the driver so the men's vehicles were never seen in the hospital car park late at night. Sometimes he'd ferry the girls back and forth when the men couldn't come to Breakmire. He was well paid, and could be trusted.'

Oonagh felt sick. Men like Harry Nugent and Graham Petrie could never operate in a vacuum. They relied heavily on other sick individuals. The waitress came back with the wine. It was surprisingly good, and, after an initial few sips, Oonagh gave up the pretence and downed the glass in one go.

The waitress's eyes widened.

Oonagh fought the urge to tell her to fuck off, but Sarah beat her to it. 'Perhaps,' she said pointing to the wall behind them, 'they should add a sign beside the nursing mums saying, "Boozing Women Welcome" and then we could all just have a guilt free lunch.'

The waitress smiled, 'Respect,' she said, giving them a thumbs-up before walking away. 'Nice one, Sarah.'

She shrugged. 'Fancy another?'

Oonagh nodded, but was keen to get back to the point. 'So, how did you start *dating* Harry?' She resisted making the air quotation marks with her fingers.

Oonagh was starting to see how things were at Breakmire. The grooming, the compliance, the subsequent abuse. It was how these things worked.

'He used to buy me things, you know?'

Oonagh nodded. It wasn't too hard to see Harry working his charm.

'But he'd never visited me at night. Harry wasn't like that. Then one day he asked me if I'd like to leave. With him. Said I'd never need to do anything like this again. Never have to have men visiting me and said he'd take care of me.' She dropped her chin onto her chest, forcing her gaze deep into her glass.

Oonagh guessed for the teenage Sarah, being treated for mental health problems, Harry Nugent had been the nearest thing to a knight in shining armour. It wasn't hard to see what the attraction of Sarah had been. She was a good looking girl, carried herself well and would make a perfect front for his sordid lifestyle. A vulnerable young girl from a broken home, she was an identikit bride, with no family to step in and realise what the hell had actually been going on. For Sarah, Harry had represented a life she could probably only have dreamt of.

'Is that why you weren't too perturbed at Harry's lack of...' she paused, not quite knowing how to put this '... the lack of intimacy between you?'

Sarah shrugged. 'Dunno. Never really thought about it, to be honest.'

Oonagh guessed that Sarah would have been so grateful for whatever lifestyle Nugent was offering, she hadn't spent too much time analysing it.

'Sarah, this doesn't bring us any closer to who the killer was, but if this goes to air the police will be back banging on your door. They'll come down on you like a ton of bricks.'

There was one thing that Oonagh didn't quite get. 'Why now? Why're you telling me all this now?'

'I'm scared. Scared they'll come for me next. And I can trust you.'

Oonagh knew by the look in her eyes that this time she was telling the truth.

45

'You know who did it, don't you?' Oonagh couldn't quite see the lovely side of Hazel Andrews that Sarah Nugent had alluded to. It was obvious now that she'd almost been like a mother figure to these girls. Or a big sister, taking them under her wing, always there for them, ready with a laugh, the only one to listen to their problems. When all the while she'd been grooming them for her own personal gain. Collecting their hearts and minds the way other people collected stamps.

'Did what?' Hazel pretended not to know what Oonagh was talking about. Gave her a blank expression when she asked again about who killed Harry Nugent, Graham Petrie and Andrew Cruickshank.

'Did they try to block your release? Is that what it was?'

'I don't know what you're talking about. Have you got any biscuits?' She was ripping the piss. Obviously knew that the last time Oonagh had visited she'd come armed with a load of bribes. Cakes, biscuits, cigarettes. Oonagh didn't even know if Hazel Andrews smoked, but she knew smokes were valuable currency in most prisons. Only she'd never got them past the front door. They'd all been confiscated at the front desk. Visitors weren't allowed to pass on stuff like that to the inmates.

'What've you got to lose, Hazel?' Appealing to this woman's better nature didn't come easily to Oonagh, but she too, had very little to lose at this point. 'I don't care who killed them.' Andrews raised an eyebrow, didn't believe her. 'Seriously, I don't. I have no intention of passing the name on to the police.'

'If you don't care, why the fuck are you so interested, then?'

'Like I say, wraps up my investigation. From what I know just now? I'm glad they're dead. They were evil. They preyed on the innocent and the vulnerable. But I need to know – did you pay someone to kill them, a professional hit man?' Oonagh knew she sounded like a tit saying that. She wasn't sure if real people used phrases like hit man, but Hazel Andrews didn't miss a beat.

The prisoner opened the little cabinet in the corner of her cell. 'See this?' She clasped the bundle of letters she'd shown Oonagh on her last visit. 'In here are dozens of people who're prepared to do anything for me.'

Oonagh struggled to believe this, but couldn't discount it straight away. She already knew the way Sarah Nugent spoke about her. That strange adoration. There might well be others who felt the same. Andrews threw the bundle down on the small table by the bed. 'Forget dying for me. I've got fans that would kill for me.'

Oonagh felt sick; the bile in her stomach started

to rise. This could be the ranting of a madwoman, but a trickle of fear in her spine said she might well be wrong.

'And why would they do that, Hazel?'

She shrugged. 'Because I'd asked them to.'

'And did you?'

'Did I what?'

She was dragging this out. 'Did you ask any of your wee pen pals to kill those men?'

Andrews sat back on her bed, suppressing a smile.

'You don't half talk a lot of shite, Hazel, d'you know that?' Andrews stiffened slightly at this change of tactic. 'Every prison letter is scanned and read and checked. D'you think they wouldn't be on to you if you were issuing orders for people to be killed?'

Andrews folded her arms hard across her chest.

'I knew you were bonkers, Hazel, but if you believe your own shite then this takes it on to a whole new ball game.'

'You think you're smart, Oonagh O'Neil. D'you know that? But you're not. You're as thick as the rest of the do-gooders who come to see me. D'you not think by now I'd have developed a code?'

Oonagh didn't know if she was telling the truth, or this was just a sick fantasy. 'Hazel, I think you've watched *The Silence of the Lambs* once too often. You're stuck in a crummy prison cell in Falkirk, for fucks sake. Half the people who write to you can hardly read their own bus ticket, let alone work out some elaborate code issuing orders to carry out three executions.'

The room was stifling and the walls were closing in on

Oonagh. She'd had enough. Enough horror and enough bullshit.

'The letters between me and my legal team aren't read.'

'Oh, so now your lawyer's involved, Hazel.' Oonagh was exhausted with it all and stood up to go. 'Give it up, love, eh.'

'I don't want to see you any more.'

This came as a bit of a shock to Oonagh. 'Why?'

'This is our last meeting. And to be honest I don't care if you believe me or not. But I'm telling you that I have people who're only too happy to help me by killing those creeps.'

46

'He was a troubled soul, Alec.' Ellie Simpson pushed the plate of biscuits on the table towards him as she stirred her tea. Alec gave that tight-line smile that said he agreed with her, but in truth he had no idea what Tommy Gallagher had been through. 'Thanks for coming though, it was good of you.'

Only three people had turned up to pay their last respects that morning, a sorry looking bunch they made, huddled under umbrellas as Tommy Gallagher's coffin was lowered into the ground. Alec had guessed there wouldn't be the usual steak pie at the local pub afterwards, but took the offer up when Tommy's sister invited him back for a cup of tea.

'I met him a few weeks ago, in the Saltmarket.' He blew on the hot tea. 'Did he tell you?'

She shook her head. 'I hadn't seen him for a few years.' Something, perhaps guilt, passed over her face. 'He was… he wasn't in a good way.'

Alec reached across and touched her hand. ''S OK.'

'I couldn't have him here, Alec.' Ellie Simpson tugged at her ear lobe. It suddenly seemed very familiar and fired up a memory in Alec; Tommy used to do the very same thing when he was worried. 'He'd be fine for a day,' she continued, 'then… I had to think of the kids and, to be honest, John was sick to the back teeth of him.'

Alec knew only too well what she was talking about. 'Sometimes we need to know when to let go too.' He wasn't sure if this would appease Ellie Simpson's guilt, but he couldn't think of anything else to say. 'He told me he'd had two kids. D'you know where they are?' Despite what might or might not have happened, they had a right to know their dad was dead.

Ellie shook her head. 'Never kept in touch after him and Alison split up.' Ellie gave a pretty cut-and-dried account of Tommy's downfall. He'd gone down to Manchester after he'd left school. Met and married a local girl, Alison. Ellie hardly knew her. Then two kids and a divorce later Tommy had been back in Glasgow, in and out of temporary jobs and rented accommodation. 'He could never settle, that was his problem. And the drink, he never seemed to be able to know when to say no.'

Ellie Gallagher was four years younger than her brother but could have passed for his daughter. Life on the streets hadn't been kind to her brother. She'd told him that Tommy had just seemed to drift in and out of jobs, getting laid off when he'd failed to show up for work, or, even worse, when he'd turned up still half-cut and reeking of booze after a heavy session the previous night.

'Your family all well?' She seemed to want to change the subject.

Alec nodded. 'Yip. Mum and Dad still in Helensburgh.' He hadn't spoken to his own brother in almost a year but couldn't be arsed going into details. 'I was sorry to hear you lost your mum.'

'Well, at least she never had to see Tommy the way he was.'

Every cloud, thought Alec, but kept his mouth shut.

'Our mam always thought he'd be a footballer. Make the big time. He was good enough, you know.' A slight note of pride touched her voice as she remembered her brother during happier times.

'Aye, better than me. I was flipping hopeless,' Alec said, and meant it.

'I blame that creep, Nugent. Pervert.'

Alec felt his scalp tighten. That wasn't what he'd expected to hear. 'Why d'you say that?'

'You know he coached our Tommy for a bit.'

This piece of information was news to Alec, either that or he'd forgotten. It was all so long ago and he'd moved to the other side of the city when he'd started secondary school and lost touch with most of his old mates. Seemed ridiculous now, with Facebook and mobile phones. But back in the day all it took was a different bus route to split up supposedly life-long pals.

'You know Nugent is dead.' Even as he said it, he knew how ridiculous it sounded.

She nodded. 'I had heard, yeah.' Then let out a hollow laugh. 'You must have a line-up of suspects as long as your arm with that one.'

'You'd be surprised.' Alec meant it. Despite the

accusations against Harry Nugent, they were no nearer to finding his killer. 'What d'you know about him, Ellie?'

'I know he was a filthy creep and I blame him for ruining our Tommy's life.'

Alec had to go easy with her. 'If you have any information, then…'

'I used to hear him crying in his bed at night. He thought I was asleep, and he'd try to be as quiet as he could. Used to think it was 'cause Dad died. But Tommy held it together for me and Mum. Would have done anything for us.' The memory gripped Ellie as she placed both hands on the kitchen table, leaning over, taking deep breaths. 'But it was always after football. Always after seeing that Nugent. I heard him being sick more than once too.'

'Did he ever talk about it?'

She shook her head. 'Not then. Then one day he came home and that was it. Never went back. My mum phoned Nugent, but he said Tommy had been caught drinking and he'd dropped him. That was nonsense. He lived and breathed football. He'd never do anything to jeopardise that.' Her shoulders softened slightly and she sat back down. The kitchen was warm but she gave an involuntary shiver. 'Anyway, Tommy was round here one night. About five years ago. Drunk, needless to say. Before he'd ended up on the streets. And it all came spilling out. He was crashed on the sofa…' she tipped her head towards the front of the house '… but he was rambling. And that's when he told me. Told me how that man used to touch him.' She clasped her hand over her mouth and gulped as the tears spilled over, splashing onto her blouse. 'It made me sick. Our Tommy.'

Alec jumped out and rounded the table, wrapping a protective arm around her shoulder. 'I'm so sorry, Ellie,' he said, and meant it. 'I wish he'd told someone. I mean, gone to the police or…' He couldn't finish the sentence. Not now. Not knowing how badly Tommy and the rest of the boys had been let down. There was a time when he'd been jealous of Tommy Gallagher and his talent on the pitch. The way the ball had just seemed to be part of him. An extension of his foot, going where and doing whatever Tommy wanted. Alec had once thought how different his life might have been had he been as talented as Tommy Gallagher.

'Things were different then, Alec.' Ellie's voice snapped him back to the present. 'Men didn't admit that stuff like that even existed, let alone happened to them.'

Alec wanted to tell her she was wrong, that the police would have been there for Tommy, that he'd have got help, that Nugent would have been put away. But he couldn't.

'D'you know, he used to make Tommy ask him for money after he'd abused him.' She was crying now, pressing the tissue into the corners of her eyes. But that last statement felt like a punch in the gut to Alec. It was exactly what Joe McLeish had said. 'What kind of sick bastard does that to a boy? He was just a kid, Alec, just a kid.'

Alec wrapped both arms around her now as Ellie Simpson gave way to her grief. He could feel the sobs go through her body and stroked her hair as she buried her face into his chest. His own tears stung the backs of his eyes as she sobbed for the loss of her brother. 'Had it not been for that man…' she straightened herself, patted Alec's hand on her shoulder to let him know she'd composed herself '… well, our Tommy would still be alive. Oh, I'm not saying he'd be playing in the premiership, but he would never have ended up the way he did had it not been for Harry Nugent.' She stood up, wiping her hands across her cheeks, then busied herself rinsing the cups. 'Tell me this, Alec, did he suffer?'

Alec gave her a look; initially thought she was talking about Tommy. He couldn't bear to tell her about the catalogue of injuries that chronicled his suffering in the months leading to his death.

'I heard his tongue was cut out – is that true?' She placed the cups in the sink and tipped her head back, looking out into the garden. 'You read so much guff on the Internet it's hard to know what's real and what's fake.'

'Between you and me, Ellie?' Alec reckoned he had little to lose. 'Yeah. We think he probably did suffer. Whoever killed him terrified him.'

'At least that's something,' she said.

The earlier rain had stopped as Alec walked to his car; it left the air feeling clean and the colours of the city more vibrant. The lump in his throat ached and he swallowed hard. It had been a long time since he'd cried, but he felt no shame for the tears that now streamed down both cheeks as he thought of the wasted lives of countless young boys. Boys like Tommy Gallagher who'd only wanted to play football, but had ended up on a slab because of pigs like Harry Nugent.

47

Oonagh knew she was freefalling her way to burnout trying to tackle this almost on her own, but she didn't trust anyone else to share the load. She had almost enough material to go ahead with the programme; once she'd compiled it she'd take it to Alan. She knew once he saw what she had he'd give her a decent video editor and the green light to go ahead.

This new information from Sarah Nugent was the icing on the cake. She'd need it 'legalled' and then she'd be good to go. There was nothing in the programme that alluded to who killed Nugent, or indeed Petrie or Cruickshank. To be honest, Oonagh had long given up caring who'd committed the deed. What she wanted to get out there was the fact that the three had caused so much suffering and they had in fact been connected with one of the most sickening cases of abuse she'd had the misfortune to cover.

She spotted Sophie at the other side of the open plan area; as usual she looked exhausted. She was shaping up to be a decent journalist, but Oonagh knew she'd need to toughen up.

Oonagh popped her head out of the door of her office. 'Hey, Sophie, you got a minute?' As ever, Sophie was eager to please and dropped whatever it was she was doing and came in and sat opposite Oonagh.

'How you getting on?'

Sophie nodded. 'Fine, yeah.' She was wearing a dark high-neck sweater, the sleeves pulled down over her hands. Oonagh wondered if this was to hide yet more bruises.

She had to ease into this, wanted to let her know that if Charlie was abusing her then she had a safe place to talk. 'Sophie, this might be none of my business, but I'm making it my business.' Oonagh tried to think what she would have wanted when she was Sophie's age. Would she have appreciated some stranger at work wading into a domestic crisis? Sophie sat on her hands and looked down, saying nothing.

'There's no easy way to say this, Sophie, but if Charlie's…' she considered her choice of words '… if Charlie's bullying you, then you don't need to stay with her.' It sounded very benign, but Oonagh didn't want to scare her off.

'She's not, she's just…' Sophie looked as though she was about to cry '… got a strong personality.'

Oonagh gritted her teeth slightly. She'd heard it called many things, but this was ridiculous. 'Sophe, I've seen the bruises. I've seen the marks on your arms. If Charlie's strong personality means she's slapping you about, then it's time to ditch her. Call the police. I'll help.'

Sophie looked genuinely shocked. 'Charlie? Hit me?'

She stood up. 'Who the hell d'you think you are?' She was crying now. 'She'd never lay a finger on me. All she does is try to help.'

'I'm sorry, Sophie.' And she was, sorry she'd upset her, but not that she'd brought it up. 'But I've seen the way she is, and I don't think I've seen you come in without a fresh bruise.'

Poor Sophie. Oonagh had seen it so many times before. Girls, women, covering for their violent partners. Admittedly, this was the first time she'd seen the scenario between two women. She didn't have a clue how the usual agencies would deal with this one. By this time Sophie's tears had spilled over, splashing down her cheek onto her jumper. Oonagh handed her a tissue and perched herself on the arm of Sophie's chair, patting her gently on the back. 'It's not Charlie. It's my brother, Jake.'

'What?' Oonagh was not expecting this.

'He doesn't mean it, but he's getting bigger and he's hard to handle and sometimes he accidentally headbutts me if I'm getting him dressed, or he'll grab my wrist and if his joints are going into a spasm he digs in and can't let go.'

Oonagh felt herself go weak. 'Oh, you poor love. I'm so, so sorry. I thought...' Shit, what a bloody wrong call that turned out to be. 'Does Jake live with you?'

'Yeah, with me and my mum. He's a great kid, honestly. He's always laughing. But he's getting heavier, and harder for me to manage.'

'I'm sorry, Sophie, really I am. Is there anything I can do to help?'

Sophie shook her head. 'No, I'm good, thanks.'

'Can you get help, or respite care?'

'A bit, but it's expensive. Anyway, we're fine, honestly.'

She got up to go and Oonagh's heart ached as she watched her sit back down in front of her PC and get to work. She was just a kid herself.

Oonagh knocked on Alan's door, then did her usual of barging in before he'd had the chance to tell her to bugger off.

'Hey, Oon, who're you noising up today?' Alan thought he was being funny, and maybe on another day he might have been right.

'Sophie…?' Oonagh gave him a moment to take in the name, but it was obvious that Alan was oblivious. Oonagh tipped her head towards the main office. 'Young girl, trainee.'

The penny dropped. 'What about her?'

'She's very good. I've mentioned her before. Anyway, I want you to give her a permanent contract.'

'Really? Well, I'll just call HR and tell them you're in charge of all personnel from now on.'

'Alan, stop being sarcastic. It doesn't suit you. What's the problem? She's a good kid, a hard worker and needs a full-time job.' They both knew what the problem was. It was cheaper all round to keep trainees on rolling temporary contracts. No sick pay, no job security and it kept them hungry and eager to put up with any shit that was thrown at them.

'No, Oonagh, that's not how it works. I'll keep her on for now, but that's about the size of it.' He made a play of sorting out some papers on his desk. 'Was there anything else?'

Oonagh stood up to leave. 'Not really.' She got to the door and stopped. 'Oh, by the way…'

Alan sighed. He knew Oonagh's style by now, knew a bombshell was about to be dropped. 'What?'

'I've erm...' she examined her nails '... established a link between Nugent, Petrie and Cruickshank.'

'You're bullshitting me, Oonagh.' It had been a long time since she'd seen Alan this animated. She had him right where she wanted him.

'Nope, I've got it all, and you'll wet yourself when you find out what they were up to.' She moved back into the room and sat on the chair opposite him.

'So.' Alan closed the lid on his laptop. 'Spill the beans.'

'I need a shit-hot video editor, and I'll have this ready to air in less than a fortnight. Can you get me a slot?'

'Fuck. Yes! You'll need it legalled, though.'

Oonagh nodded; that wouldn't be a problem. Suddenly Alan seemed to forget that he'd given the story to the senior crime correspondent, who was still using all his favours with the Glasgow gangsters to find out what happened.

'I don't have a clue who killed them,' she said, 'and as far as I can see neither do the police. But nothing in the programme alludes to that – it's a background piece. A very detailed background piece that'll blow the lid on the whole thing.'

'If I jumped up and kissed you right now would you report me for sexual harassment?'

'No, but I might be a little bit sick in my mouth.' She'd known Alan a long time.

Alan was grinning. 'I suppose you want Sophie as your researcher on this.' He knew how she operated. How Oonagh knew how to get her own way.

'No, Alan, that ship has sailed.'

He folded his arms, clearly wondering what was coming next.

'I want her on a permanent contract and a raise. And I want you to give it to her as a cash expense payment every month so she's not hammered by tax.'

'Have you lost your marbles?'

'An extra fifty quid a month. That's peanuts to you.'

'Absolutely fucking not. D'you have any idea how many girls, just as good, if not better than Sophie, are battering on my door each week offering to work for nothing, just for a chance to get their foot in the door?'

'I do, Alan, and that's what's wrong with this fucking industry. It preys on people's insecurities and bleeds them dry until they end up washed up, with no home life, popping pills and downing the booze just to stay afloat.'

'It's a tough gig, Oonagh, but that's just the way it is.'

She stood up to leave, and leaned against the wall as she gripped the door handle. 'I'm putting my money where my mouth is here. Give her an extra fifty quid and I'll match it.' Oonagh knew the difference a clear hundred quid a month would make to someone like Sophie. It wouldn't solve all her problems, but it would make life a wee bit more palatable.

Alan shook his head. 'Absolutely no way. I'll give her a six month contract.'

'Suit yourself.' She opened the door. 'Shame, I think the network would have liked my programme.'

'What the fuck's that supposed to mean?'

'I mean, Alan, I'm not handing it over. Instead I'll punt

it.' They both knew Oonagh had enough contacts in this industry to approach a rival station with this, and they both knew they'd bite her hand off for the chance to air this. 'Sky'll pay silly money for this.'

'Can I remind you that, under the terms of your contract, everything you make here is the property of the station?'

'And can I suggest you check out my workload and input over the past few weeks. I've met every deadline and worked every shift I was assigned to. Alan, I put this together in my own time, using my own equipment.'

'Oonagh, d'you just get up in the morning and plan to totally piss people off?'

'I knew you'd see sense. Listen, don't tell Sophie that I'm chipping in some of the money.' She was halfway out of the door, then popped her head back into the room. 'You'll need to invent some expenses grant.'

She didn't wait for an answer. She had more things to worry about and only had a matter of days to knock this programme into shape. Alan might have agreed to get it on air, but she reckoned he'd make her jump through a few hoops first.

48

Oonagh slipped the car into first gear and followed the private cab as it left Houston and then joined the M8 near Paisley, heading east. Her initial thoughts were that it was heading for the airport, but it passed junction twenty-eight and continued on to the south side of Glasgow, veering off at just past Plantation. Factories and industrial units, some long deserted, flanked both sides of the motorway. This stretch of land south of the river had once belonged to a wealthy banker who'd owned sugar and cotton plantations in the West Indies; he'd decided to rename the entire area Plantation to advertise his success. Some believed it had seen better days; Oonagh struggled to regard Glasgow's link to the slave trade as such. Enormous canvas backdrops covered some of the tired buildings informing every driver that there was indeed office space to rent inside.

Rain smeared the windscreen and cast a grey light over the city. Oonagh kept a safe distance from the cab she was following; it was unlikely her car would be recognised, but, just to be on the safe side, she allowed two more vehicles to nudge in front as the Uber driver took a right turn at the roundabout and then doubled back onto the motorway, taking the slip road onto the southbound M77. She had no doubt now where it was going.

Ash had called her earlier that morning. At first she thought she'd forgotten to pay him, but his voice had an unfamiliar sense of urgency. They'd agreed to meet again at the same tea house as before; he'd arrived before her and jumped up as soon as she entered.

'What's the emergency?' she'd asked.

He'd been wearing the same green cords as last time and was tugging at the sleeves of his red anorak, wriggling his shoulders free from it as she'd leaned over to give him a quick peck on the cheek.

'I didn't realise at first…' He'd been even more animated than usual; bouncing his right heel off the floor, which had been really annoying. 'You know when you asked me to look over these accounts, I'd never heard of Harry Nugent.'

Oonagh had nodded; she could well believe it. Over the years she'd come to realise that Ash could recite the back catalogues and lyrics of every Japanese jazz album ever produced, or so it seemed, but he'd never heard of the Spice Girls, *EastEnders* or Frank Sinatra. It had come as no surprise that the name Harry Nugent would have sparked the same vacant expression and lack of interest.

'But you have now?' Oonagh had replied. 'And that's important because?'

Ash had looked round, apparently to ensure no one was listening, but apart from a woman inhaling the scent of her tea before each sip and a frazzled looking hipster desperately trying to ignore her small child tugging at her sleeve, there had been no one close by to care. 'He's been killed,' Ash had said in an exaggerated hushed tone. 'D'you know that?'

'Yes, Ash.' Oonagh had struggled to suppress a smile. 'Yes, Ash, I do.'

A guy sitting at the back of the room had got up to leave. He'd looked out of place in the tea house and weaved his way through the tables, deliberately slowing down as he passed. 'You'll be going home soon.' The comment had been directed at Ash.

'You our Uber driver, then?' Ash had looked him straight in the eye, not missing a beat. It was only then that Oonagh had seen his *Make Britain Great Again* badge. He'd shaken his head in apparent disgust, then stormed out of the door.

If the comment had bothered Ash, he hadn't let on. But he'd still worn that worried expression that puckered the skin on his forehead. Oonagh had leaned across and patted his thigh. 'Anyway,' he'd added, getting back on track, 'I thought I'd have another look.' He'd sat back and drummed his fingers on his thigh. 'And was somewhat surprised by something.'

'Oh?'

From what looked like nowhere he'd produced a mini laptop. Oonagh had been impressed; it was a decent piece of kit, tiny screen, portable enough to slip inside his jacket, and looked good too. She could only wonder in amazement as to what else Ash had tucked away in the inside pocket of his anorak. He stood up and rounded the coffee table, plonking himself down beside Oonagh so they could both see the screen at the same time.

'Look.' He'd spread his hand across the front of the

screen. Clearly Oonagh had been meant to see something startling.

'You may have to explain this to me, Ash.'

The rain was coming down heavier now, and, despite the grey clouds overhead, it picked out the vivid green of the grass verge as she left the thick of the city behind and headed south. The motorway stretched out ahead with just a smattering of vehicles and Oonagh felt more comfortable now, allowing a greater distance between her and the cab. She followed it to Newton Mearns and prepared to pull over as it slowed down at the end of the road. Sarah Nugent paid the driver and walked the few hundred yards to the art-deco flat before pressing her fob on the side of the wall to open the gate. She had no cases with her, just a small black handbag, which fell to the ground as she jumped when Oonagh approached her.

'Sarah?' She spun round and Oonagh was shocked to see Sarah's sister. She'd gone through the same transformation as Sarah had: new haircut, same style of clothes.

'Sorry?'

'Oh, I thought...' Oonagh braced herself. 'Where's Sarah?'

'Sorry, do I know you?'

This was getting tedious. 'Listen, love, don't get cute with me. Yes, you know me, I'm the one you told to fuck off when I went to see your sister a few weeks ago. Remember now?'

The other woman raised an eyebrow, but said nothing.

'So where's Sarah?'

'I have no idea.' She stuffed the fob back into her bag and made to walk away when the gate clicked into life and a voice from the intercom told them both to come in.

Oonagh took the lead and walked up the path, making her way to the double doors at the entrance to the block of flats. Like before they opened automatically and she didn't bother waiting for the lift, rather took the stairs, taking care to pace herself. She stopped at the first landing and fished her inhaler from the zipped pocket of her bag. The last thing she wanted was to arrive at the top panting and out of breath. The ping of the lift on the landing above told her that Gill had already arrived. Muffled voices spilled down the stairwell, and she wondered how warm her welcome would be this time.

There was no luggage or clichéd stack of suitcases sitting in the hall that Oonagh had expected as she entered the flat. But then maybe Sarah Nugent didn't know she'd need to be making a run for it any time soon.

'Come in, why don't you?' Oonagh detected more than a hint of sarcasm in Sarah's voice, given that she was already well past the threshold.

'Gill…' this time she was addressing her sister '… I need a few moments here.' She held her car keys out and Gill snatched them from her, making a huge play of looking pissed off as she slammed the door on her way out.

'You two planning a double act on *Britain's Got Talent*?' Oonagh nodded towards the door.

Sarah smoothed down her hair self-consciously, shaking

her head slightly. 'Gill's always copied me. Even as teenagers she'd want the same style I had.'

'So you're not planning any wee identity swaps or using her as a decoy?'

Sarah looked genuinely confused. 'Eh?'

'You look extraordinarily alike, and she left your house this morning pretty much disguised as you.'

Sarah's eyes widened. 'Disguised?' She let out a very slight laugh. 'She's my sister, we've always looked alike and she's staying with me for a few days.' She paused as she made her way through to the living room, then turned and looked at Oonagh. 'Sorry, what is this?'

Oonagh realised she'd made the wrong call. Her mind had been racing after meeting Ash and when she'd mistaken Gill for Sarah her mind had gone into overdrive. She'd put two and two together and come up with five; certain that Sarah had been planning to make a run for it and use Gill as some sort of decoy. Not for the first time, she felt like a total tit.

'Sorry, my mistake.' She held her hands up in a stop sign. 'I thought…' Oonagh didn't bother finishing. Her thoughts on this weren't something she felt like sharing at this time.

'Why're you here, Oonagh?'

'Can I sit down?'

Sarah nodded towards the white leather settee. Despite the fabulous looking design, this sofa was not built for comfort and Oonagh perched on the edge of the square edged cushions.

She looked at Sarah and a mix of emotions washed over

her. Here was a woman who'd been either used or abused her whole life, yet, despite that, Oonagh knew that she'd also facilitated covering up her husband's reign of abuse over others and that was something she was finding hard to stomach. She wasn't quite sure where she was going with this.

'Why d'you do it, Sarah?'

'Do what?' Sarah sucked hard on her vape, blowing the sickly sweet scented smoke back across her left shoulder. It left a pall of grey mist resting in the air.

'Kill your husband?' Oonagh pondered the question for a moment. 'Actually, can I rephrase that? Why did you wait so long?'

'Seriously? You think I killed Harry? For God's sake, why the hell would I do that? The police have interviewed me – I'm not a suspect, never was. But you barge in here with your half-arsed theories.'

'Sarah, I'm glad Harry is dead,' Oonagh admitted, 'and I actually don't know how to feel about this.' It was true. Oonagh liked to think of herself as the champion of the underdog, someone who liked to see justice prevail. She was no vigilante, but could shed no tears over the deaths of Harry Nugent or his cohorts. 'I've no intention of going to the police with this,' she said, and meant it. 'I don't want you or anyone else to suffer any more than you already have done. But, please. Cut me some slack here. Help me tie up some loose ends.'

'Seriously? I've told you everything I know.'

'But you stand to get the lot.'

'And that's news because?'

'No, Sarah, I don't mean the nice house in Houston and Harry's legitimate business interests.'

Oonagh's meeting with Ash this morning had left her reeling. He'd delved deeper into the business accounts. The spider's web of properties and sham businesses that were used as a front for the brothels couldn't immediately be linked to Harry Nugent, but he was the main shareholder of each of the smaller businesses that made up the larger portfolio. The junior shareholder was Graham Petrie. Although his share was a fraction of what Nugent was worth, Petrie had been creaming off a tidy wee sum each quarter that would have made a very welcome supplement to his pension. There was a beneficiary clause tucked away. In the event of Harry's death, then the portfolio would automatically transfer to his widow. There was a sub-clause, however, that in the event of no living beneficiaries, then Graham Petrie stood to get the lot. Oonagh had guessed Petrie had drawn up most of the papers, and had added this clause as some added insurance.

'I'm not altogether shocked that you had Harry killed, Sarah. I just can't work out why you waited all this time.'

'I don't care if you believe me or not. I didn't kill Harry.'

'Was Harry on borrowed time? Was that it?' Oonagh knew there had been murmurings about Harry's abuse. It had only been a matter of time, in this current climate, before it all came out. Sarah would have known that, had he been investigated and found guilty, she'd have been left with nothing. His assets from the brothels would have been frozen and most likely everything else until the police could be sure they weren't from illegal activities. Sarah would have been left high and dry. 'Did you get someone to help you?'

It was already documented that Sarah had been away from home that evening. She had a boiler-plate alibi. According to the toxicology report, Harry had been drugged, so it wouldn't have needed any brute force to wrap that noose round his neck. The police knew he'd climbed the stairs; whoever had been there forcing him to hang himself must have known he wouldn't or couldn't fight back. Oonagh wondered if Sarah's sister, Gill, had done it, or, more likely, her bruiser of a brother, Chaz. But it seemed obvious who gave the command to attack. Sarah.

'I'll never get that image out of my head.' Sarah rubbed her eyes. 'Him swinging from the balcony.' She looked at Oonagh. 'You're right, I didn't love Harry. But I had a decent enough life with him, and, you may find this hard to believe, but he was good to me.'

Oonagh pondered that one for a moment. People were rarely as cut and dried as that; good or bad. It was easier back in the day. When she'd sit on her dad's knee watching an old western on the telly of a rainy Sunday afternoon. The good guys always wore white hats, the baddies wore inky-black from head to toe, as they charged into town astride their horses. But this wasn't the movies, this was real life and things were more complicated than that. Sometimes evil men could do nice things, or just not be evil for long enough to make someone like them. Perhaps that was what Harry Nugent had been like.

'Sarah, the laptop. D'you honestly expect me to believe a man as careful as Harry Nugent would leave a laptop lying around with those images of child abuse on it?'

The colour was draining from Sarah's face. The slash of red lipstick now a harsh line across her pale complexion.

'Sarah, did you plant those images on Harry's laptop?'

'You going to tell the police?'

Shit. Oonagh slumped back and braced herself against the firm leather of the settee. The sudden stab of fear in her chest told her this wasn't one of her better moves: spilling her half-baked theories out to someone she believed had given the order to have her husband executed.

'No, Sarah, I won't go to the police. But, let's face it, if the images have been planted recently, it won't take them long to find out.' Oonagh had no idea if she was convincing. No idea whether she even knew herself if she was telling the truth. Her head began to swim as her heart raced. The faint murmur of traffic in the distance gave her a sense of comfort. They weren't so far from civilisation that her screams wouldn't be heard. Surely there would be residents in the adjoining flats too. Also, the fact Sarah had chased her sister away suggested she wasn't going to get violent.

'I didn't plant those images, Oonagh,' she said, pausing for just a moment, 'but I know who did.'

Suddenly Oonagh was scared of what she was about to hear. Tingles of fear tightened across her forehead.

'Graham Petrie.'

'Excuse me?' Well, that came from left field and took Oonagh completely by surprise. 'What the fuck? I mean, why the hell would he do that?'

'He contacted me after Harry was... after Harry died. This might sound strange but I'd actually forgotten about him. I hadn't thought about him in years. But as soon as I saw him it came flooding back.'

By all accounts Sarah had been one of Petrie's favourites. He'd groomed her with the help of Hazel Andrews, then sold her on to his most discerning clients.

'I'd no idea about Harry's other…' she held out her hands, searching for the right words '… businesses. I certainly had no idea of his involvement with Petrie. You've seen the accounts. This was money on a scale I'd never even imagined before.'

Oonagh was getting lost with all this. 'So why did Petrie come and see you?'

'At first he claimed he wanted to help. Told me that Harry had other business interests that weren't public knowledge and he could help free up the capital.'

From what Sarah told her, Graham Petrie had got greedy. With Harry out of the way, he'd thought he could get a bigger slice of the action. Offered to help Sarah, banking on her dumb blonde routine being the real thing. Apparently, he'd offered to help her for a whopping 60 per cent of the business.

'As soon as he started his spiel, everything began to slot into place. I suddenly realised the comfort women had never gone away. They might have closed down Breakmire, but the place was rotten and the stuff that went on in there continued. Only this time the stakes were higher. Everything had been scaled up and streamlined and…' The words choked in Sarah's throat. 'I wanted nothing to do with this. It sickened me. The very thought.'

'Why didn't you go to the police? Tell them what this pig was doing?'

'The following day the police seized Harry's laptop, and I knew Petrie had planted it and tipped them off. Harry was a total fucking creep. But he was careful. And I'm not excusing him, but what they found, that sort of stuff didn't interest Harry.'

'Why would Petrie do that?'

'To let me know that he could. To warn me off telling the police. Make me keep my mouth shut.'

'So why didn't you say that to the police?' Oonagh already knew the answer.

'Listen, Oonagh, they'd never have believed me. And, let's face it, Petrie might have had his own wee stash of dirt planted on me too, for insurance. Anyway, the type of people Petrie had dirt on? He had a get-out-of-jail-free card for the rest of his life.' She began to sob. 'It was a living nightmare.'

Oonagh suddenly felt an enormous amount of sympathy for Sarah Nugent. 'Oh, I'm so sorry, Sarah. I can see why you felt so trapped.' She waited a moment, but was eager now for Sarah to continue. 'So what happened? What did you do?'

'I had him killed.'

'What?' Oonagh had heard, she just couldn't quite believe it.

'Chaz knows enough people,' Sarah continued, as though this type of thing was commonplace. 'You'd be surprised what some guys would do for the price of a pint, let alone the money we offered.'

'Sarah, but…'

'I didn't kill him because he was blackmailing me. I killed him because he was an abusive fucking bastard.'

Slowly the pieces started to slot into place.

Sarah sat down. 'Are you going to tell anyone? Because, d'you know something? I don't fucking care any more.'

Oonagh's mind was racing. She needed to know the full story; running to the cops wasn't the first thing on her mind right now. 'And Andrew Cruikshank?'

Sarah nodded. 'It just seemed easier with him out of the way too. We dressed it up as a gangland execution. The connection to Harry would be obvious.'

'So you didn't kill Harry?'

'No, I've told you.' There was a tinge of impatience in her voice. 'And I have no idea who did.'

'You know the police have been looking at a gambling ring, match rigging, all sorts.'

Sarah nodded. 'That's what we'd planned.'

Oonagh had a million questions. 'But, Sarah, apparently some guy's claiming he knew who did it.'

'Yes, and the cops'll chase down a few gangs for God knows how long. They'll be on the wrong track and then hopefully the case'll go cold. You need to understand. These men were scum.'

'But you can't just take the law into your own hands, Sarah. It's not right.' As she said it Oonagh remembered the way she'd dealt with Ross. There had been other incidents peppered throughout her life, but she'd never actually killed anyone, so it wasn't quite the same. Was it? 'You can't let an innocent man take the blame for this. No matter how much you're paying him. Anyway, the police'll find out and they'll hang him out to dry when they discover it's a pack of lies. He'll be convicted of...'

Sarah raised an eyebrow. 'D'you think? Anyway, these guys are career criminals, Oonagh. They're in and out of jail all their lives. They know the system. They'll easily take a two year stretch if the money's right.'

Oonagh suddenly realised she lived in a very different world. She knew Glasgow had its reputation as a mean city, but had never known it to be this mean.

'What're you going to do with this information?' Sarah was biting her bottom lip, and scratching a faint line on the arm of the cream leather chair.

'I don't know, Sarah – honestly I don't.' And she didn't. Oonagh felt the soft leather of the cushion as she worried her thumb along the seam. She stood up quickly, suddenly aware of what might have gone on in this flat. What poor young guy Harry might have abused under the guise of subtle seduction. The sickness began to rise in her gut and she had to breathe deeply to keep the swell from her throat. Outside life went on as before. She stood by the picture window; the roofs of the post-war bungalows outlined against the grey sky. The rain had stopped. There were too many loose ends.

'What I don't get, Sarah, is why you gave me those accounts. You must have known they'd throw up something like this.'

'Don't get me wrong, I knew Harry wasn't squeaky clean. I knew he liked young guys, was never interested in me. But d'you think for a minute, had I known he was running these brothels…?' She stopped and checked herself. 'I know what it's like. To have no choice. I thought Harry was my knight in shining armour when he took me away from Breakmire. That was my chance to make something of my life.'

Oonagh could well believe it. For someone with the shitty childhood that Sarah had had, perhaps living with a creep like Harry Nugent might have seemed like a good deal at the time.

'I know how that must sound. But the other two, they were just kids, Chaz was still at primary school. They'd been through enough shit. In and out of care might seem awful to someone like you, but for us it actually meant the chance of being washed and fed and taken care of.' She hugged her arms tight around her waist. 'I know what the girls at school said about me behind my back. Called me smelly. Wouldn't speak to me.' Oonagh reached out her hand but Sarah shook her head, didn't want her sympathy. 'And they were right. The house too. Always filthy. And cold. Never any food. One of the neighbours used to shove a slice of toast into my hand when I left the house in the morning. I don't think she knew what else to do. It wasn't Mum's fault. She was just too fond of the booze. I blame that fucking G.P. Every time she went to him he'd just up her pills. She was a mess.'

'Where was your dad?'

'We were told he was on the rigs. He'd plan to visit when we were at the home. The staff would have us all washed and ready for him. He never showed up. The one time he did he was so spaced out they had to phone the police. Dad was never on the rigs. He was a junkie that didn't give a shit about his weans. I know what you must think of me. Living with Harry Nugent. Marrying a man like that. But we were taken care of,' she stabbed her index finger into the arm of the settee, 'I made sure of that. He gave Chaz a chance in the ring, he never amounted to much, but Harry made sure he wanted for nothing. And Gill, you've seen her house. All I had to do was play the dutiful wife.'

'That must have been awful for you.'

'Honestly? It was a cake-walk compared to some of the shit I've had to deal with.'

Oonagh barely trusted herself to speak. 'You gave up a lot to take care of your family.'

'Fat lot of good it did me. Look at the mess I'm in now.'

'I'm in no position to judge anyone Sarah, especially you. And I'm not going anywhere with this. This is between you and me.'

'Thank you.'

Something still burned at the back of Oonagh's mind. 'But I need to ask, why did you hand it all over to me?'

'After Petrie was dead, I didn't really know what to do with the information. I was terrified. There were no names, but I knew there were a lot of big noises enjoying what Harry and Petrie had provided. I didn't trust the police. And they might have thought I'd known about it all along.'

It suddenly clicked. Sarah had wanted Oonagh to find all this out. 'Sarah, you've told me this much, please, just tell me the truth. D'you know who killed Harry?'

She shook her head. 'No, I swear. But now that I know what I do about him, I'm glad he's dead.'

This was getting too much for Oonagh to cope with; she had to think fast with this one. 'The programme'll be aired in the next week or so. The police may get their own forensic accountant to look more closely into Harry's affairs. That means they're going to ask you more questions.'

'That's fine. I'm ready. I swear I didn't know any of this.' She caught a look in Oonagh's eye. 'Me knowing that Harry liked nineteen year old rent boys is a different thing entirely.'

It was obvious Harry had deliberately not covered his tracks with his predilection for teenage boys. He'd wanted Sarah to find out, as though *that* had been his big dark secret.

Not the fact he'd been abusing young boys and offering underage brothels to sick rich bastards with enough money to pay for whatever their depravity called for.

'What the fuck is wrong with men?'

'Not all—'

'Oh, I know, Sarah, I meant some men – most men are lovely.' Oonagh was ashamed of her sweeping statement. For the most part, the men in her life had been lovely. And those that hadn't, she'd had no problem kicking them in the balls.

'No, I mean, it wasn't all men. There were women too.'

'What?'

'Not many. And they mainly just watched. But some would join in.'

Oonagh couldn't take any more of this. She could feel her stomach heave. 'Sarah, I need to level with you. When this programme goes out the shit will hit the fan. I'll make sure of it. There'll be such a public outcry there'll be calls for the killers of those three bastards to be given a special commendation in the New Year's honours list. But the police will still have to investigate, and you may find yourself in the frame as a suspect.'

The programme was almost done and dusted, but Oonagh knew she'd need one final interview. 'Will you go on camera again?'

'No.'

'Please hear me out. You need to say out loud that you knew nothing about this. Otherwise it'll be trial by media. You'll be hung out to dry, Sarah.' Oonagh hoped the advice she was giving was as good as it sounded. But she knew how these things worked. 'The fact that you handed over the accounts to me shows that you wanted this out in the open. But this'll be added insurance. Also...' Oonagh hesitated; it went against every journalistic bone in her body to coerce an interviewee, but this had to be done '... I'll coach you. You need to say you fear for your life. That there are people out there who want this kept under wraps. It's the best way for you to stay alive.' Oonagh knew from bitter experience how these things operated; a tragic accident, a grieving widow overdosing on sleeping pills, or a complicit wife ending it all to hide her guilty secret. 'Meanwhile,' she added, 'is there anywhere you know you'll be safe?'

49

The digits on the bottom right hand side of the screen counted down to zero then froze. Oonagh switched off the monitor. It was hard to know if the churning in her stomach was the familiar nerves of watching a new feature being shown in advance of its official airing, or the fact DI Alec Davies was sitting on the sofa next to her. She felt the tension in his body bleed through to her.

He rubbed the corners of his eyes with his thumb and forefinger. 'Why didn't you come to me earlier?'

Oonagh eased herself up from the sofa and walked over to the chair by the window, perching herself on the arm. 'You'd have tried to steer me clear, stop me from going any further. Slapped an injunction on me.' Oonagh felt a swell of pride in the programme. It was good and she knew it. It made no reference to who might or might not have killed the three men, and it posed more questions than it answered. But it set up a platform that left Police Scotland no choice but to investigate some of the most high profile names in the country.

When Sarah Nugent was speaking about her time as a teenager at Breakmire, her face had been silhouetted out and Oonagh had got one of the production assistants to voice her words, but her sentiment and pain were real. When questioned by Oonagh, she said some of the men who used the brothel were well known names, even claimed one to have been from the Scottish Office. But her final piece to camera as Harry Nugent's widow was in full view. Her statement about her dead husband. And once again the camera loved her. The new hairstyle and more subtle make-up made her all the more appealing. Oonagh had also used one of the best cameramen she knew to make sure the image was just right. His soft focus and getting Sarah to speak slightly off camera was a work of art.

'I handed over these documents because I had reason to believe that my husband was involved in something that sickened me.' Oonagh had ensured that it was clear Sarah Nugent had willingly brought this story into the open and stood to lose everything if her dead husband's assets were frozen by the courts. *'I didn't go to the police as I was scared and feared for my life,'* she'd said. *'And,'* she'd added, *'I don't want a penny that has come from other people's misery. All I want is justice for those who've suffered.'*

'I take it you've had the lawyers give the OK on this?' Alec let his shoulders drop as he slumped forward, resting his head in his hands.

Oonagh nodded. 'Of course.'

'Well, thanks for letting me see it first. I suppose that's something to be grateful for.'

He looked shattered. She got the impression it was more than this case that weighed heavy on him right now.

'Alec...' There was so much she wanted to say to him, but didn't know where to start.

'Will I need a warrant for any of this?' He meant her research, her journalist's notes into her own investigation on this.

'No,' she said, 'it's all yours. Just don't let anyone down with this. These people deserve better.'

Alec smoothed his hands over his face; the dark circles under his eyes were back, and he'd lost weight. 'I'm getting too old for this, Oonagh.' He was far from old, not yet fifty, but she knew what he meant. He was tired and weary. 'I'm sick of being on the side of the good guys when I can't even help.'

'Alec, you're not responsible for every crime that's gone undetected, for every bad thing that's happened in this city.'

He wiped the back of his hand across his mouth. 'But it never ends. This...' He pointed to the screen, which was now blank. 'This level of abuse is probably happening in another city right as we speak. It's endemic, yet who the hell is there to help?'

'I'll get you a drink.'

'Booze.' His voice followed her through to the kitchen. 'Is that your answer to everything?'

'Pretty much,' she said, and handed him a glass. 'Ice, no water. 'S'at right?'

He smiled, seemed happy that she knew how he liked his whisky. He leaned back on the sofa. It had grown dark outside, and the sodium orange of the street lights split through the blind, leaving a slash of colour on the wall behind his head.

Oonagh sat on the seat opposite, hugging her knees to

her chest. The programme was good; there was no doubt about that. Sophie had been given a permanent contract and by all accounts had been delighted with her bumper pay rise. She'd rushed in to tell Oonagh that morning. But there was no happy ending to this and she felt like shit.

'How d'you cope with the misery, Alec? The shit you have to deal with every day?' Oonagh was no stranger to a horror story, but at least for her there were breaks along the way. Long periods of respite when she'd fronted soft news programmes, human interest features, daytime chat shows. During those times the misery had lingered in the background. Just out of reach. But now it seemed to descend on her like a blanket.

'It's my job, Oonagh. I *have* to cope.' He took a sip of his whisky; she saw his shoulders visibly relax as he swallowed. 'When's this going out?' he said, referring to the programme.

'Scheduled for next Monday. Plenty of time to get a decent press release put out.' Oonagh was one step ahead of him. She knew that Alec would need to be ahead of the game with this one. Couldn't look as though his department had been caught on the hop.

The implication in the programme was that senior public figures had used the services of the comfort women, and those senior figures included politicians, celebrities and members of the police force.

'There'll need to be an internal investigation, of course.' Alec held the glass to his lips and tipped his head back.

Oonagh knew that the new Police Investigations and Review Commission had come under fire from officers who claimed it was too heavy handed. It had set out to show that it would not tolerate any misconduct and that dodgy cops knew their days were numbered, but had instead found itself at the other end of bullying allegations.

'And they'll take no prisoners, believe you me.' He placed his empty glass on the table by the settee.

'I take it you'll still be investigating the abuse at the Boys' Club?'

'Oh, yes. Make no mistake. That bastard didn't operate alone. There must have been senior figures on that board who had his back.'

Nugent, it appeared, had had enough dirt on enough people to pretty much do as he pleased for as long as he wanted. Oonagh wondered who he'd stretched his luck with just once too often to end up swinging from a rope with his tongue sliced off. 'Have you spoken to Jack Nesbit?'

'He was one of the first. He was being palmed off as a senile old man, but he gave us names. Enough to go on to question several fairly prominent figures. I can assure you, Oonagh, I'll have their fucking balls for this.'

Oonagh started slightly; she'd never heard Alec speak like this. There seemed to be a shift in him. A change somehow that she couldn't quite put her finger on. He leaned back and closed his eyes, just for a moment.

'Listen,' he said, straightening up, looking at his watch, 'I need to get going. It's late. Let you get to your bed.'

It wasn't yet eight o'clock, but Oonagh could see he was dog tired. She got up and sat next to him, leaning her back against the arm of the settee, her bare feet on the cushion between them, her toes just shy of his thighs. He reached over and gave her arm a gentle pat. 'You're lovely, Oonagh O'Neil, d'you know that?'

'So they tell me.' She grinned, but he didn't laugh. She

thought for a moment. 'You don't need to go home, Alec.' She waited for a reaction, but his expression didn't change. 'You can crash here.' She glanced at the settee, giving him a get-out clause in case she'd made the wrong call. He said nothing. Then she raised her eyebrows, tipping her head towards the ceiling. 'Although I hear the master bedroom is far more comfortable.' She let out a laugh; despite how she felt about him, she wanted to let him know there were no expectations.

'You might hate yourself in the morning,' he said, and for the first time that night she thought she saw a glimpse of a smile.

'Oh, I'm sure sleeping in until lunchtime would sort that out.'

EPILOGUE

Was it possible to envy oneself? She slipped the photograph back into her purse. A relic now. A reminder of happier days, when they were all together as a family. That had been so long ago. She wished she were that person again. That once again she could become who she'd been.

Vivienne Gray took the stairs to the third floor, blinking against the sunlight beating through the full length windows. It belied the bitter cold outside and she felt its scorching heat settle on her head as she smoothed her hand across her hair. She stopped on the second landing and rested her forehead on the glass for a moment. The clattering noise from the corridors filtered through to the stairwell, but the sounds were muffled and for a few moments she felt safe and quiet. Outside students hurried to and from lectures, heavy backpacks slung casually across their shoulders, eyes glued to mobile phones. A slight pang of fear for the future pricked her thoughts. A future where students too doped up on social media would forget how to fight for what they believed in.

She made her way back up the stairs and through the double doors that led onto the main corridor. The lecture theatre at the end faced north. It was her favourite; the light was always so blue, with little shadow cast throughout the day. She eased a crick in her neck as she walked slowly, allowing the few stragglers to get to class before she did. Her students knew by now she did not suffer fools gladly, and latecomers were more than aware of her 'three strikes and you're out' policy.

Tiredness tugged at the corners of her eyes. These last few weeks had taken their toll, but it was getting better, as she'd known it would. For the first two weeks sleep had been a luxury denied to her. Nights had been spent pacing the floor, begging for the relief morning could bring. Even closing her eyes for a moment had brought back the memory of his dying breath. His sobs as he'd begged for mercy. The smells as he'd lost vital control towards the end. But slowly that had been replaced by his last words. She knew now what it felt like to die. Or at least what Harry Nugent had felt as he was dying. He'd felt scared, she'd known that even without him uttering a word. But once he'd accepted that there was no way out, he'd seemed to surrender himself. He'd taken several minutes to pass out. That must have seemed like a lifetime to a dying man. All the while, she'd held the knife close to his groin, the tip piercing the soft fabric of his chinos, edging its way closer to his balls as he'd given in to her demands to narrate his dying thoughts. He'd known that at any time she could have cut the rope around his neck, but that would have been worse. For then he truly would have died in agony. This way, it had been more peaceful.

She made her way along the corridor, only vaguely aware of the colourful posters crammed onto the noticeboards at either side. She paused for a few seconds before entering the lecture theatre. A quiet sense of calm had descended on the corridor and she took a deep breath, allowing her thoughts about Harry Nugent to subside.

She'd thought that killing him would solve her nightmares of the past two decades. The agony of not knowing what her darling Hannah had felt in the last few hours of her life had haunted her every waking moment. Had her baby known that the cold would seep in and take her life as she fell into a final sleep? Vivienne wrapped her arms instinctively around her stomach and remembered those precious months before Hannah was born. Those beautiful moments when it had been just the two of them inside one body. When her baby had been snuggled up in her womb. Where she'd kept her safe. Had Hannah cried out for her in those last few moments?

The thought of her daughter's final cries had haunted Vivienne for over two decades. Images of her final moments replayed in her imagination. Each image growing more painful as time had worn on. Then when she'd discovered what had happened to her daughter a new nightmare had emerged. One where Hannah was begging for mercy. Crying out for her as those men abused her.

Now those nightmares were slowly being replaced with the final cries of Harry Nugent. Her memory as she watched him take his final steps, remembering how he lowered himself from the balcony. Too terrified to jump. Clinging onto the edge with his fingertips before his strength gave way to his body weight and he finally fell, dangling by the rope around his neck. That was what filled her nightmares now. But at least they were of a different sort. At least now they weren't of Hannah, and for the first time in a long time Vivienne Gray felt her daughter was at rest.

AUTHOR'S NOTE

In September 2018, I had just starting on this book when I got chatting to a Glasgow taxi driver. On the short journey into town, David Gordon told me he'd been a promising young footballer in his day, but tragically his career had been cut short – he'd been abused by his coach, turning his whole world upside down. Four decades later he can still recall every detail.

Jim Torbett was jailed for two years in 1998 – David's testimony along with the other boys helped put Torbett behind bars. It also encouraged others to come forward and in November 2018 Torbett was jailed for a further six years.

The characters and storyline in this book are totally fictitious. David's generosity in sharing his experience with me helped shape part of that story – but it is entirely fictitious.

Thank you, David.

ACKNOWLEDGEMENTS

As ever this book is a team effort.

First and foremost my husband, Jeremy Fellick – for his love, enthusiasm and lack of grumpiness.

Everyone at Team Aria, especially Hannah Smith, Vicky Joss, Sue Lamprell and Rose Fox – and not forgetting my lovely agent Nicola Barr. They all deserve a huge hug – but would probably rather champagne!

A whole host of experts pitched in: D.I. Dougie McKinlay (retired), Crime Scene Manager of Strathclyde's finest; Chief Superintendent Stewart Carle; Dr Margaret Balsitis and Andrew MacLeod. Their collective expertise ensured I didn't look like too much of an eejit – any 'errors' are down to my poetic/dramatic licence. (I'm an author – I make stuff up.)

While I'm on the subject – I used a bit of leeway here & there. The old Glasgow city mortuary is no longer on Saltmarket St and although Strathclyde Police is now part of Police Scotland there's no equivalent term for 'Strathclyde's Finest.' But *coorie* IS a word, and a *close* is the common entrance to a block of tenements.

Fellow writers who've supported me – too many to mention – but Shari Low, Denzil Meyrick and early readers Douglas Skelton and Brian Hannan deserve a special thumbs-up.

Sandy Murray who let me use his name and didn't mind being described as grumpy.

Every reader, blogger, bookseller, librarian – anyone who loves books enough to breathe life into characters and make this all worthwhile.

And a very special thank you to David Gordon, a lovely man who shared his story with such quiet dignity.

ABOUT THE AUTHOR

Theresa Talbot is a BBC broadcaster and freelance producer. A former radio news editor, she also hosted *The Beechgrove Potting Shed* on BBC Radio Scotland, but for many she will be most familiar as the voice of the station's *Traffic & Travel*. Late 2014 saw the publication of her first book, *This Is What I Look Like*, a humorous memoir covering everything from working with Andy Williams to rescuing chickens and discovering nuns hidden in gardens. She's much in demand at book festivals, both as an author and as a chairperson. *The Lost Children* was Theresa's debut crime novel.

Hello from Aria

We hope you enjoyed this book! If you did let us know, we'd love to hear from you.

We are Aria, a dynamic digital-first fiction imprint from award-winning independent publishers Head of Zeus. At heart, we're committed to publishing fantastic commercial fiction – from romance and sagas to crime, thrillers and historical fiction. Visit us online and discover a community of like-minded fiction fans!

We're also on the look out for tomorrow's superstar authors. So, if you're a budding writer looking for a publisher, we'd love to hear from you. You can submit your book online at ariafiction.com/we-want-read-your-book

Printed in Great Britain
by Amazon

45618473R00201